Antimacassar City

Born in Birkenhead to Scots parents, Guy McCrone grew up in Ayrshire. He was educated at Glasgow Academy and Pembroke College, Cambridge.

He wrote several novels but the *Wax Fruit* trilogy was by far the most successful, especially in the USA where it was a Book of the Month Club choice (under its American title *Red Plush*). First published in 1947, *Wax Fruit* has remained one of the best known of all Glasgow novels and was brought to a new audience when it was televised in 1975.

Guy McCrone was actively involved in Glaswegian cultural life, especially the Citizen's Theatre and the Glasgow Chamber Music Society.

He was always fond of the Lake District and towards the end of his life he made his home near Windermere, where he died in 1977.

The other titles in Guy McCrone's
Wax Fruit trilogy available in Pan Books

The Philistines
The Puritans

Guy McCrone
Antimacassar City

Book One of the *Wax Fruit* trilogy

Pan Books London and Sydney

First published in Great Britain 1947 by
Constable and Company Ltd
as Book 1 of *Wax Fruit*
This edition published 1978 by Pan Books Ltd,
Cavaye Place, London SW10 9PG
© Guy McCrone 1947
ISBN 0 330 25288 7
Made and printed in Great Britain by
Cox & Wyman Ltd, London, Reading and Fakenham

To Glasgow Readers

No. You must forgive me. But I did not
have the impertinence to draw for you portraits
of your grandparents and their friends.

Book One
Antimacassar City

Chapter 1

1

Why were the dogs whining?

It was Doon and Nith that were making the noise. Clyde, who was the oldest and was most attached to her father, must have trotted off after the trap when her mother and he had driven off this evening.

The strong moon, coming through the skylight, made a dazzling oblong on the wall opposite the little girl's bed. Although she herself lay snug, the attic room was so cold that she could see her breath when she puffed in the direction of the beam of light.

'Haud yer tongue, Doon! Keep quate, Nith!' That was her brother's voice. She could hear his heavy boots cracking the frozen puddles of the farm close.

What time was it? Nine or ten o'clock? Late for Ayrshire farm folks, anyway. Her instinct told her that her parents were not yet come home from their visit. There was still a sense of waiting. That must be why the dogs were restless.

She knew all the farm's lightest sounds. She could tell their meaning. She could hear the movement of hoofs as the Clydesdales shifted the weight of their great resting bodies from one leg to the other.

But the lighter taps of the pony's hoofs were wanting.

A suppressed excitement took hold of her. It was not quite anxiety, though she was beginning to feel that too. This odd child of ten was beginning to hope, almost, that something was coming to her. For, though she did not know it, she was of those strange people who must have experience, even though it be tragic – who, even in catastrophe, are able to stand back and appraise.

She climbed out and threw some bedclothes about her. Dragging the one chair in the room beneath the skylight, she climbed upon it and pushed the glass frame wide open. The air, cold as a knife, met her round warm cheeks, but she did not care. She could now get her head through.

She could see the shape of the buildings – the barn, the cart-shed, the stables, the byre. And beyond, the stacks in the stack-yard, then the gate to the road. In the strong moonlight, and rimed with hoar-frost, everything was colourless. Everything had

9

been reduced to planes and angles of velvet blackness and silver-white.

But for the occasional shuffling of the beasts in the stables and the cowshed, there was silence now. The collies must have followed her brother, wherever he was.

No, there they were, back again, wheeling about the yard like phantoms. Now they were whining the low, restless whines that had awakened her.

'Nae sign yet?' A farm-hand's voice was speaking.

'No' yet.' Her brother's voice again.

'Whit time is it?'

'Ten.'

So they *were* late. The farm usually went to sleep at eight. This tension was exciting. There were little thrills all over her. It wasn't just the cold creeping up from her bare feet.

2

Were these the steps of a pony now? She listened intently.

Her brother and the man emerged from the shadows and, crossing the yard, hung over the gate.

Were these the familiar hoof-claps? They must be. But she couldn't understand. She knew the weight and ring of them. But she could hear no wheels, and the hoofs clattered together at times as though the pony were dancing hysterically on a leading-rein.

Where was the trap? And where were her father and mother? She could feel her heart thumping in her body.

The dogs had run forward to the gate too, barking excitedly. Her brother turned on them and again shouted at them to be quiet. Suddenly something ran through them. It was her father's dog Clyde. Paying no attention, he came down to the centre of the yard. In the strong moonlight she could see the handsome long limbs of the old collie trembling. His bushy tail was clapped down tight over his thin buttocks. His ears lay as though he were in pain. For a moment he stood shivering, turning his long, elegant muzzle this way and that, looking about distractedly; then, balancing backwards, one thin front paw off the ground, he threw back his head and uttered a long, low howl.

The child had never heard anything so heartbroken. The other dogs seemed to get his meaning, for they were circling round him now, copying his low-sung note of woe.

Her brother paid no attention to them, for the pony, impatient at being led by a strange hand, was dancing sideways through the opened gate.

The three men were talking together excitedly. Suddenly her brother broke from them and ran towards the house. Now, inside, she could hear him calling, though she could not catch what he said.

She jumped from her chair and listened at her door. The house seemed to be stirring. She could hear the door of the servant-girls' room bang.

All this was very exciting. It was horrible to be missing anything. Should she go down to ask what it was? She did not dare. Her brother would order her back to bed, for he was strict with her, as their father was.

Now she could hear heavy steps coming to the foot of the attic stair. They began to ascend. She jumped into bed and covered herself up, ready with the pretence of sleep.

In another moment the catch was lifted and her brother stood in the doorway. Was it the moonlight that made him look like this? His aspect gave her a sensation of intense interest. So people looked like that if something dreadful had happened? He was struggling to seem calm. She could see that his deliberation was merely to give himself time.

She sat up abruptly, as though she had been shocked out of a deep sleep.

'What is it?'

His voice was even stranger than his looks as he told her.

Chapter 2

I

Mr and Mrs Arthur Moorhouse, of Ure Place, in the City of Glasgow, were already half-dressed by seven o'clock.

Arthur was standing in his best trousers pouring out his shaving-water from a shining copper can. For though, in this year

1870, hair on the face of the male was considered more orna-
mental than in later days, there was still a certain amount of
shaving to be done. Arthur limited his natural decoration to
mutton-chop whiskers. He was wise, for their blackness lent his
strong features, his black eyebrows and the natural paleness of his
skin an added distinction.

'There was no need for ye to get up so early, my dear. It's
a bitter morning.' Arthur drew out his razor and tested the
edge.

Bel Moorhouse, wrapped as well as was possible against the
Arctic chill of the bedroom, was running her comb down
through the thick ripples of her hair. Its waved fairness shone
bravely in the light of the two gas-jets above her head.

'Nonsense, dear. You've got a long, cold day in front of you. I
must see that you get your breakfast properly.'

Bel went on with her combing and Arthur took up his shav-
ing-brush.

These foregoing words do not seem, in themselves, very preg-
nant, but their overtones were many, and to each of these young
people betokened more than a perfunctory demonstration of
affection on a cold morning.

Bel should stay in bed and take care of herself, Arthur was
implying, because she was his precious wife, only lately acquired
after many tedious years of looking after his own none-too-
thankful family. And in addition – and of still greater importance – he was delicately reminding her that her body was a frail
casket bearing within it their first child, to whose birth both were
looking forward with the keenest pleasure. In his heart Arthur
knew that Bel was as strong as a horse. But the strength of horses
is not romantic, except perhaps in the horses themselves. Certainly it was not considered so in a twenty-four-year-old matron
of mid-Victorian days. Politer to assume that any puff might
blow her away, though you knew perfectly – and were thankful
for it – that her agile young body would stand a hurricane.

And Bel's answer had been just as full of meaning. 'You must
be fed and tended, my dear husband,' it implied, 'by the only
person who really knows to a hair's-breadth all your needs,
physical and mental. You must be fortified against all dis-
comforts of the body and of the mind. Today you are to be with
relatives who for the past fifteen years have done nothing but
worry and annoy you. You are going to bury your old father –
for whom I personally never cared – and with him, a second wife

twenty years younger than himself, whom he should never have married. It has all been very sudden and annoying, coming in this the eighth month of our marriage and just before Christmas. But I am much too fine a woman to complain. With my charm, my profound affection and, above all, my great good-sense, I shall throw myself between you and your annoyances. In a word, I shall be to you the perfect wife.'

Each comprehended the meaning of the other perfectly. Which all goes to show that Arthur Moorhouse and his wife were on excellent terms.

By half past seven Arthur was warming himself before a crackling fire in their pleasant red-plush dining-room. The breakfast-table looked cosier than ever from the fact that the room was still in gas-light.

Bel, all pride and importance behind the teacups, was looking up at her slim, thirty-three-year-old husband, more dark and effective than ever in his long black coat. And Arthur, looking down upon his glowing wife, decided that black suited her fairness almost better than anything else.

'When is your train, dear?' Bel asked as he took his place.

'Half past eight.'

'Then you won't be going down to business first?'

Down was the right word, for on their marriage the Arthur Moorhouses had set up house here in Ure Place, a quiet and pleasant little square with trees in the middle, set on the side of a steep hill. Up there they were in the City of Glasgow, but not quite of it. Yet in little better than five minutes Arthur's long legs could drop him down Montrose Street and into the Candleriggs, where he conducted with diligence his business of wholesale provision merchant.

Arthur finished his last spoonful of porridge and held out his hand for his plate of ham and eggs.

'No,' he said, 'I've no need to go down. David is going to let me know if there's anything.'

'That's good,' was all Bel said, but in her mind she wondered if Arthur's young brother would really trouble himself to go. He was such an unreliable creature.

'There's time to send one of the maids for a cab,' she said presently.

'Nonsense. I'll walk across the town. If I leave at eight I'll have lots of time.'

But Bel was insistent this morning. She even went the length –

Junoesque though she was – of pretending, a little, to be pathetic, and thus, conquering her lord and master, she succeeded in having the cab ordered.

2

At five minutes to eight, Mr and Mrs William Butter arrived.

Mrs William had been Sophia Moorhouse. Before her marriage, some eight years ago, she had kept house for Arthur. Arthur at the age of eighteen had left his father's farm and come to Glasgow to make his fortune. One by one his brothers and sisters had followed him, with the exception of the oldest brother, Mungo, who remained a farmer. Sophia had been the first.

Sophia was not perhaps one of Bel's favourites. For, of all the family, she exploited Arthur with the least shame. Even now – from habit – Bel wondered for a moment what Sophia and her stolid husband could be wanting that they should call in on their way to the station; for they lived in a flat in Grafton Square, further up, across Cathedral Street, or the Stirling Road as it then was, and there was no reason whatever why they should come to Ure Place.

'Good morning, Bel dear. What a cold morning! How cosy you both look! Could William and I possibly have another cup of tea? Or would it be a bother? We were so hurried at breakfast. Little Wil and Margy were so sure we would be late for their grandpapa's funeral, they kept running with gloves and things. William nearly died laughing.'

As their sister-in-law pulled the bell – with the shallowest appearance of hospitality – to have more teacups brought, she could not help wondering what William looked like dying of laughter.

For, although William was only thirty-three, he was fat and square, and as much of his face as possible was covered with hair. Her gay young brother-in-law David had once described William Butter to Bel as a fat, hairy man who stood. You might as well connect the expressing of emotion with the Tolbooth Steeple as with William. Perhaps it was the hair, Bel pondered. But after all he could emit sounds. And this he didn't do either, much. No, if you shaved him clean, there would still be little or no movement of his facial muscles.

'Not that they aren't very sorry about grandpapa's death,' Sophia was going on. 'But as they've only seen him twice – or was it three times, William?'

William said nothing.

'Yes, that's right, three times, and then only for a little; they can't remember him very well. This tea's putting new life into me, Bel dear. We must get some like it. Mustn't we, William?'

William said nothing.

'It's time we were getting to the station,' Arthur said, pulling out his watch.

'What about your bonnet, Bel dear?'

'Bel's not coming,' Arthur said irritably.

'Why? Oh, of course. How wise. I was forgetting.' She patted Bel's hand knowingly, then apropos of what appeared to be nothing, looked about her and said: 'Delightful to think—'

'I've arranged to go to the station in a cab. Would ye like a lift?' Arthur said, with no attempt at grace in his invitation.

'That would be a great help, wouldn't it, William?'

William did not seem to hear.

And at last it broke upon Bel why these two had come down to them this morning. Young David had christened them the Emperor and Empress of Cadge. David, Bel reflected, was not far wrong.

It was bitterly cold as Bel opened the front door for them. She saw her husband into his thickest overcoat and tied a woollen muffler of her own knitting about his neck.

Arthur went down the front steps, said 'Bridge Street Station, please,' and got into the cab without further ceremony.

Sophia bade Bel an effusive goodbye and regretted not having her company in the train.

Bel, having decided that William's hand was a little inclined in her direction, grasped it and shook it.

Holding the cab door open, Sophia turned. 'Bel dear, as you're not coming, could you *bear* to send over for the children today? After all, it *is* Christmas-time. Poor wee mites. We can hardly expect them to feel our sorrow very deeply. They looked so forlorn when we said goodbye.'

Bel succeeded – just in time – in looking vague and saying something about devoting the day to her mother.

'Well, anyway, if you can— Come along, William, don't keep Arthur waiting. Do you know what the time is now?'

But William did not bother to tell her the time. He merely followed his wife into the cab.

3

As they drew up at Bridge Street Station, they could see the slim black figure of Arthur's youngest brother, David, turning into the entrance. His hands were deep in his overcoat pockets and his shoulders were hunched against the cold.

The noise of the cab attracted his attention and he turned with a beaming smile to hold the door for its occupants. David was always delighted to see everybody.

Arthur bounced out, paid the cab, then turned to David, saying: 'Anything from the office?'

'I didn't go in this morning.'

'Why the devil didn't you? I told you to. Have you got your ticket?'

'No.'

Arthur said no more. But, going to the ticket office, bought his own and his younger brother's. By this time Sophia was hovering.

'Come on,' he shouted. 'I've bought your ticket.'

Sophia's gentle expostulation, 'But, Arthur dear, William didn't mean you to,' was cut in two by Arthur saying: 'I haven't got your tickets, Sophia. Just David's and my own,' as he disappeared into the inner station.

His second brother-in-law George was pacing the platform. George McNairn Esquire, as David always called him, was a large, elderly-looking man of thirty-five. If ever a stomach was made to support the chains of office – if ever shoulders were made to carry municipal ermine, these belonged to Mr McNairn. He seemed infinitely large as he moved, slow and important, up and down.

He did not go to meet his brothers-in-law, but rather allowed his stately progress to converge with their more abrupt steps. He shook their hands with ceremony and, looking beyond them, spoke impersonally as though he were addressing the back gallery of the City Hall. His words could be heard all over the station.

'Good-morning, Arthur. Good-morning, David. Well, this is a melancholy duty – a melancholy duty.'

Arthur returned his handshake quickly. 'Good-morning, George. Where's Mary?'

'At the fire in the waiting-room. She's feeling this very badly, poor girl – very badly.'

Arthur hurried on to find his younger sister.

Mary was sitting solitary on a hard chair before a new-lit fire that was, as yet, giving out no heat. Her wide black dress was all about her and a thick veil hung over her face. Her hands, in their black gloves, were folded on her lap.

Arthur went to her and greeted her in a business-like way. 'Hello, Mary, how are you? Cold, isn't it?'

Mary raised her veil to allow her brother to kiss her.

'Good-morning, dear,' she said, in a voice that was controlled and gentle. You could never quite determine just how much this tone was assumed and how much of it came naturally to her.

Mary Moorhouse was a beautiful woman of thirty. Her face was oval, her brows clear and serene, and her eyes da Vinci-like and candid.

Mary was in danger of becoming a saint. Consciously, that is. For there was a conscious, thought-out quality about everything she did. Like most saints, she was not above staging herself a little. And, again like most saints, she was quite devoid of humour.

At this point Sophia flooded into the waiting-room, embraced her sister and gave her good-morning.

'And how are the boys, Mary?' she gushed to her sister, who was settling down again like a lake after a sudden squall.

Mary knew that Sophia was only asking after the children that she might make for herself an opening to begin talking about her own, but she put this unworthy thought from her. Besides, she had something to tell Sophia.

'Georgia and Jackie are having a little tea-party this afternoon, dear. Not anybody in, of course, but I baked some cakes. I felt that they should be happy at Christmas-time. They're too small to understand about their grandpapa.'

Before she could say more, Sophia had broken in. 'Mary, I wish I had known! My children could have gone there today. Their Auntie Bel wants them.' (In the background Arthur grunted at this.) 'But still, it would have been nice for the children to be all together.'

'I've arranged for a cab to go for them, dear,' Mary went on serenely, knowing in her heart what she was saving Auntie Bel and not feeling the less saintly for the knowledge. 'One of George's clerks had just been down to take any orders we might have to give him, so I told him to see to it.'

In the matter of worldly gear, Mary had done better than her sister. She lived in a neat, front-door house at Albany Place, near Charing Cross. And her husband conducted a flourishing manufacturers' agency in Queen Street.

Sophia, to do her justice, was not really jealous of her sister's greater prosperity. But her motto in life was: If there's anything to be had, then have it. And there was so much to be had from and in connection with Mary.

She turned to her husband, who was standing mute behind her. 'William, aren't you delighted? Wil and Margy are going along to tea at their Auntie Mary's.'

At this point Arthur, who had been looking out of the doorway, shouted, 'Hurry up and get into the train.'

So William Butter did not appear to feel it necessary to add to his wife's expressions of rapture. Or perhaps he was just standing.

4

They were all in the train now and settling down to a melancholy, and what promised to be a cold, journey.

George, by dint of impressing with his majestic presence the man with the trolley of warming-pans, had two put into their carriage instead of one. But these, they reflected regretfully, would not remain hot for long upon so cold a morning.

The train jogged slowly out towards Paisley. In these days all trains going to central Ayrshire went by Paisley, for the direct line to Kilmarnock was not yet available, and the journey, for this reason, was more than an hour longer.

Arthur sat huddled, trying to read his newspaper, but the constant chatter of Sophia – about her children, about her house, about her maids, about a misunderstanding with a lady in the church – became too much for him and he laid it down, thrust his hands into his coat-pockets and looked at his brood, pondering.

For in a very real sense they were his brood. He had put them all where they were. In a sense he had taken the place of their father.

Fifteen years before, feeling that life at the Laigh Farm could offer him no future, he had taken himself to the City. The first years had been hard. A man with whom his father dealt had taken him in as a clerk. Pay had been meagre for the eighteen-year-old lad, but Arthur was country-bred and wiry. His health had stood up to long hours, airless quarters and none too lavish food. Presently he had found himself with better wages and more responsibility. It was inevitable, for he had health, character and a sound village education, and his own mother, though a farmer's wife, had been anything but crude. The others had not come to Glasgow until their father's remarriage to one of his own servants eleven years ago had scattered them. The girls had felt their situation worst. Sophia had come to him almost at once. For a couple of years he had made a home for her; then, to the satisfaction of all, the high-mettled William Butter had lost his head at a church *soirée* (or perhaps Sophia had taken matters into her own hands) and claimed her for his own.

It was then that Mary came. For much the same length of time she had been with him. She had always been calm and distinguished. Though she was country-bred, she took on the refinements of the town at once. It was as though its gentler, more genteel ways had called to something in her blood. Arthur had been sorry, a little, when George McNairn had taken her to his majestic bosom. For Mary, in her quiet, self-conscious way, was a highly capable person.

That left only David to come – for Mungo, the oldest of them all, remained a farmer. At the time of his father's remarriage, David was a child of twelve.

He had better make himself responsible for David, Arthur had decided. He didn't want the boy to live in a house where he might feel himself a stepchild. And so, for David's sake, he had persuaded their aunt – a sister of their own mother – to put herself beneath his roof, to keep house, and to bring up his youngest brother.

As he sat now looking at David, he doubted if he had done the right thing. Would it have been better had the boy been brought up in the country? He had been delicate and their aunt had spoilt him. And now that he was twenty-three he was all too well acquainted with the town's ways.

David was slack.

Arthur had him in the business now and was trying to knock some kind of discipline into him, but it was uphill work. He might have done better to leave him to his father and his stepmother.

Why had they taken such a hate to this Highland woman that their father had married? After eleven years they still knew nothing against her, except that she had been a hired servant and was almost illiterate. Mungo, the only one who really knew her, had liked her well enough. Had they been unfair in keeping away so much from the old man? They had felt it, perhaps, a desecration of their mother's memory. But had that been reasonable? And now, they hardly knew their little half-sister Phoebe.

Bel had asked what was to become of her. She had even suggested she should be brought to live at Ure Place. He wondered if he ought to let her come. His habit of taking responsibility for everybody told him he should. Bel had maintained that the child could not stay on at the farm with only Mungo and a household of crude farm-women.

5

The train was jogging on through the frost-bound country. He looked out across the wide Clyde valley. The Kilpatrick Hills and, further away, the Campsies stood peppered with snow. In the rosy-morning distance a white cone stood out. That must be Ben Lomond. He and Bel must make a trip to Loch Lomond sometime. And there were the buildings of the new University on Gilmour Hill at the extreme west end of the town. In the far distance they looked almost completed. He had heard about the difficulty the builders were having with the spire and wondered what they intended to do about it.

Yes, it had been nice of Bel to think of taking in his little half-sister. But he felt reluctant. He felt he had done enough for everybody. Or was he the kind of person to whom everybody would always turn for help? Would he never be able just to lead his own life, be able just to look after his wife and his children and bother about nobody else?

He had hoped he had come to an end when, before his marriage, he had seen David settled in rooms, sold the flat where they had lived alone together – for their aunt had died – and, with the help of his wife-to-be and her mother, had furnished the pleasant house in Ure Place.

That was only eight months ago. And now suddenly his little half-sister was an orphan.

Well, they would all have a look at her today. And this evening, back again at tea in his own house and with the help of his sisters and their husbands, the future of Phoebe would have to be thrashed out.

The carriage jingled on the points and came to a standstill.

'Dear me,' Sophia was saying, 'this is only Paisley!'

Chapter 3

1

Punctually to the minute, old Mrs Barrowfield was roused to consciousness by the housemaid re-laying her bedroom fire.

This began every morning on the stroke of eight. Old Mrs Barrowfield saw to that.

'A body's not much worth, if she's come to the age of sixty-five and still lets her girls get the better of her.'

Mrs Barrowfield's two girls had not sought to get the better of her for a long time now. They had been with her for more years than any of them cared to remember, and the discipline of the old lady's much-betasselled and upholstered flat in Monteith Row had long since ceased to chafe. Time had been when they had not been above an exchange of wit with young men at the door on the back lane. But their hair was grey now and their bodies had long since lost the fluidity of youth and had, like the body of their mistress, turned unalluring and rotund. And young men had, somehow, ceased to be witty.

Mrs Barrowfield awoke with a sense of uneasiness. She had fallen asleep worrying over her only daughter Bel.

She raised herself on her pillow a little and looked about her.

'Wipe yer hands, Maggie, and draw back the curtains.'

The respectful, respectable woman rose to her feet and did as she was bade. From her bed the old lady looked out on the slow winter dawn.

'Is it still frosty?'

The maid at the window cast her eyes over the wide expanse of Glasgow Green – to the winding banks of the Clyde – to the belching chimneys on the further side. On the south-east, the rising day was still red, made redder than it should be from particles of smoke. One or two stragglers, huddled in overcoats, were hurrying quickly along the carriage-way in the park. Distant buildings loomed indistinct in the morning haze.

'Aye, it's still frosty, Mam.'

Mrs Barrowfield let Maggie go back to her work and lay watching her get the fire going. She did it deftly and quickly, according to minute instructions long since given and long since learnt.

Bel. Bother the girl with all her highfalutin nonsense.

Mrs Barrowfield was proud of her twenty-four-year-old daughter. Indeed, it would not be too much to say that she lived for her – that is, when she was not living for her own immediate and highly organized comfort. But, as Bel's mother often assured herself, she would be no proper parent if she were blind to her child's faults. And to high falute was one of Bel's worst ones.

Mrs Barrowfield lay considering. Of course, the girl had got it direct from her father, the lamented Doctor Barrowfield. A little decorative pomp had been no bad thing in a doctor with a good-class practice, where bedside manner was everything. But it was merely irritating in the doctor's daughter. Besides, Charles Barrowfield had always managed to high falute without incurring obligation. Which was just precisely what his daughter was not doing. She was threatening to take on a responsibility that might be a trouble to her for years. That might, indeed, threaten her married happiness.

But here Mrs Barrowfield's sense of comfort intervened. This worry was spoiling the nicest hour of her day. The crackling fire. The newspaper. Tea, toast, and ham and eggs (the eggs just soft and no more, or cook would hear about it).

She would try to dismiss Bel until she had got up.

The maid was standing now, scuttle in hand, preparing to go.

'Bring up my *Herald* now, Maggie. And you'll have to light the gas. It's dark these mornings.'

Maggie was surprised. The old lady usually lay contented until her breakfast came up punctually at half past eight. But she did as her mistress told her, helped to arrange her in bed, found a shawl for her shoulders, and gave her spectacles a rub.

Mrs Barrowfield – to show defiance, perhaps, to her own uncomfortable thoughts – snapped the paper open.

2

The *Glasgow Herald*, Saturday, 24th December, 1870.

It was her habit to look through the paper systematically. This morning she started fiercely at the top left-hand corner of the front page.

The *Glasgow Weekly Herald* was advertising itself. Special Hogmanay Stories. 'A Loveless Marriage', by A Young Lady. 'The Fate of Baby Daisy, the Village Beauty'. How could people read such trash? People, that was, who had business to attend to. For herself, seeing that time lay in plenty on her hands, she might go the length of a penny to see just in what respect the marriage had failed, that it had become loveless.

The new Theatre Royal, Hope Street. The pantomime, 'Sinbad the Sailor', the cast including King Wangdoodle of the Chickorybony Islands. Pity Bel had to be in mourning for her father-in-law, otherwise she might have taken the young couple to see this. Not that she approved of theatres much, but of course the pantomime was different.

Hengler's Circus. Herr Holtum would exhibit his wonderful powers of juggling with cannon-balls. The circus was for children. She laid down her paper smiling and looked about the much-upholstered room, which was becoming lighter with the growing day. Well, Bel was making a start. In May there would be a grandchild.

And say in five more years he – she was determined it should be a *he* – would be ready to go to the circus. The prospect of this grandchild enchanted Mrs Barrowfield. She would, she pondered, be able to give the little boy lots of good advice.

If only Bel didn't go and— Mrs Barrowfield snapped up the paper and went on reading.

Pretty Baby Things could be had at Mrs Fyfe's shops in Argyle Street and in Sauchiehall Street. She must remember that for Bel. She would look into the Argyle Street shop. There was no need of her dragging up into the West End where things were bound to be dearer and not a whit better.

Great Bargains! Smart clothes for genteel assemblies. She was past genteel assemblies and Bel didn't feel like them just now.

The Argyle House was overflowing with French and German fancy goods. Just imagine that now! With the Germans and the French fighting each other as hard as they could! You would wonder that they had time to send fancy goods anywhere.

Wine advertisements. She could do with a bottle or two of that Marsala for odd guests on New Year's Day.

She turned a page.

Reviews of Books. They all looked as dry as dust.

Letters to the Editor. Women's rights. Dear me! What was making them start that nonsense? Signed 'Dejected Brother'. Did you ever? What was he dejected about? Because these modern hussies expected all the chivalries from the male sex and yet expected to be on equal terms with them. Rights had never worried Mrs Barrowfield much. She didn't know what they were talking about. But there would be nothing dejected about *her* treatment of these shameless besoms: A good skelping from their fathers was what they were all needing. That behaviour like this should be happening in what was nearly the year 1871! She would just like to know what the Queen thought of it all!

Criminal Judge of London Court deprives two pickpockets of their Christmas dinner. And quite right too.

War Victims' Fund. A Glasgow meeting to raise funds to help the women and children of France in their terrible plight had met with discouraging response. Poor things! It was terrible for them. Mrs Barrowfield immediately forgot them as Maggie appeared with the breakfast.

She sat up yet higher, buttered her toast, poured out her tea and took a sip.

Serious Railway Accident at Port Glasgow. Dear me! That was terrible too!

Nice ham they were getting just now.

The War. Great Battle in the North: Sortie from Paris. What was a sortie? Additional details. This war news was really very difficult to follow. Besides, she was perfectly certain the newspapers exaggerated it just to get more sales.

The Mont Cenis Tunnel had been completed for a distance of 12,215 metres. (Why couldn't they say yards or miles or inches?) And only five now remained to be pierced. A banquet was to be held in the tunnel to solemnize the completion of the event. Fancy! In a tunnel. Had they no nice hotels at one end or the other where they could sit down in comfort? But you never knew with foreigners what they would be up to.

The stock market was very quiet, but prices were steady. That was good. Consols were at 91¾ per cent. Railways were firm.

She took a last look through the pages.

Last Days of the Art Union Draw. She had three tickets. It would be nice if she got a picture. She would give it to Bel for her new house. Young marrieds couldn't afford things like pictures.

Mr Charles Hallé, pianist, and Madame Norman Neruda, violinist, were giving a recital in the Queen's Rooms. Well, she would *not* be there. No one would catch her going right away up to the very edge of the town to sit among the hoity-toities from Park Circus and Royal Crescent. She liked a bit of music you could tap your toes to. But these devil's trills were not for sensible people. Bel and her husband had gone once or twice when they were courting. It was nice to think of them going. For her Bel could hold her head as high and look as fine as any of

your newfangled ladies in the West End! And very plain porridge they had come from, some of these very ladies! Mrs
Barrowfield smiled to think what some of them would have
thought of their grandfathers.

3

While she was dressing comfortably before her fire, a note was
brought by a messenger.

DEAR MAMA
The funeral is today, as we expected. Arthur and all the others have
just gone. I offered to go too, but Arthur wouldn't hear of it. He said
it would be much too exhausting for me at present. I have invited
them all to come here for tea, but I shall be alone all day before they
get back. Would you like to come up and have dinner with me – just
the two of us alone? Or are you still busy with your Christmas
shopping? Try to come.
Your loving daughter,
BEL

Mrs Barrowfield had had every intention of going to her daughter this morning, but the letter pleased her. It was affectionate
and, from its tone, she judged that Bel would be amenable to
reason.

And it said nothing about her husband's little half-sister,
Phoebe Moorhouse, who was the cause of all the trouble. Perhaps
Bel was now taking a less emotional view of the child's situation.
After all, children had been left orphans often before. And in
much less pleasant circumstances.

Mrs Barrowfield hurried into her clothes, intent upon walking
across the town to Ure Place where her daughter lived.

At ten o'clock she was out on the pavement in front of Monteith Row, wondering which way she would take. There was
bright winter sunshine now. The Green was white with hoar-
frost. Windows here and there glittered in the sunlight. Mrs
Barrowfield stood for a moment looking up and down the Row
itself – that handsome block of flats and front-door houses – that
had, when she was yet a growing girl, been built to be the most
exclusive terrace of Regency Glasgow, overlooking Glasgow's
Hyde Park. But now the prestige of the Row was sinking. The
industrial princes had forsaken it twenty years ago, escaping into
the prevailing west wind from the smoke of these, their own
factory chimneys. And the famous Green itself, that had played
so great a part in Glasgow's story, was sinking too. Covered with

smuts, it was fast turning into a mere lung in the centre of an ever-growing mid-Victorian City.

But Monteith Row had not yet fallen to nothing. For middle-class people who liked a well-built place and were not too snobbish – for people like old Mrs Barrowfield, in short, who put comfort and convenience before an exclusive address – it was, at this stage of its history, just the right place.

On this bright morning, however, many uglier corners of the town had taken on a glamour. The frost and the sunshine had, for the time, obliterated all suggestion of smoke and squalor. In spite of her preoccupation, Mrs Barrowfield's spirits rose. She set off briskly. She was a big woman who had, as yet, lost none of her vigour. Iron-grey curls and a bonnet tied with broad flying ribbons. Rather too pronounced, masculine features. Large hands thrust into a small, tight muff. Swaying crinolines, for she refused to be new-fashioned. A sealskin jacket, elastic-sided boots. She moved along the pavement, a galleon in full sail.

At the end of the Row she wondered if she should continue along London Road and thus go direct, but sunshine like this was rare in winter, so, deciding to remain in it longer, she turned along Greendyke Street.

No. She had made up her mind to talk to her daughter straightly. Why should Bel rush to take little Phoebe Moorhouse into her home? She wasn't even her husband's full sister. Indeed, Arthur hardly knew her. It was after he had left the farm to come to Glasgow that his father's second marriage had taken place. And, so far as she knew, none of the Moorhouse family had ever liked their stepmother. Arthur had told Mrs Barrowfield what he knew of her. She had been a wild Highland woman of forty – handsome, lithe and silent – who had come to the farm as a housekeeper. In a year she had married old Moorhouse and in a year more had borne him this daughter.

And now, only on Wednesday, driving home from a neighbouring farm late in the night, old Moorhouse's pony had bolted and hurled the couple to disaster. The old man was killed at once. The woman had lived until Thursday.

And Bel hearing of the disaster in her mother's presence – and what to Mrs Barrowfield was much more serious, in the presence of her brother- and sisters-in-law – had exclaimed: 'This is terrible! And poor wee Phoebe! Listen, Arthur, I won't hear of anything else. Phoebe's to be sent up here to me. I won't allow the child to be without a mother.'

Mrs Barrowfield had known it was no use talking at the time – indeed, it would have been unseemly – but she considered that Bel's heroics had been simply ridiculous. Moreover, she had seen the momentary glint in Sophia Butter's eye. As though to say: 'Bel, dear, that's the kind of highfalutin that takes a lot of getting out of!' And Bel's mother knew that Bel hated climbing down, just as Bel's father had done.

4

Old Mrs Barrowfield stamped furiously along Greendyke Street. Why should Bel take the child? The farm would go to Mungo, the oldest brother, of course. The child could go on living there. What was to stop her? He was thirty-five and a bachelor, but probably he would marry now, and his wife would have to look after the child. Why should her handsome daughter Bel, for whom she had every ambition, be worried by a gawky farm-child? It was all very well being sympathetic. But there were limits. She preferred to think of her daughter sitting fragrant and Madonna-like, awaiting the advent of her firstborn. Not fagging round after what might turn out to be a very troublesome girl of ten.

She had left the Greendyke now and had come into the Saltmarket. So intent was she upon her thoughts that she was quite unaware that a barefoot urchin had emerged from a vennel and was following her, begging.

'Gie's a ha'penny, lady. Gie's a ha'penny.'

At last she noticed him. Barefoot on this cold winter morning and filthy. The people in this neighbourhood were almost beasts! Drunken, brutish and undersized. It was, indeed, only on bright mornings such as this that she would venture up the Saltmarket. On rare occasions when she spent the evening at Bel's or elsewhere, she took care to come home in a cab – or at all events accompanied by a man. Ladies always avoided the wynds and vennels, of course. It was not genteel to know much about them. But this old woman's husband had told her. A doctor must go where others did not.

'Gie's a ha'penny, lady.'

She walked on.

Suddenly memory flared up vividly in the mind of this rather smug, not very imaginative woman.

She saw her husband sitting exhausted and beaten after a long and indescribably squalid midnight confinement in one of these terrible places. It was not his custom, as an established doctor, to take such work, but this time – to help an overworked younger colleague – he had gone.

'I tell ye, ma dear, it's an abominable blot on the honour of the town. It's a wonder the Lord God doesn't strike all the well-to-do folks of Glasgow with His thunderbolts of wrath!'

'Gie's a ha'penny, lady.'

Well, it was Christmas. And, when you came to think of it, this child beside her must be human too. She took her purse from her muff and gave him a sixpence. Without a word, he snatched at it, thrust it into a filthy little waistcoat pocket, turned a cart-wheel with the agility of an ape and disappeared.

Mrs Barrowfield walked on, indignant for a moment at the conditions that should bring such a gruesome little creature into existence, only to become a danger to more worthy people. Why did they allow these places? Glasgow was rich!

But the conscience of this comfortable Victorian city was stirring. The City Improvements Trust had come into being and was taking thought. And more potent still than conscience, perhaps, vested interest, in the shape of a railway company, had thrown a bridge across the Clyde and was continuing its arches over the Briggate and through the very worst of these dens, forcing much to be pulled down that should long since have gone. The Royal Hand that signed away the old College of Lister, Watt and Kelvin to make a drab goods station, was also signing the death-warrant of scores of these earthly hells. And now there was talk of a great terminal station on the north side of the Clyde, with an hotel of a luxury unparalleled in Scotland, facing St Enoch's Square. That would inevitably demolish a great many more of these places.

At the Cross the old lady halted, looking about her. The clock in the Tolbooth Steeple stood at the quarter past. People were lounging about in the sunlight. As there was but little traffic, she crossed over to look at the Christmas display in the windows of Millar's warehouse on the corner of the Gallowgate and High Street. Presently she turned and looked up, wondering if, on her way to Ure Place, she should go on up the hill past the doomed College, or along past the Tontine and up Candleriggs. She took the latter course. There were shops in the Trongate she might have a look at. As she passed the equestrian statue of King William III, she smiled to herself, remembering that her son-in-law's brother David Moorhouse – who thought himself a wag – had

28

told her that the King's horse was a wise beast, that, bronze though it might be, it knew to wag its tail at every Irishman.

But presently her thoughts were on Bel once more. No, it was preposterous. The child might have a very bad influence over the grandchild who was coming. Country children were so coarse and uncontrolled.

'Guid-day, Mum.'

She was in the Candleriggs now, passing the business premises of her son-in-law.

'Oh, good-morning.' She cast an appraising eye through the open door. Everything very neat, she must say. The stock was carefully arranged and tidy.

'Mr Moorhouse would not be here this morning?' she said, to make a moment's conversation with Arthur's man.

'No, Mum. It's terrible aboot his faither.'

'Yes, terrible. The funeral's today, of course. Good-morning.'

'Guid-day.'

At first she hadn't much liked the idea of Bel, a doctor's daughter, marrying a wholesale cheese merchant. But Bel had been twenty-four and it was time she was marrying someone. She, her mother, had had to suffer all the disgrace of spinsterhood until she was thirty-nine (she still regarded it as an intervention from heaven that she had emerged triumphant in the end), and she had had a horror at the thought of her daughter being among the unwanted. She herself had known everything there was to know of patronage from securely wedded and copiously fecund.

Besides, the Moorhouse boys, although they were farmer's sons, had a strange air of breeding. As though a lacing of blue blood flowed in their honest Ayrshire veins. Perhaps a young aristocrat a generation or two back. But if there was a story Mrs Barrowfield had never heard it. Victorian propriety forbade.

5

At the head of the Candleriggs she crossed over to the pavement in front of the Ramshorn Kirk, reflecting for an instant that her own parents were buried over there in the churchyard. In a second or two more she was in Montrose Street and making her way up the hill.

She was breathless as she rang her daughter's door-bell. For the upper part of Montrose Street was very steep and Ure Place was almost at the top of it. It had once come into her mind that her son-in-law had fixed his house in a place that was difficult of access to an elderly woman so that he need not see too much of her, but her common sense told her that Arthur's mind could not jump to such subtleties. He was much too straightforward.

Five minutes more found her sitting by the fire in her daughter's pleasant plush parlour, sipping a glass of sherry wine and eating a piece of black bun. Her bonnet, with its dangling ribbons, was laid aside with her sealskin jacket and muff and she was looking pleasantly about her.

'Well, dear, it's nice to have ye to myself for a day. What a terrible hill that is! I'm all peching.'

'Yes, Mama. But it's convenient for Arthur up here. He can drop straight down to his work. The steepness is nothing to him.'

Mrs Barrowfield smiled at the bride's pride in her husband's vigour.

Bel was looking wonderful. Her tall fairness was enhanced by the unrelieved black of her mourning. In her wide, unrevealing dress she was still elegant. Admiration and ambition for her prompted her mother's next words.

'I hope before long you can move out to the West.'

Bel, though she was fully at one with her mother, merely said: 'It's very far away for Arthur.'

'Nonsense. I hear Menzies is running his Tartan Buses to the Kirklee now. I'm not suggesting as far out as that, of course. But you could go out to the Great Western Road somebit near the Kelvin Bridge. You could even go up the hill into the Hillhead. And with the new University being nearly finished out there, it's bound to turn out a very nice district.'

A vision of polite calls and pleasant, intellectual converse in professors' drawing-rooms rose for a moment in Bel's mind.

But 'We'll have to make more money first,' was all she said as she settled down on the opposite side of the fire from her mother. 'Besides,' she went on as she took up her sewing, 'the people out there would be much too grand and brainy for Arthur and me.' She did not say this because she believed it for one moment. For Bel had a fine conceit of herself. It was merely to fish from her mother a little comforting praise.

But all she got was a complacent 'Not them'.

Mrs Barrowfield had no fears for her daughter's social abilities when they should be put to the test. Had not Bel been sent for years to a very reputable establishment for young ladies in St Andrew's Square? If she herself still held in part to the speech and homely manners of earlier days, she had seen to it that her child should speak pure English and observe the modern elegances.

She noticed that Bel was making something for her baby. A good moment to appeal to her, perhaps. But she approached the topic warily.

'So the funeral is today?'

'Yes.'

They spoke of this for some moments. How the accident had happened. How the pony had stumbled, then, frightened, had dashed ahead, out of control, along the ice-bound road. Arthur's stepmother had been able to explain before she died.

Mrs Barrowfield listened to these things with perfunctory interest. Old Moorhouse and his wife were nothing to her. At length, at what she deemed to be the right moment, she said:

'You didn't mean to take Phoebe, did you, Bel?'

'Yes, Mama, I think so.'

'Whatway, can she not stay at the farm?'

'I can't allow Arthur's sister to grow up like a farm-servant.'

Her mother's inward comment was fiddle-de-dee, but she said: 'She's got her brother, Mungo.'

'He's a single man. Besides, although he's the oldest, Arthur and I are really at the head of the family.'

There was Bel at it again, giving herself airs. Her mother looked across at her severely. 'Bel, mind, you've got yourselves to think of. And what's more, you've got your own bairns to think of. For all you know, Phoebe Moorhouse may be a thrawn wee besom. Have you thought what you're doing?'

'Yes, Mama. I've thought. And besides, the old man made Arthur her guardian because he was a business man and knew about money.'

The old woman pricked her ears. 'Money? But the bairn has no money.'

'Well, of course, it would make no difference if she hadn't, Mama, but as it happens she has. It won't be much, but enough to educate her, we expect. The old man had little outside his farm stock, but what there was goes to her.'

Mrs Barrowfield was deeply interested. Perhaps Bel was nearer her house out West than it might appear. All her worry had, perhaps, been over nothing! With the girl's money—

'And you see how it is, Mama. Arthur has the responsibility for her anyway. It would be much better if we had her here under our eye.'

A benign smile suffused Mrs Barrowfield's features.

'You're your father's bairn, my dear. Aye thinking about doing good to somebody else,' she said.

'Actually, it's to be settled this evening when they all come back,' Bel said.

Chapter 4

I

It was all strange and very unnatural. Yet little Phoebe Moorhouse was by no means struck down by her double bereavement. As was the custom, her elders thought it right that the child should be taken to look upon her dead. The first time, her oldest brother Mungo had taken her by the hand and led her into the eerie, familiar room where her parents lay. Her father's face frightened her at first. He looked so old, so pinched, so yellow. But her mother lay like serene marble, with her white, well-shaped face and her raven-black hair parted in the middle as she had always worn it in life.

Phoebe had clung to Mungo's hand.

But soon she had gone back into the room with her friends, the women servants, Gracie and Jean, who had wept a great deal, and, Phoebe could not help thinking, with a contemptible lack of control. And presently she found herself taking those who came to pay their respects into the chamber of death without any emotion other than a feeling of importance.

The physical aspect, the appearance of her parents as they lay there, quickly came to have no effect upon her, for already, at the age of ten, this country child had seen the death of so many animals, just as she had seen their birth, and she had long since accepted both phenomena without being unduly stirred.

In life, her father and mother had been so remote, so for each other, that the pulsing existence of the farm, with its friendships and quarrels, had, for the great part, gone on without them. Even their daughter had not broken through the invisible ring that seemed to be about them.

Phoebe had grieved more bitterly when the beloved servant into whose charge she was given as a baby, who had tended her in her first years, had finally married and gone away.

Now, in the darkened farmhouse in her new black dress, she tiptoed about, feeling her consequence as the chief mourner, and accepted all the abnormal petting and notice she was receiving with pleasure and complacency.

Then Mungo told her that these other half-brothers and sisters that she scarcely knew were coming to the funeral.

She had only had fleeting looks at them, and that, not for a year or two. What each looked like was half-imagined, half-remembered. It would be exciting to see them again. She had caught herself wondering recently why they did not come often. Indeed, she had gone the length of asking her mother, but the Highland woman had merely laughed, a remote, wry laugh, the meaning of which this child of ten could not guess. But now she was to see them and she was all agog.

2

They arrived. Some with Mungo in the trap, some in the only cab that served the village station. She had pushed back a lowered blind and watched the two vehicles coming in the winter sunshine up the ice-bound road. By the time they had gained the top of the hill and were rounding the farm buildings to come into the more convenient yard, Phoebe, if she had dared do anything so unseemly, would have danced with excitement.

Then, suddenly, she felt shy.

'Here, they're comin'. Come on.'

Jean had come to look for her. Phoebe was glad to take the dairymaid's large red hand as they both went together to the door opening on the yard.

Arthur and David were in the trap with Mungo. They were all jumping down. A farm-hand was holding the pony's head. How pale and distinguished these brothers from the City looked, with their shining top-hats, their long black overcoats and black gloves!

Arthur looked like a white-faced, fine-boned Mungo, with his prominent, well-cut features and his mutton-chop whiskers. Mungo's muscles were lusty and developed from a life of labouring in the open air. His body was burly and strong, with no claims to elegance. Sun and wind had given his face a dark, enduring tan. Yet his likeness to this brother, two years younger than himself, was very definite.

David was quite different. At twenty-three he still looked boyish. Phoebe noticed that his light hair curled pleasantly beneath his black hat, and when he took this off and bent down to kiss his little sister, she saw how clear his skin was and how attractive his eyes.

Arthur kissed her too and said: 'Well, Phoebe, how are you?' Then seemed to think of nothing else to say. But the awkwardness could not last, for all three brothers must turn to help the ladies from the cab.

Her half-sisters were very grand ladies indeed. Far grander, say, than Miss Smith, the retired schoolmistress in the village where Phoebe, along with a dozen other well-to-do children, was sent for morning lessons in preference to the rough-and-tumble of the village school. Far grander than the banker's daughters, who helped with the singing in church. Grander, even, than the minister's wife, who was old and – for a little girl – intensely uninteresting.

Sophia got out first and came straight across to her.

'And is this wee Phoebe? How are you keeping, dear? You know, the last time I saw you, you were only half the height. About the height that Wil and Margy are now.' Sophia bent down too and kissed her little sister. It took Phoebe a moment to remember who Wil and Margy were.

Mary pushed back her black veil and bent down too, putting her arms round her. How calm and blue her eyes seemed! And she smelt of lavender. 'Well, deary? Here are your big sisters to look after you.'

Mary was so elegant in her well-made black clothes and her furs. And indeed – by what Phoebe knew of elegance – Sophia did not come so far behind her.

She suddenly became acutely conscious of her black serge dress, hastily put together by the village dressmaker, her home-knitted black woollen stockings and her sturdy country boots.

But the child's steady little mind was not long in summing up her sisters. Sophia was big and fussy and chattered without ceasing about her own children. But somehow she seemed more spontaneously kind than Mary, whose more ostentatious goodness appeared to be so consciously controlled.

Of their husbands, Phoebe took little note. They were just stolid male things in black that you shook hands with, then dismissed from your mind.

There was hot soup for all the travellers and a 'dram' for the men, for the midday meal would take place later, after the funeral. But before they had this, the brothers and sisters requested to see the last of their father.

The child, lynx-eyed and curious, followed them into the room. Mary and Sophia were weeping dutifully, bending over his face as he lay ready in his coffin. Arthur and David stood solemnly by, with set faces. Mungo, accustomed, stood behind merely waiting.

Suddenly a flame of resentment flared inside Phoebe. They were all looking at her father. Not one of them was thinking of her mother as she lay there so quiet, calm as she had always been, and, to her thinking, beautiful. On the woman's breast lay a posy of very early snowdrops, grown under a frame in a sunny corner of the minister's garden. The minister's wife had sent them to Phoebe, who had tied them up together with some ivy leaves and put them where they lay. It seemed an affront to herself that they should appear to take no thought for her mother. She was still too young to understand their embarrassment.

Tears sprang into Phoebe's eyes – tears of pride and resentment. For a moment she stood alone beside her mother's coffin, weeping.

It was Arthur who noticed first. He took her tears for uncomplicated childish sorrow. But he came to her, put his hand in her own, and thus remained beside her until the others were ready to go.

From this time on, it was to be Arthur Moorhouse who was to be first of all the family in his half-sister's strange affections. Even before Mungo, whom she had known all her life.

3

People were coming for the service now, and presently the minister and the laird, Sir Charles Ruanthorpe, were there.

The service took place in the Room. This was the sitting-room of the farm – a room of tassels, horsehair, stiff chairs, antimacassars and Cupid ornaments. Unlike the other rooms of this prosperous farmhouse, the Room did not pulse with life. It was merely a dead ceremonial chamber where, in the days before their father's remarriage, the two sisters had given occasional formal tea-parties for such friends as were too genteel to eat in the much

35

more welcoming kitchen. Where, if the laird or his lady called, they were thrust to sit uncomfortably looking about them, while the farmer's wife flew to tidy herself and to look hastily into her supplies of cake and wine. For years it had given Phoebe much quiet rapture to tiptoe into the darkened Room – the blinds were always down to keep things from fading – and to stand solemnly admiring its aloof splendour.

But now the Room was full to overflowing with black-coated, white-tied men – most of them neighbouring farmers and known to her.

She felt herself wanting to run about to see everything that was happening, but Sophia and Mary sat by the kitchen fire and seemed to expect her to do the same.

At last, when all were there, they rose and, each taking one of her hands, led her into the Room, where places had been kept for them. But Phoebe did not want to sit between her sisters. She wanted to sit between Jean and Gracie, who were wiping red eyes with the backs of their great hands. So, ignoring the chair that was set for her, she wedged herself between her two friends, and, as this was no time nor place for remonstrance, succeeded in remaining.

Except that the minister kept talking about 'these, our dear brother and sister' or addressed the Divinity concerning 'these, Thy son and daughter', Phoebe decided that the whole thing was rather like church, only at home.

Yet, when the service was over and the child, watching once more from a window, saw the coffins borne out, the procession of mourners forming up and the whole beginning solemnly to move away, she ran to her room, threw herself down on her bed and wept bitterly.

Chapter 5

I

Bel had sent her mother home in a cab as it began to get dark, which at Christmas-time in Glasgow is before four o'clock in the afternoon. In these days there was no question of an elderly or, indeed, any lady walking alone at night in any of the streets that converged at Glasgow Cross. The wretched creatures from the wynds and vennels poured themselves forth from their dens, and, as something like every third shop in such streets as the Briggate and the Saltmarket was a drinking-shop, most of them were drunk. Some of them roaring, some fighting, some of them collapsed in huddled masses in the gutter – men and women.

The better people tried not to think of them. And succeeded on the whole very well. You did not go near a sewer. Why be contaminated? It was the passionate, imaginative few who tried to effect changes for the better. It was those afflicted with highly uncomfortable consciences who could not but see these poor victims of a too hastily improvised industrial era as the possessors of bodies and intellects that nature had once intended to be sound and wholesome like their own. These conscience-ridden people, pointing the way back to the most elementary common sense, have since done away with the worst of Glasgow's slums and raised the descendants of these human vermin to something nearer decency and normality.

Bel was quite aware that her mother was not too anxious for her to take her brother's little half-sister into her house. But she had been careful not to say a word that would tie her in one way or another. Her mother and her sisters-in-law had heard her first, quite unconsidered outburst of pity for the little orphan. And she was determined to leave it at that meantime.

On the doorstep, the old lady, remembering that Phoebe's future was to be discussed by the Moorhouse family that evening at Bel's, and tortured to know whether the amount of money coming to the child would make it worth while Bel taking her or not, had kissed her daughter and said: 'Now don't do anything in haste, Bel.'

'Do you mean about Phoebe?'

'Yes.'

'I'll do whatever's right, Mother. Goodbye, dear. Arthur and I will come down in the morning and bring you your Christmas present before we go to church. Don't keep the poor cabman waiting. It's so cold.'

When people – especially highfalutin people like her own daughter – said they were going to do whatever was right, there was no use talking to them, old Mrs Barrowfield reflected, beaten. Whatever was right left a vast margin for doing what you, personally, wanted to do. You could, she reflected further, call almost anything right, if you argued hard enough.

But Bel was quite determined not to be dominated any more by her old and domineering mother. It was much pleasanter to be dominated by a husband. She had had twenty-four years of the first kind of domination, and was determined to have no more of it. She was still recently enough married to feel a pleasant feminine thrill – a subtle flattery of her womanhood – when Arthur laid down the law to her. It was, she felt, as though she were fulfilling a wifely function.

She stood at her open door now, looking after her mother's cab. In a few seconds it turned back up into the Rotten Row, for the driver could not trust his horse to go down the steep, slippery cobbles of Montrose Street, and had determined to choose one of the streets further west, where the incline was less abrupt. She took a few paces along the pavement and looked down Montrose Street itself. The hum and lights of the City came up to her. The noise and traffic of George Street. The view of endless roofs. The roofs of the Athenaeum. Hutcheson's Hospital. The roof of the hotel on George's Square where the law lords lived when they came to Glasgow. The spires of the Ramshorn Church and Free St Matthew's, and, further over, the Tolbooth Steeple. Yet further the spire of the Old Merchants' Hall. It was getting dark, and there was some fog. She hoped the train from Ayrshire would not be held up by it. With a little shiver she turned back and shut her front door. The house was cosy and pleasant. It still gave the eight-month bride a little thrill to feel it was her own – its decoration, its arrangement, everything – for Arthur was a busy man and had left things in her hands.

She must go and see what the maids had done about the tea-table, for in these days – as indeed still, for the greater part of middle-class Glasgow, though its social status keeps ever sinking – high tea, elaborate and triumphantly lavish, is the focal point of the day.

The table was groaning with bread, several kinds of scones,

cakes, large and small, fancy and plain, a variety of jams, and much else, all of which were to follow two sumptuously rich cooked dishes.

Bel cast an appraising eye about her. Well, it would be as good a tea as ever Mary produced out West at Albany Place, and certainly more lavish than Sophia's efforts across at Grafton Square. She had no intention of being outdone by her sisters-in-law.

She felt very pleased with herself. It was nice to remember that she was a doctor's daughter, and that Sophia and Mary were the daughters of a mere farmer. It was nice for her to think that Arthur had certainly taken no step down by marrying her. What if her mother was a little downright? You didn't expect your parents to have the polish they had been able to give you. And when it came to the education of her own children, she would see to it that their advantages would well exceed what her own had been.

Like all middle-class Glasgow at this time, Bel – like a thousand other Bels and Arthurs in the City – was on the up-grade.

2

Mary and George arrived first with Arthur. They came direct from the station, since the McNairns had decided that it would take too long to go out to their house at Albany Place and then come back again into town. But, on the platform, Sophia announced that she would be quite unable to touch her evening meal, until she knew her children were back home from their visit to the McNairn cousins and safe. There had, she said, been so many cases lately of children being waylaid and robbed of their clothing. So, in spite of protests from Arthur that nothing could befall them in that quarter of the town, and escorted as they would be, and that there was no possible reason for keeping waiting several people fatigued by cold and hunger and the emotional trials of a long day, she went, taking her inarticulate husband with her.

'I won't really be any time at all, dears,' she had clucked. 'And it would be a comfort to you too, wouldn't it, Mary dear, to know that Wil and Margy had left your children well and happy?'

Mary felt that, somewhere, there was the sting of a reproof hidden in these words – a hint that she was showing a lack of interest in her own children, but though she was exhausted like the others, and a little out of temper, she controlled herself,

39

merely smiled with that saintly smile of hers, and said with a voice that was all kindness: 'Of course. But don't be any longer than you possibly need to be, dear. The boys are hungry. Besides, I don't think we should keep Bel waiting,' and thus, having re-established herself as the soul of consideration for everybody, she preceded two impatient brothers and her own large, portly boy into the cab that was to take them to Ure Place.

'We might have taken Sophia and William part of the way,' she said, when once the four were fairly started.

Her own husband said nothing. But Arthur snapped: 'Not at all. It'll do the Butters no harm to pay for themselves once in a while. Besides, it serves Sophia right for being a fool.'

So, apart from drawing David's attention to the reflection of the moon on the river as they crossed Glasgow Bridge, Mary said no more. If the poor boys were tired, she, the most understanding of women, would certainly be the last one to worry them with talk.

Bel, all concern for their comfort, received the four of them with roaring fires, and, what was better still, she had mixed a bowl of toddy which was fragrant and hot, and which did wonders in soothing everybody's bad temper. Even Mary was persuaded to have a sip or two, and as the colour came back into her beautiful calm face, she was pleased to find herself thinking how, in spite of minor defects, perhaps her new sister-in-law was just the very wife for Arthur, and was turning out splendidly.

Her husband, George McNairn, taking rather more than his share, actually revived enough to joke ponderously with his sister-in-law, and determined that Bel was a damned fine-looking young woman, full of life and mettle. He regretted to himself a little that his own wife – while flinching in no way from her duty – should always be so passive and saintly in their more conjugal moments.

David put his arm round Bel's shoulder, kissed her and said she was a dear, and Arthur glowed with pride and satisfaction.

In other words, Bel's toddy quite dissipated the exasperation these tired and hungry people were beginning to feel at the prospect of being kept waiting by Sophia's over-developed feel-ings of maternity. Indeed, its success was such that Sophia and William – themselves exhausted and breathless – were finally shown into a room where, though all, of course, was decorum, a distinct atmosphere of conviviality reigned round an empty bowl. And their annoyance was not lessened by the fact that no sooner had they arrived than the starched housemaid, Sarah, rang the tea-bell in the hall, and Arthur said: 'Come on, everybody, there's tea,' giving Bel no opening whatever to make amends for the toddy being finished.

'Wil and Margy enjoyed themselves very much, Mary.' Sophia looked at her sister coldly as she took her place at the table.

'I'm glad, dear.' Mary was positively benign.

Sophia waited in a condition of extreme self-righteousness to see if Mary would really not bother to ask after her own children, and, finding that she did not, she said triumphantly: 'Jessie, my new girl, who went with them, said that your children were looking splendid, Mary.'

'They were looking very healthy this morning, Sophia – vulgarly healthy,' George McNairn said, wolfing his food with relish.

But Bel, detecting wisps of venom floating in the air, called upon Sophia to decide upon the relative merits of tappit hen and steak pie – and if she cared for neither of these, then the cold ham was on the sideboard – and thus succeeded in clearing the atmosphere for the time being.

3

'Do you know, it's funny to think,' she began presently, when her guests had emerged from their meal a little, the first hunger sated, 'but I've only seen Mungo once, and that was at my wedding, when I wasn't in a fit state to notice anybody very much. And little Phoebe was ill then, and didn't come. It's queer that I should know you all so well, and yet that you should have a brother and sister I don't know at all.'

'Mungo's coming up in the first week of the New Year. He's bringing Phoebe with him. They're coming here,' Arthur said.

'I'll be delighted to see them,' Bel said, knowing well that two pairs of feminine Moorhouse eyes were upon her.

'We would have been delighted to have them, Bel dear. Are you sure – situated as you are? Arthur hasn't said anything to me about this,' Mary interposed.

'No, of course they'll come here. I expect you've family business to discuss with Mungo, haven't you, Arthur?'

Arthur said, well, yes – there was some business to discuss.

'Of course, any of us would be delighted to see them.' Sophia came in comfortably at the end of the race.

But all the reply she got from Bel was: 'Now try one of these sponge cakes, Sophia, they're very light.'

'I thought Phoebe wasn't very well behaved today. Didn't you think so too, Mary?' Sophia said, having embarked upon a sponge cake as she was bidden.

'A little unfriendly perhaps,' Mary answered – agreeing, but softening the accusation.

'Well, considering what was going on, you could scarcely expect her to behave as usual,' David said.

'It wasn't that,' Sophia continued. 'No. She didn't seem particularly upset, which was queer too, now I come to think of it. But there were Mary and I, her own sisters, ready to be a comfort to her, and yet she seemed to be always trying to get away from us.'

'She struck me as rather a cold child,' Mary added. 'But of course it may have been shyness.'

'Why should she be shy of us?' Sophia said.

'Because, if you had any sense, Sophia, you would see that sisters or not sisters, you were perfect strangers to her,' David snapped.

Sophia ignored this. 'Do you know,' she went on, turning to Bel, 'she wouldn't sit with us during the funeral service, although there was a place for her, of course.'

'And where did she sit?' Bel asked. She had been listening to this conversation with great interest.

'I don't know,' Sophia said aloofly.

'She stood between two of the servants – byre-women, I think they were,' David said. And as Bel seemed to want him to say more, he added: 'One of them had an arm round her. The other was holding her hand.'

A look of gentleness on Bel's face thanked David for making the situation clear. Her young brother-in-law had given her a vivid, moving picture of the little girl. Why had the Moorhouse men so much more intuition than the women? Had Mary, with all her ostentatious goodness, been unable to see that the child was trying to find comfort from familiar people, to steady herself in the face of the great change that had come into her life?

'The bairn was feeling it. Don't you make any mistake,' Arthur said.

'Well, I would be sorry to think that Wil and Margy would behave like that if anything happened to William and me. While we were waiting for the men to come back from the cemetery, she went to her own room and wouldn't come out of it. They could scarcely get her to come and say goodbye,' Sophia went on.

'When *my* father died' – Bel's voice sounded a little tart – 'Mother tells me I missed him very much, and the way I showed it was by being very naughty.'

'Our stepmother was a strange, cold sort of woman.' Mary felt she didn't quite see the point in Bel's naughtiness being put forward in defence of Phoebe's.

Bel was angry now. Mary was just as lacking in understanding as Sophia. There were moments in life when you had to take definite steps – whether they turned out rightly or wrongly. Moments when the hand had to be stretched forth to a fellow-being without counting the cost. This child was needing mothering – needing understanding – more understanding than her two smug half-sisters could give her. Bel's impulsiveness got the better of her once again. The colour was high in her face when she spoke.

'Well, at any rate, I've been thinking about Phoebe,' she said. 'I don't see how the child can stay at the farm without a woman of her own kind to look after her. If Arthur wants it, I'll be delighted to have her here.'

Old Mrs Barrowfield would have called this more highfalutin. She would have said: 'Let the child go to a sister.' 'Let her stay with her farmer brother.' Mary and Sophia, because, perhaps, they had been made to look mean and cold through their sister-in-law's offer to undertake a duty that both of them were determined to avoid, called this speech of Bel's – in their hearts – a mere piece of show-off.

But Arthur was glad that his wife should show his family that her blood ran redder and warmer than theirs, that prudence did not block the channels of her sympathy.

So Phoebe's future was settled without any discussion, after all.

Bel had taken the plunge, everybody felt, and good luck to her. Another five minutes of steady, reflective munching persuaded the McNairns and the Butters to drop any rancour their hearts might still hold, and decide that everything had been settled for the best.

'What perfectly delicious black bun!' Sophia said presently. 'Do you think, Bel dear, I could have a wee bit cut off to take home? William's old uncle and aunt are coming in for tea to see the children tomorrow and I haven't a scrap of black bun in the house. I don't know why we've been too busy to make it. But you know what old people are. They expect, at a time like Christmas, just to find all the usual things. Perhaps if you could spare—?'

Chapter 6

1

The winter afternoon was getting on as the train containing
Phoebe and Mungo beat its way along the last lap of the journey
towards Glasgow. Phoebe had never been in a train before. The
nearest she had got to it was when she went in the trap to the
station to meet her father or Mungo coming home from the
markets in Ayr or Kilmarnock. She had asked her mother if she
might not go with them one day, and her mother had put her off
by telling her that they would take her soon. But soon had gone
on receding ahead of her and nothing had happened. Once she
had driven in the trap some ten miles to Ayr, and her mother had
taken her down to wade in the sea, while her father had bought a
new cart-horse. That had been her furthest and most thrilling
journey.

Now she was on the way to Glasgow, large, magic and unknown, and she could not sit still for excitement. It was fortunate
that they had the carriage to themselves, for now that they had
passed Paisley and were speeding across the flat to the great City
– where her grand half-sisters and brothers lived, where, she had
been told, you could walk and walk and never get to the end of
the streets – she kept running from window to window, looking
at this and that, as her train went by. Distant spires. The boats on
the Glasgow–Johnstone canal – this house – this building –
everything excited her. Mungo sat staring a placid farmer's stare
out of the window, his handsome, weather-tanned face lighted by
the setting sun, and let his little sister jump to her heart's content.

Phoebe had left the farm with a mixture of feelings, but by far
the greatest of these was curiosity at what lay before her. She was
a child avid for experience, and she had so far known little of
fear. Gracie and Jean had packed her little black tin box for her.
Her simple and few things were washed and mended to per-
fection. For, decent souls, they were determined that that Mrs
Arthur to whom Phoebe was going should find nothing amiss in
the way they had tended her.

The child had hopped about, watching them. She kept asking
them endless questions. What would she do in Glasgow? What
kind of school would she go to? Would meals be at the same
time? Would she have to help Arthur with his business? That

would be fun – she would like that. Did it rain in Glasgow? No, they told her. There was a very large umbrella that the Lord Provost put up every time it rained, so that the town was always dry. She laughed at that. But who was the Lord Provost? And so on her questions went.

Strangely, she seemed to think little about the familiar things she was leaving. She had asked if she could come back on holiday, and Mungo had assured her that she might. That appeared to satisfy her. It was Glasgow that engrossed her.

But at their early midday meal today she had scarcely eaten anything. And when her box was lifted into the trap and she had made to jump up after it, suddenly the sight of Jean and Gracie weeping at the door into the drugget aprons had touched her, and she had run back to them as they stood there and clung to them one after the other, inhaling from them the familiar farm smells of cows and chopped winter feeding, of soap and their own wholesome bodies.

Yet presently she was done with all that and was waving to them valiantly as the pony clattered along the road, causing the farm to shrink into the distance.

2

Now she was at the station. Mungo was buying tickets. Third-class tickets. One for himself and – oh, unbelievable thrill – one for her. What were the glorious people like who travelled first- and second-class? Now the porter had rung his big brass bell. Now the great engine was bearing down upon them. Now the carriages came alongside. This time she was to have a place and was to be allowed to climb in. Now they were off! Trees and houses were rushing past her. Suddenly everything was wiped out. Darkness! The Mossgiel tunnel!

The railway tunnel that pierces the rolling uplands of a farm that once was ploughed by the hand that wrote 'The Cottar's Saturday Night'. But to Phoebe it was just 'the tunnel' she had heard them talk of. In the darkness she sat close to Mungo. Now another station, a different porter, a different bell. Now Kilmarnock where the men came to market. How busy it was! How anxious people seemed to get themselves into the train! There was another girl of her own age. What nice clothes she was wearing! Phoebe wished she would come in so that she could have a look at them. 'Looking for the first-class, Mum?' A porter spoke to the lady who was with her. 'Further up the train, Mum.' So it was people like that who went first-class. Should she herself be looking like that? Would Bel, whom she had never seen, object to her wearing such a plain black dress? But she liked Arthur. She felt Arthur wouldn't mind. Besides, Arthur had seen her in this very dress at the funeral. Here was another station. There was a sheet of water. What was that, Mungo, a loch? Yes. A loch. Now Paisley. Busy and much like Kilmarnock. Now they were away again. They would soon be in Glasgow. Was the station at Glasgow bigger than the ones at Paisley and Kilmarnock? Yes. Mungo thought it was. Now houses and streets and endless backyards. There was fog a little and endless strings of lighted lamps. Was this Glasgow now? Yes. The train was slowing down. It had stopped. A porter was running along opening all the doors. A big porter with a bushy beard shouting in an accent that was Highland, like her mother's, 'Bridge Street'. He offered to help with the box, but Mungo paid no attention. He reached up and got it down for himself.

Everybody was getting out. Was she to get out too? Yes, of course. Jean had told her to see that she kept her gloves on. That it was more genteel. She had taken them off, but now she hauled them on again over paws that were dirty from the carriage. Little black ones that Jean had knitted herself. She jumped out. What crowds! What a noise of puffing, of steam! What shouting! A fat lady had come to meet another fat lady! What a fuss they were making! *There* was the child she had seen at Kilmarnock! Yes. Her clothes *were* nice. But her face looked petted – or, as Jean would have said, thrawn. Here was Arthur running up the platform! He was all hot with running.

3

'Hello! I thought I was going to be late.' He was giving Mungo his hand and bending down to kiss her. Once more she liked the look of this brother, and felt reassured at the thought of going to stay with him.

A porter had seized her black box and was marching down with the main stream to the entrance. Phoebe looked up at the flares of gas burning in the station, although the daylight was not yet altogether gone. Suddenly she realized that she was walking under great roofs of glass! She could count three of them! She was walking in a great glass-house! They were through the barrier. What a wide stair leading down into the street! And what a busy street! Arthur said it was Clyde Place. And there was the

Clyde! He called her attention to two great steamers, their paddle-boxes gleaming with golden paint, lying against the other bank. That was the Broomielaw, where the steamers were. One of them, he said, went all the way to Ireland. Behind them were high houses. She read the words 'Lord Byron Hotel'. Why did people go to hotels? Because they had no friends to stay with?

But Arthur was debating with Mungo what to do with Phoebe's box. 'We'll have to get a cab for this,' he was saying.

But Mungo seemed annoyed with the extravagance. 'Not at all. We've good legs. Can ye not get a barrow? There's a laddie there.'

A boy no bigger than herself but much older-looking came forward and tugged at the glossy skip of his dirty cap. He pointed to a little flat hand-cart. 'Tak' yer trunk, sir?'

Arthur nodded, and Phoebe was amazed to find with what agility and apparent strength he swung it up and on to his little cart. Arthur waved a directing hand, said 'Across the town', and away he went, keeping to the street just in front of them, while they followed on the pavement. In a few moments he was turning to the left over Glasgow Bridge.

Phoebe was glad that her brothers had so much to say, for she was enraptured with what she saw and wanted to be left alone. There was the great river stretching away to the west, the water glittering in the sunset. A steamer was turning round. Churning her paddles in midstream. And down beyond on both sides the shining waters were fringed by forests of sailing-ship masts, interspersed here and there by a steam-ship emitting clouds of smoke and steam. Distant tugs and ferries and even rowing-boats looked like water-beetles against the light. She had come indeed to a place of magic. The very bridge she was walking on was lit by handsome lamps, set high on the balustrades on either side. The gas-flares inside them looked like pale jewels against the fading eastern sky.

She made to dart across to look at the river on the other side. Mungo caught her shoulder. She was to stay where she was! Now she was in the town, she must learn to be careful. Did she want to get herself kicked to pieces by the bus horses as they rushed past? Phoebe walked on, sobered for a moment. She did not like to ask which were buses, for she was not sure. But presently she decided to ask Arthur. Was that big thing with three horses in front coming up to the crown of the bridge a bus? Yes. That was a bus. She watched it as it passed. How funny! She would like to have a ride on that, especially on the top, where things like two summer seats were arranged, back to back. People were sitting sideways, huddled in their winter coats. She was surprised that they did not appear to be enjoying their exciting position. And how funnily the sides of the buses were painted, with criss-cross colours to represent tartan!

Now they were on the other side. The shops were beginning. First, right on the corner, facing the bridge, Thomson's, clothier and outfitter. The boy with the barrow was well ahead of them now, hurrying up Jamaica Street, so that they had no option for the moment but to take the way he had gone – for the brothers had no intention of letting him out of sight. So Phoebe was able to enjoy herself, casting hurried glances at the lighted shop-windows, as they passed up.

Now they were at the crossing of Jamaica Street and Argyle Street. They halted for a moment, shouting to the barrow-boy to turn to the right, along Argyle Street. Phoebe had never seen anywhere so busy. She counted four of these tartan buses crossing in different directions while they stood. And there were several cabs, two or three men on horseback, a huckster with a donkey, and endless people. Where could everybody be going to? It was getting darker now. To the left, beyond Anderston, the sunset was deepening to a lurid crimson.

Argyle Street, as they went along it, was gay and busy. Phoebe wondered that so many people dare walk about in the middle of the street, with so much traffic on the move. The sound of horses' hoofs was never out of her ears. The shops were ablaze with gas-flares and most of them still had their Christmas and New Year display of goods and decorations. As they passed the opening to St Enoch's Square, Arthur pointed out to Mungo the position that the great new railway station and hotel were to occupy.

4

And now, after much walking, they were going up a narrower street. Phoebe was able to read its name on the corner. It was called Candleriggs. She had heard them talk of the Candleriggs. She asked if that was the same thing. They told her it was. It was a cheerful street. Through open doors men were working in the gaslight, moving boxes and bales, or perched at high desks writing in books under a single flare. This was the street where Arthur worked, she was told. Here he had his business. She would like to come and work here too. Would Arthur allow her?

The brothers laughed heartily and said here was Arthur's warehouse. Phoebe, a little sulky, said nothing more. She looked up and read: ARTHUR MOORHOUSE AND COMPANY. What was there to laugh at? She had always worked about the farm, and liked it, for she was a managing little body. Besides, her elders had seemed to expect her to help.

Inside the place was spotless. Great cheeses were ranged on scrubbed shelves. Packing and expediting were in full swing, for, though it was four o'clock and almost dark, there were still several hours of work before the warehousemen. Phoebe walked about with her hands behind her, concealing her intense interest under a business-like air.

Suddenly, in a little gaslit den at the back, she came upon the backs of two men perched up, writing. A fire burnt in a little black iron fireplace, making the place hot and stuffy. The men were working with their jackets off and their sleeves rolled up. One of them wore a wide black tie encircling a high collar. Over the edge of this crept the thick chestnut hair of her brother David. Phoebe walked primly round to the side of his desk and said: 'Hello, David.'

David looked down upon her, smiled quizzically, and shut one eye.

He was untidy, his face was dirty and his fingers were stained with ink. He was not at all the grand young man she had seen on the day of the funeral. She liked him much better as she found him now.

'Jimmie,' he said to the elderly clerk at his side, 'this is my sister.'

'The Maister wis sayin' ye wis comin' tae Glesca, Miss.' The man climbed down and shook hands.

Phoebe had never been called 'Miss' before. For a moment it made her feel very important. Presently she said goodbye with dignity and went out again, bent upon seeing anything else there was to see.

Mungo and Arthur seemed to be having an endless discussion with Arthur's head man on the subject of cheese. Finding nothing further of vital interest, Phoebe went to the door.

The boy was sitting on his barrow beside her trunk, waiting. He looked a thin, depressed sort of boy, Phoebe thought, but quite good enough to have a conversation with.

'What age are you?' she said, sitting on the barrow beside him.

'Seeventeen.'

'Yer ower wee fur yer age. Are ye no' weel?' she said, looking at him critically.

'A'm fine.'

'Dae ye get enough tae eat?' she said presently, still unconvinced.

'Whiles,' was the fatalistic reply.

She was quite unconscious that she had fallen into the broad Scots of the Laigh Farm. It was natural, for the boy's replies to her were in Scots too. But while Phoebe spoke with the clear, as yet uncontaminated peasant accent of Ayrshire – little changed, probably, from the accent of the poet Burns – her companion's tongue had all the slovenliness of the Glasgow underworld. This difference, however, went unremarked by the two young people sitting on the barrow. Indeed, the boy wondered that such a well-put-on little girl should speak a tongue so like his own.

They were great friends, exchanging many confidences, when her two elder brothers re-emerged from the warehouse.

'Well,' Arthur was saying, 'you know the way. I'll be up in about an hour.' And, giving the boy directions how to go to Ure Place, Phoebe and Mungo set off behind him up the Candleriggs.

Chapter 7

I

Bel realized at once that her mother was merely being naughty when she called at four. She knew that old Mrs Barrowfield had for once let her native inquisitiveness get the better of her. For, on this particular afternoon, little Phoebe Moorhouse was expected to arrive, escorted by her brother Mungo. Bel felt that her mother might have had sense and seen that her hands would be full.

The child's room had to have its last touches – you couldn't leave everything to maids – and the best room had to be got ready for Mungo.

Besides, Bel was just a little defiant about Phoebe. Her mother and even her sisters-in-law – though much more cautiously, lest they themselves should become involved – had felt it their duty to warn her more than once that the child might be far from easy to put up with. But Bel's honour was already committed. There was no getting out of it unless, of course, she hauled down her colours – a thing she never even thought of doing. So, by way of retaliation, she had highfaluted and insisted that she would stand by Arthur's sister, whatever she turned out like.

No. She felt her mother had come out of sheer curiosity, to see the child whose arrival she was prepared to resent. And she could very well have done without her.

But Bel was a woman of quick resentments and just as quick repentances. She chid herself for an undutiful daughter and rang for a cup of tea.

'When are you expecting them?' the old lady asked, pouring her tea into her saucer and sitting complacently with both elbows on the parlour table, holding up the tea and blowing upon it.

This habit of her mother's was a great cross to Bel, who considered it vastly ungenteel and did not like even her maids to see her do it.

'Any time now,' she said with that gentleness in her voice that goes with controlled annoyance. 'Arthur must have taken them round by the warehouse or they would have been here long ago.'

'Bel dearie!' The door had burst open. 'I just dropped in for two minutes to see wee Phoebe!' It was Sophia.

Bel, for a bewildered, ashamed moment, had an idea of standing between her mother and Sophia, so that Sophia should not see the old lady in the act of saucering her tea, but Mrs Barrowfield, who hotly resented that Sophia should have come at this moment to bother her daughter, finished her saucerful at one gulp and, placing her teacup upon it, got up and said very stiffly:

'Good-day, Sophia. Phoebe's not here.'

'Never here yet? Oh, well, anyway, I'm not sure that I can stay. I promised Wil and Margy to be back.' Then, looking about her: 'I couldn't have some tea, could I, Bel dear? I've been down town trailing round the Polytechnic. I'm nearly dead.'

Bel went to the embroidered bell-pull and gave it a convulsive, irritated tug.

'You haven't been up to see us for such a long time, Mrs Barrowfield. Wil and Margy were just talking about Auntie Bel's mother the other day. What did you think of their wee thank-you letters for your Christmas presents? I showed them to William. He said he thought they were lovely!'

Wil and Margy's letters had each betrayed signs of having been written by grubby little paws that had been shakily guided by their mother's hand – the only really original additions being inky fingermarks and a blot or two. But Mrs Barrowfield, downright though she was, dared scarcely remark on this. Besides, she was waiting for Sophia to say that it was very kind of her to think of sending toys to Wil and Margy at all. For, after all, her connection with them was slight. But as Sophia said nothing more on the subject, and as the pause was becoming noticeable, she said:

'They're wee to be writing letters.' This, at least, she felt, was a remark.

But Sophia, who was still ranging the room, did not appear to hear her. The door-handle turned. 'Ah!' she exclaimed. 'Here's my cup!'

But instead of the parlourmaid, Mary McNairn came in. Her calm demeanour and her gentle, controlled tones were almost more exasperating to Bel than Sophia's fussiness.

'Bel dear, just for a moment. I brought these little books for Phoebe. I know she's coming to the dearest sister-in-law in the world. But the child will be lonely and have a sore heart sometimes. No matter how good you are to her, and no matter how brave the wee body is. So I thought perhaps these might help her. They're little books of comfort and good conduct and things.'

Bel was far from feeling the dearest sister-in-law in the world. There were moments when Mary's saintliness made her sick. And this was one of them. Besides somehow, as often with Mary, her words had left a sting. The very use of the word 'sister-in-law' had somehow implied that the child was coming to a house where inevitably she would be unhappy and misunderstood.

But now she felt beaten. Let them all come! It was a pity, she told herself, that she did not have another dozen sisters-in-law and another half-dozen mothers to see Phoebe's arrival.

Her maid had followed Mary into the room with Sophia's cup. She bade her bring another for Mary.

As the girl returned with this, she turned to Bel. 'I think that's them, Mam. There's a gentleman like Mr Moorhouse comin' up the brae. I looked out for a minute.'

'Was there a little girl too, Sarah?'

'I didna see right. There was a barrow wi' luggage.'

'She must be there.' Bel got up. At her own front door at least she herself would receive them.

2

'Listen! We'll all go to the door and give them a grand welcome!' Sophia exclaimed.

Bel gave up. The spark that had dared to revive within her was immediately extinguished. It was no use trying to be a separate person this afternoon. So everyone trooped outside the door to where they could see the travellers coming up the steep incline of Montrose Street.

'Where's Phoebe?' Mary asked.

In the light of the street lamps they could discern Mungo coming up on the pavement, carrying his own carpet-bag. His strong body was inclined forward against the hill. His natural farmer's stoop was accentuated by the effort. Out in the middle of the street a little hand-cart with a black box was being pushed upwards. On one side they could discern the face and ragged cap of the youth to whom the cart presumably belonged. They could see his shoulders rise and fall with his steps as he pushed it upwards. Suddenly a little girl's head appeared from behind the box. She was shoving and pushing just as hard as he was. It was Phoebe.

'Good gracious! There's Phoebe, and look what she's doing!' Sophia exclaimed.

'Mungo ought not to let her. If the boy has a barrow, surely he must be able to push it himself,' Mary said.

Bel didn't like it either. After all, if Phoebe were coming to live in a refined quarter like Ure Place, she must learn to behave with dignity. Bel, at this stage, was very much of that social cast that allows its life to be ruled by the nameless critic lurking behind the neighbouring lace window-curtains. She was mortified, too, to feel that the eyes of her sisters-in-law were emitting furtive gleams of triumph.

'I can see you'll have to be firm with her, Bel dear,' Sophia said with relish.

'I'm sure your little sister means to help the poor boy,' Bel retorted with the shadow of stress on the words 'your' and 'sister'.

But the old lady, who had had her beginnings in an age that was much less genteel, when prim refinement had not been at such a high premium, was pleased with the little girl. She liked people to have what she called 'smeddom'. And this child obviously had it. The box had to be pushed up the hill, so, without thought of dignity, Phoebe was giving a hand. She could not have chosen to do anything better to put herself into old Mrs Barrowfield's good graces.

And yet, if Mrs Barrowfield had stopped to think, it was precisely this unfashionable straightforwardness that she had striven to eliminate from the behaviour of her own daughter. She had paid high fees at an establishment for young ladies, so that Bel should be taught to seem – in public at least – as frail and useless as possible.

Now they had arrived and were standing before Bel's front door under the lamp. After all, perhaps, it had not been such a bad idea of Sophia's that they should all go out together and greet the new-comers. It was cheerful and fussy and it helped to cover up shynesses. She was pleased to see Mungo, whom she knew so little. He was a shy man, but he had that placid force about him that is to be found in many farmers. He was very like her husband, but bigger, ruddy and physically stronger. But his mind seemed slower, and he did not have the quick, appraising eye of the merchant and townsman.

'Bel, this is our little sister Phoebe,' Mary was saying.

Bel bent down and kissed this child about whom she – and all the others – had thought so much. She seemed a well-grown, sturdy little girl in her black country-made clothes. Her round apple cheeks were glowing with the effort of pushing the barrow. Her blue Highland eyes were large and penetrating. As the little girl looked up at her, Bel could see shyness and curiosity in them.

'What a lot of people all at once, isn't it, Phoebe?' Bel said, keeping her arm about her. 'It's terrible to have your sisters and brothers all so old that they might be your uncles and aunts!'

Phoebe's face relaxed into a vague smile. It was impossible to make out what the child was feeling. Had her words – said at random – conveyed the goodwill that she, Bel, had intended? Or had Phoebe thought them a little silly? She couldn't tell. Nor could she say whether she liked or disliked the child in these first moments.

Phoebe's eyes kept turning towards the boy who was waiting with the little hand-cart. She seemed anxious that he should get whatever was due to him. Mungo was standing talking to his sisters and Bel's mother, paying no heed. At last, breaking away, Phoebe went to him and touched his arm.

'Mungo, the boy's money.'

Queer little thing. She seemed almost worried over a slum waif who could mean nothing to her. Was it kindness of heart? Was it self-importance? Was it a premature habit of responsibility?

Presently they were all inside the house.

3

Phoebe had taken off her little round black hat. Her sister-in-law was better able to examine the child's face under the light.

Apart from an impalpable family look, the child was unlike her brothers and sisters. Her face was round and undeveloped. But her eyes were fine and set like a foreigner's, as Bel thought to herself, meaning that strange, high-cheeked, almost Tartar look that you meet here and there in the Highlands. Her colour was glowing and vivid, though a little too countrified to Bel's way of thinking. Her hair was raven-black and glossy.

Bel insisted that everyone should come and have tea before Phoebe and Mungo should be settled, as she put it. She wondered at herself a little for doing this, considering her annoyance at her mother, Mary and Sophia ten minutes ago. But the truth was, perhaps, that she wanted to postpone for a little longer being left alone with these unknown relatives of her husband. The slow, ponderous farmer and the puzzling little girl.

But in a very short time Mary stood up. 'Sophia, we've taken too much of Bel's time. But you can understand how much we wanted just to get a glimpse, Bel dear. You'll come to see us of course. Bel, when can you and Arthur bring Mungo?'

Mungo hastened to say he would only be staying two nights. Bel protested politely at the shortness of his visit, then Mary went on: 'Well, tomorrow for tea at six. And we'll arrange for you to come and see the children very soon, Phoebe.'

Phoebe didn't say anything. She was not used to being kept apart with other children. She had always eaten with her elders in the big, cheerful farm kitchen. And when Mary finished by saying: 'Now, dear, remember to be a good girl, and do everything Bel tells you, for it's very kind of her having you here,' it made her feel infinitely bleak for a little, and somehow her feeling towards her elder sister did not grow any warmer.

Sophia was able to regret with a clear conscience that there would be no time, then, for Mungo to come and have a meal with herself and William. William could not be counted upon to come to their midday dinner, so *that* was no use.

Sophia and William must come to them too, then, Mary the saint insisted.

Might they? Was she sure it would be all right? Mary was sure it would be all right. Thereupon the sisters prepared to go. Mary kissed Phoebe and told her how pleased she was to have her where she could get to know her, and Sophia likewise kissed her fussily, arranged for her to come to see Margy next morning, and to everybody's amazement gave her half a crown.

And Phoebe's ten-year-old summing-up of Sophia was that she was stupid but quite nice.

In another ten minutes Mrs Barrowfield's maid, Maggie, acting on previous instructions, arrived to see her mistress home. Maggie, breathless and not so much younger than the old lady herself, was allowed by Bel's young and smart housemaid to sit and wait for her mistress on a chair in the hall. At which she was furious. For a cup of tea in the kitchen would have made all the difference. Arrived home, she reported to her neighbour this discourtesy of Miss Bel's girl – said that servants nowadays were newfangled besoms, and opined that that one would come to no good anyway.

4

It had been a strange day for Phoebe. Later in the evening, hand-in-hand with Bel, she climbed to the top of the house to the little bedroom that was to be her own. For Bel, even though she had not entirely given her heart to Arthur's little sister – she was not a child who responded with quick, open warmth – was, after all, a womanly woman. And it would have taken someone much less motherly than she, to be insensible to the fact that the little girl should, at this time, want some show of affection and sympathy. Bel, like everybody else a person of mixed motives, was determined to do her duty. But the motive that moved her to her duty at this moment was one that made her duty easy, and its name was kindness.

Phoebe, although she did not show it, was very impressed with Bel. There was much about her she could not understand. Bel's quiet voice. Her restrained way. Her – as it appeared to the child – lack of insistence in everything she did. In the country her elders had behaved quite differently. At the farm, if you had guests, you fussed, you insisted on them eating, insisted on them having the Chair at the kitchen fire. You talked and laughed, often about nothing, until your voice boomed loud and heartily all over the kitchen and resounded on the stone floor and scrubbed pans in the milkhouse.

Here it was different. Everyone was quiet in comparison to the Laigh Farm people. They seemed to try to make as little noise as possible. And Bel was the most restrained. She wondered at first if it was because they were in mourning, then decided it must be the way people behaved in Glasgow.

As for Bel herself, she was the most beautiful person she had ever seen. Her shining fair hair, her neat, well-cut mouth, that now and then expanded into a smile that was charming. There was something so elegant about Bel's smile. Phoebe made a mental note to practise smiling like that before the mirror. And she had sat so well-poised and splendid in her beautiful black dress at the head of her own tea-table, saying in that curiously quiet way of hers, things that seemed incredibly suitable and right to Phoebe, who was used to abrupt manners.

She had seen at once that Bel was going to have a baby. The wives of the two ploughmen at home were for ever having babies. The little girl was perfectly used to it. The cows had babies; the mares had babies; the ploughmen's wives had babies. This child, even in these mid-Victorian days, looked upon the births one and all as things of great interest, rejoiced and asked questions.

Now she was enchanted to think that this glorious person who was sitting on the edge of her bed watching her undress was also to have a baby. It would be a very special baby, she decided. And she would be here to help to nurse it. The idea took hold of her. Bel, helping her now to brush out her almost blue-black hair, saw her reflection in the mirror and wondered why, suddenly, she looked so pleased.

Finally she was ready for bed in her long flannel nightgown. It was not very elegant, but it was new and clean, Bel decided, and highly suitable for a little girl.

Bel bent down and kissed her.

'Now I'll put out your gas and you can say your own prayers and go to sleep.'

Phoebe was grateful to her. She had said nothing about being good nor about trying to be happy. And it would have been embarrassing to be 'heard' her prayers.

Yet Bel waited for a moment. There seemed to be a question hanging on Phoebe's lips. It came.

'Bel, will you allow me to nurse the baby when it's born?'

Bel, brought up to genteel reticence like every other young woman of her class and period, was so taken aback at such words coming from a ten-year-old girl that she could only say, 'What baby?'

'Your baby, of course!' Why not? Young things at the farm had always fascinated her. This young thing would be the most enchanting of all.

'But who told you, Phoebe?'

'Nobody.'

For a moment Bel actually felt angry. But her fundamental sense came to her rescue, though of necessity she must remain a woman of her time.

'Phoebe,' she said, 'you mustn't say things like that.'

'Why?'

'Because it's wicked.' What nonsense Bel knew she was talking.

'Wicked?'

'Well, no, not wicked. Unsuitable.'

'But I don't see—'

Bel, fast getting out of her depth, must use her wits.

'Well, come here and I'll tell you something. There *is* going to be a baby in May, and if you don't say a word about it to anybody between now and then, I promise you'll be allowed to nurse it sometimes.' And with that she turned off the gas and quickly took herself out of the room.

Phoebe pondered for a long time, sitting on her bed. Why? It would have been nice to think and talk about the baby.

Truly Glasgow was a strange place.

For a moment she leant from her window, looking out across the town. The glow of the street lights had caught the smoke hanging over the great city, giving it a luminous, dusky cover. Endless roofs! And did all these spires mean churches? What a lot there must be! In the near distance she could see indistinctly the shape of Sir Walter Scott's statue standing silhouetted in the haze. She could see a part of the column too, although she could not see its base in George's Square. Who could that be? She must remember to ask Arthur.

She turned back, filled with curiosity and excitement and with an avid desire to go on living. Yes, it had been a strange day.

And now her bed was strange. Not at all like the bed at the Laigh Farm. Her room was strange. Bel and Arthur were strange. But what, on this first evening of her new life, was not strange?

She must lie quiet, listening to these strange town noises, and think about everything.

But in five minutes more Phoebe was asleep.

Chapter 8

I

It was just dark as Mungo said goodbye to Bel and Phoebe at the Arthur Moorhouses' front door. In the morning Phoebe had asked Arthur if she might cross the town to see Mungo off, but she had been told no.

Now he had turned to raise his hand to them for the last time and was striding giant footsteps down the incline of Montrose Street. A few drops of rain fell upon his face.

Neither Phoebe nor he had shown any emotion at parting. But his thoughts as he paced quickly downwards, impelled by the slant of the hill, were with his little half-sister. On very few nights of her life had he and she failed to sleep under the same roof. For he had been scarcely ever away from the Laigh Farm, and she never. He was fond of her, he supposed, as he was fond of any of the other young creatures growing up about the farm. He wondered vaguely how she would settle into this new existence. Then he reflected that all the rest of his brothers and sisters had done so, and that they seemed busy and happy.

For himself, two days of it were about enough. He wasn't built for all the fripperies and politenesses of the town. Bel had been very kind and had left no stone unturned in her anxiety for his comfort. But he had felt the constraint of her braw house and her starched housemaid. He had, indeed, been afraid to be left alone with his sister-in-law. For their thoughts and interests were such poles apart. Very quickly he had found conversation hard going. It wasn't that he couldn't get on with fine ladies on occasion. Finer ladies than his own relatives, if it came to that. Miss Ruanthorpe, the daughter of his laird, often hung over a gate and talked to him for half an hour on end, when he came across her, which, now he came to think of it, was not infrequently. And she never made him feel ill-dressed or awkward as he stood in his rough clothes. But then she talked his own language. She could talk of ploughing and reaping and sowing. How the young beasts were promising. She had a good idea of prices. Once or twice she had come to beg his advice about her ponies or her dogs. This had flattered him, for it showed that she considered his advice of more weight than the advice of the grooms or the keeper. And Mungo was well aware that she was right. He knew that he had a growing reputation as a farmer, that his help was of value.

But Bel and Sophia and Mary. They lived in a world of gentilities for which he could raise no enthusiasm. He supposed all town ladies must be like that. Endless tattle about dress. He had heard a great deal about bustles, which were just coming in about this time. What was to be got in the shops. Meetings of this, that and the other kind in connection with the church, at which so far as he could gather – especially from Sophia – you had as many misunderstandings as possible with other ladies. Indeed, the church seemed to be the hub of their universe. Sewing meetings. Missionary meetings. Prayer meetings. Tea meetings. He caught himself wondering just what good all that did. He had always thought of church as a place to go to at twelve o'clock every Sunday. Where you sat in peace and reverence. Not as cockpits of social strivings. Well, he supposed it kept town women out of mischief and prevented a great number of them – especially the unmarried and therefore unwanted – from turning into those sluts who were so much to the fore just now; who claimed that women should have votes and stand equal with men in the world; who had the effrontery to call themselves the New Women.

He had taken his way down the Candleriggs in order to bid his brothers goodbye, and now he was at their door. Arthur was hard at it, directing his men. David was in the back office, sucking the end of a pencil.

He gave them both a hurried farewell, for he saw that Arthur was preoccupied. And he invited them both to come and see him now he was to be by himself. Especially David, for he thought he looked none too robust in his stuffy little counting-house.

No. He didn't want their kind of life. He knew that Arthur was building up a good business, and he admired him. He knew that his brother's name was one which was slowly gaining respect in the City, and he honoured him for it. But he had no desire to stand in Arthur's shoes. The very thought of eternally working in the Candleriggs was abhorrent to him. Packing-cases. Straw. Gas-flares. Account books. The never-ending clatter of dray-horses' hoofs. The oaths and the shouting. No. Never.

It was raining more heavily as he hurried along Argyle Street. The muddy street was shining in the lights. Several times the wheels of the passing buses splashed him, for in his hurry he tried to keep to the less-crowded outside of the pavement. Filthy urchins were calling an evening paper. Hucksters of various kinds were calling their wares. Fresh herrings. Mussels. Caller oysters. Here and there at the turn of a side-street, a barrow of vegetables. John Anderson's Royal Polytechnic was a blaze of light.

Now down Jamaica Street and across the Glasgow Bridge. It was raining heavily. He bent his head as the rain struck against his face. A steamer boomed in the darkness. Above the sound of the traffic he could hear the beat of paddles as another steamer pounded itself against the force of the black, muddy river into position along the quayside of the Broomielaw. Its bow was almost under the bridge.

But here was Clyde Place and the Bridge Street Station steps. In a moment more he was under shelter.

In a few minutes he would be out of it all. And a good thing. For he was a countryman, and he was going back to the country.

2

The rain lashed in bitter bursts against the windows of his carriage whenever the train was free from the covering protection of the station. The raindrops glistened and sparkled on the panes as the train, working its way outwards across the points, moved past street lamps and lighted shops and houses.

Two stout women, with large, uncomfortable bundles on their knees, sat and stared before them in the pale gaslight, bothering neither to speak to one another, though they were obviously together, nor yet to place their bundles on the seat beside them or on the rack above. But Mungo did not think this odd, for, without actually considering them, he rightly took them to be country-folk like himself. And it is the habit of such when on the move to sit clutching their belongings. Indeed, all three of them now sat forward, swaying with the lurches of the railway carriage, in that almost inanimate state of waiting that belongs to peasant people of all lands. It is impossible for townsmen to tell whether they are patient or impatient – whether, indeed, they have sensations of any kind.

At a side-station after Kilmarnock, the two stout women bundled themselves out. Mungo came to life enough to help them with their packages.

He did not move again until the train had roared through the Mossgiel Tunnel. Then he stood up stiffly and got down his bag.

The rain was falling, soft and steady, as he stepped out on the station platform. Here he halted – alive again, breathing familiar air and bidding one or two local people good-evening. This rain was good after the coldness. It would take the frost out of the ground and let him get on with his ploughing.

Outside the station, one of his men was waiting with the trap. The pony, standing in the wet with hung head, suddenly came to life at this known step, shook himself in his harness, put forward his ears and screwed his head round to look at Mungo. Mungo passed his hands down the front of the animal's nose and over his quivering nostrils. Then he greeted his man, jumped up and took the reins. The high-mettled little beast, pleased with the feel of its master's guiding hands, stretched his back and trotted sharply off on the road homeward.

Mungo was happy now. The country round about him was shrouded in darkness. By the help of his own gig-lamps he could see the road a little. That was all. Yet he and his beast knew every turn by instinct. If a black shape passed over his head, he knew it was a certain branch of a tree, which tree it belonged to, and how it looked in the daytime. The very echo of his pony's hoofs told him where he was.

He chatted in a desultory manner with his man. Everything was, of course, as he had left it two days ago. There was nothing to tell. Yet it was pleasant to speak of his own things after the trivialities of the town – to smell the wet, wintry earth and horsy odour from his pony.

In his own farmyard the two dogs, Nith and Doon, were circling and baying with joy. They followed him barking into the glowing firelit kitchen, where Jean welcomed him with a quiet show of country pleasure.

How was Phoebe? she asked. Phoebe, he told her, was fine. Was she going to be happy in the town? He said he thought so. The woman was bursting with questions. About Phoebe. About Mrs Arthur's grand house in Glasgow. About Glasgow itself. For to her it might just as well have been Paris or St Petersburg and almost as remote. But Mungo looked thoughtful and she dared not bother him.

It was queer to see only one place laid. For so long there had always been at least four. And often too the inside servants, if they were at liberty, had sat with them. There had always been his father, his stepmother and Phoebe as well as himself. Often, apart from his father calling for a blessing on their food, little or nothing had been said. If Phoebe had been talkative sometimes, she had been told to be quiet. For a mealtime is not always a social event among those who labour heavily. It is a time of rest. Now they were all gone, he missed the strong sense of companionship.

But for his own dogs, he was alone. It pleased him to be at home again in these surroundings, yet he was lonely. He found himself wishing that his little sister were with him.

When, after he had finished and had taken down his pipe and filled it and seated himself in his father's chair, the woman came in to clear away, he was glad to exchange a word or two with her – even to tell her a little about Glasgow – although he had scarcely ever bothered to speak to her in his life before.

Presently everything had been taken away, washed, brought back and put in its place on the shelves of the scrubbed dresser. His heart was strangely empty tonight, but it was pleasant to sit again with his jacket and collar and tie off, and his sleeves rolled up at ease in the Laigh Farm kitchen.

Nith and Doon had settled down in peace in their own separate corners of the room. They were never allowed nearer to the fire than that.

Mungo did not know how long he had sat thus ruminating over his pipe when he heard a thin whine at the door. He got up with slow deliberation and opened it. It was his father's old dog Clyde, gaunt and shaky on his legs, for now, since the loss of his master, he would not eat. The animal showed no pleasure; he merely cast his cloudy eyes about the kitchen as though he were looking for someone. Mungo bent down and patted him. In two days his ribs had become more prominent.

One of the men had said: 'That dug'll no' dae nae mair guid, wi' yer faither awa'.'

He had been quite right. The dog was doing no more good.

'He's no' here, Clyde. He's no' here, lad.' Mungo ran his hand over his ears.

The old dog looked about him stupidly. Mungo tried to bring him into the warmth, but he whimpered and wanted to go out again, so he let him go. He himself came back to his chair by the fire.

No. They were not here.

On a sudden impulse he called his other dogs. They sprang to their feet and came to him. He laid down his pipe and ran his hands down their sleek, long muzzles. This was unheard-of spoiling for creatures who must work for their living. But dogs are tactful beasts. One soon had stretched himself across Mungo's feet and the other sat, resting his head on his master's knee beside his hand.

And so they remained for a long time. Long enough, indeed, for coals to fall in the great open fireplace, and for the cheerful glow from the ashes to sink and dwindle.

But Mungo Moorhouse did not notice. He was asleep.

Chapter 9

I

Bel set David's small white tie with all the care of an arch-conspirator.

'There. Now let me look at you.'

David straightened himself, and tugged at the front of his brand-new tail-coat.

'Now turn round slowly.'

He turned. When he could see himself full length in Bel's bedroom mirror, he halted.

The reflection showed him the picture of a handsome young aristocrat, with a wealth of chestnut hair and side-whiskers trimmed with restraint and refinement that afternoon by Glasgow's Greatest Tonsorial Artist.

'You don't think they've cut my waistcoat too high?' David looked down dubiously at his trim black waistcoat.

Bel cast her mind back to a recent performance of 'Astonishment' at the Theatre Royal and to the aspect of the handsome Mr Kendal who had, in flawless evening clothes, so brilliantly led the company, in partnership with his talented wife. Bel and Arthur went very seldom to the devil's playbox, but an influential customer had kindly given Arthur cards, which, presumably, he could not use himself. Thus, much to Bel's delight, pleasure had, for once, become a matter of business. For Arthur could not dare tell anyone so important that he had not cared to profit by his kindness.

But Bel did not say anything to David about her mental picture of the brilliant Mr Kendal. She wanted rather to give her brother-in-law the impression that she was more than used to that kind of thing, to convey to him that she was a woman of the world. That David – as a near relative – knew all about her did not damp this hope. So she looked at his waistcoat critically and said, 'No, I think it's just right as it is.'

She was pleased with the appearance of David. To her eye, at least, he looked as though he might be anybody. In things social Bel and David were allies. They both had ambitions. David's – to rise in the world generally: not so much by hard work as by getting to know the people whom he considered to be deserving of that elusive qualification right. Bel, while quite approving of the right people, was directing her aims at a handsome house situated out West. The increasing unfashionableness of Ure Place and the increasing prosperity of her husband had created within her the desire to move.

It was Arthur's stubbornness and lack of understanding that had driven Bel and David into this alliance. Couldn't she be happy where she was? her husband asked every time they touched upon the subject. There were moments when really he was infuriating. Couldn't he see that this quarter of the town would, in time, become impossible? Now that he was the father of a boy of three, and a little year-old girl, he really ought to think of a suitable environment for them. And there was Phoebe, nearly fourteen. In a year or two she would be a young lady. She knew Arthur wanted to do well by his sister. She did too, if it came to that. Were they only to have Mary McNairn to depend on for getting to know nice people? (Mary's possession of a wide, if somewhat pious circle, did not increase Bel's affection for her.)

But now, a month ago, David had come to her with a beautiful gilt invitation card asking him to a Dancing Party in Dowanhill. What should he do?

Bel looked at the card. 'Mrs Hayburn and Messrs Stephen and Henry Hayburn request the pleasure of Mr David Moorhouse's company,' and so on. 'Dancing.'

' "Dancing" means that it's a full-blown dance?' David said uncertainly.

Bel turned the card about admiring but thoughtful, and said 'Yes.'

'That will mean full evening dress,' David said, feeling his way. In the Moorhouse circle none of the men had evening dress. (Except Mr McNairn, of course, who, now one of the City's Baillies, was really forced to get it. Mary had explained: 'You see, we have so many wearisome official functions, dear!') No, they were entertained and returned entertainment – the ladies in what might be called semi, the men in a dark suit.

Bel still went on twisting the card and pondering. It had ceased to be a card in her hand. It was the thin edge of a wedge.

'Who are the Hayburns, David?'

'They're very rich. Their father died last year. Hayburn and Company. Something to do with iron. I know Stephen. There are two sons. They live with their mother near the Botanic Gardens.'

'Where did you get to know him?'

David was ready for this. His first encounter with Stephen Hayburn had been at the White Bait Music Hall in St Enoch's Wynd. They had struck up a friendship, and finding, like many another pair of sparks, that they had frivolity in common, had met there again or at Brown's Music Hall Restaurant or some other convenient free-and-easy. Then, in the summer, while the house in Dowanhill was closed and Mama Hayburn and her maids were by the sea, David had invited his friend to share his lodgings for a week or two. He knew that he dare not say the words music hall, even to his ally Bel, nor could he say that he knew Stephen in business, for any business David did was from Arthur's office.

'As a matter of fact,' he said, 'he had rooms at my digs in the summer, when his mother was at Kilcreggan.'

'It's queer you never told us about him.'

'As a matter of fact, I've really got to know him better since then. I meet him sometimes.'

'Have you been to his house?'

'No. But he introduced me to his mother last week. We met her coming out of Wylie and Lochhead's in Buchanan Street. She was just getting into her carriage.'

David had, knowing and sharing Bel's weakness, aimed the carriage direct at it. It hit its mark.

She tried to look as matter-of-fact and sensible as possible. 'Well, David,' she said, 'I think it's perfectly ridiculous that a young man like you with a steady position in a good business should not have the proper clothes to wear when nice people invite him to things.'

And so it came about that David was standing, in full warpaint for the first time in his life, turning himself about, in front of Bel and her mirror.

'Yes. Very nice. Have you got your gloves?'

'Yes.' He produced them – white and immaculate kid.

'Wait a minute.' Bel went to a drawer and produced a white rose from a little paper bag. It had cost her a bit, for the month was November. And hot-house blooms were hot-house blooms in these days. It was a perfect half-opened bud too, set in maidenhair fern, wired and finished off with silver paper. She showed David where and how it should be fixed when he arrived, and returned it to its paper bag.

David grinned a little sheepishly and thanked her.

2

'Are you saying good-night to the children?'

'Of course. Arthur's not back, is he?' He looked a little anxiously at the little bedroom clock.

'No. No. Of course not. He had a church-meeting, otherwise I wouldn't have asked you to come and show yourself off.' Church-meetings had other uses than merely religious ones. But if Arthur would be so stubborn and silly about the uses of polite society, what could his wife and his brother do?

Firm, still childish, purposeful tinkling was coming from the drawing-room piano. Phoebe had finished practising and was amusing herself playing a waltz David had bought her. It was called 'Come to my Pagoda'. He had heard it first at Brown's, and Phoebe's innocent strummings evoked memories of the spangled, if a little overblown, charms of the lady who had sung it. He had thought it better to buy an edition with the words left out.

'Hello, Phoebe!'

Phoebe spun round on the stool, and said 'Hello!' She looked little different for her four years in Glasgow, except that she was bigger. There seemed nothing of the woman about her so far. And yet you felt that she was approaching the borderline. That any time now she would take a fit of growing, and, before you knew where you were, you might have a slim and elegant young lady for a sister.

'Like that tune?'

Phoebe nodded.

'Some day I'll sing the words to you.'

'Why not now?'

'Oh, I don't know – I've got to go away. Good-night.'

She came to David and took his hand. 'Come upstairs and look at Arthur the Second.'

'I couldn't possibly.'

'You must!'

'Don't tease her, David,' Bel said, coming in and overhearing this last piece of talk. 'And don't wake the babies up.'

All the family knew that Phoebe had a passion for her little nephew. Every moment she was allowed to give to him, that she gave. Perhaps it was that she felt she had established a special claim upon him on that very first night that she came to Ure Place, and forced Bel to tell her that the baby was coming. Perhaps her heart had seized on the tiny new-comer and filled its empty places with him, in that first difficult year in Glasgow.

For it had been a difficult year. Both for her and for Bel. There were many times when Phoebe had been naughty, and Arthur and Bel were at their wits' end. At moments it had only been pride and fear of the derision of her sisters-in-law that had kept Bel from asking Arthur to send her back to the Laigh Farm. Often she had to remind herself of what she had said to Mary and Sophia – that a child could show its sense of bereavement by being ill-behaved.

But now in four years she had settled down to be a quiet child – strangely reserved, observant and impartial. One wondered what went on behind those quick, deep-set eyes. She seemed to care little for any of them, even Arthur her brother, though for him she appeared to have respect. The single exception was the little boy, for whom she had this extraordinary attachment.

Bel had never been sure if she liked her little sister-in-law much, but, being on the whole a sensible woman and quite un-morbid, she had long since accepted Phoebe as part of her duty, and left it at that.

David was dragged tiptoe into the nursery where Arthur Moorhouse, junior, slept in one cot and Isabella Moorhouse slept in another.

'Look at him, David,' Phoebe leant over the little boy.

Arthur had all the enchantment of any pretty, sleeping child of three. There was nothing more. The strange thing to David was the intensity of Phoebe. She seemed as though she could devour him. He crossed over and looked at his niece, Isabel. To him she was just as pleasing in her way. But Phoebe scarcely bothered to look at her.

David turned and came out of the nursery.

'Good-night, David.'

'Do you know what about you? You're a curiosity. Good-night.'

Phoebe did not know what he meant. Nor did he bother to explain.

Bel was holding the handle of the front door. At the carriage-stone a cab was waiting.

'I'm treating you to this cab,' Bel said. 'There and back. It's all arranged.'

'Bel, you're too good to be true.'

'Good-night, David. Have a good time. And come in whenever you can and tell me all about it.' She kissed him and patted his shoulder, as one might pat the bread one is about to cast upon the waters.

She stood on the step and laughed to herself a little, as the cab disappeared round the corner. A cab from the middle of the town all the way out to beyond Botanic Gardens! When there were excellent horse-buses running, that would take you at a mere fraction of the cost! This was an expense that would have to be discreetly sunk in her house-keeping money! But, after all, David was a nice boy; why shouldn't she stand him a cab? Bel did not care to own up. Even to herself.

It was a good thing that Arthur was now an elder of the kirk and had to attend meetings!

3

The cab jogged its way westward. Cathedral Street, Bath Street, Bath Crescent. The further end of Sauchiehall Street.

David, though he was now twenty-seven and considered himself a man about town, was beginning to suffer from social panic. Each street, as he watched, sitting forward in his seat, seemed to have become incredibly short. The very outline of the new University seemed majestic and forbidding; seemed to belong to a world that was not his. Now he was outside the boundaries of the City of Glasgow.

What was this strange compulsion that made timid, sensitive people drive themselves into company that knew nothing of them? What was this strange determination not to be left out of things? Stephen Hayburn was familiar enough to him now – and good fun. But why hadn't he left it at that? Why should he, David Moorhouse, force himself to enter Stephen's house? Because Stephen would be offended if he didn't come this evening? Perhaps. But that was the mere shadow of a reason. And David knew it. No. It was something that went much deeper. Down into the roots of him. Meanwhile the damned cab was bringing him remorselessly nearer. And as the distance lessened, the hollow weakness that occupied that part of him where his stomach was usually to be found, seemed to grow in magnitude.

The Hayburns occupied one of the many newly-built mansions in Dowanhill. This pleasant preserve of the wealthy was coming into being. It took the cabman some time to find the house. For Dowanhill was then no less confusing than it is today. David, paralysed with shyness, hoped he would have to go on searching for ever. But at last the house was found. Now he must descend, preserving as best he might the outer semblance of a man of the world.

The door was standing open. Flaring gas-jets cast their mellow light. Discreet and pretty parlourmaids directed him onwards and upwards to the gentlemen's bedroom. A handsome room, with a fire burning in a large iron fireplace, littered with black overcoats and scarves. There were a number of other young men. All, David thought, looking intolerably self-assured and appearing to know each other unnecessarily well. One of them, with cascade moustache, was, he gathered, staying in the house for the night, as his home was so far out in the country. He came from somewhere near the village of New Kilpatrick. He had a great deal to say about the duck-shooting in the ponds not far from his home. He was giving the others in the room pressing invitations to visit him.

David, having said good-evening, and having received in return very formal good-evenings back, left it at that. He picked up the great silver brushes on the dressing-table, and brushed his already perfectly macassared hair. He brushed his shoulders and his sleeves. He sat down and adjusted his brand-new elastic-sided boots of glacé kid. In every way he could think of he did things to himself so that he might remain behind by himself in the bedroom. Up here he was far from comfortable, but the thought of it was heaven to facing the people downstairs.

The young men went, leaving him alone. Then he wondered if he ought to have followed them down. It would have been easier, perhaps, to have gone in and been received with the crowd. He hung about, looking at the bedroom pictures.

There were two handsome engravings of stags and mountains, taken from the work of Mr Landseer, hanging against the rose-trellised wall-paper. Another of a Greek lady embracing an urn. They were very striking and interesting, David told himself falsely.

Strains of music came up from down below. So they have a violinist and some wind instrument as well as a pianist! The sound of the several instruments increased his panic. It would have been easier – less alarming – if there had been only a piano. His throat was very dry. He remembered a little box of perfumed cachous Bel had given him, and took one.

4

He was leaning on the mantelshelf gazing into the fire, when a 'Hello' behind him caused him to jump and turn round.

A tall, spare boy of nineteen or thereabouts with big, puppy bones that made his clothes look ill-fitting came forward.

'Hello, are you David Moorhouse?'

'Yes.'

'I'm Henry Hayburn.'

David had grasped this from the family likeness to his friend, Stephen. Though Stephen must be quite five years older, and was handsomer and more mature.

They shook hands.

'Stephen said he thought he had caught sight of you going upstairs. Are you all right?'

'All right?'

'Yes, I thought you were looking a bit seedy when I came in just now.'

'Oh, no. I'm all right.' David smiled into the boy's pleasant pug face.

'Perhaps you were just feeling like me, that all this kind of thing is just an awful nuisance.'

David did not know what he meant. 'What kind of thing?'

'All this dancing and nonsense. Turning the whole house upside down. It's not as if we were a family of girls, and had to set to work to find husbands.'

David could find nothing to say to this. He smiled vaguely.

The boy seemed to take for granted that he agreed with him. 'But there you are, Mother and Stephen are so infernally socially minded. And as usual there were far more women expecting to be asked than men. If you only knew the hunt we've had for anything in trousers!'

It was fortunate that the exact meaning of this remark in so far as it applied to himself did not penetrate to David's flustered reason. For he liked this boy. He was friendly and unaffected.

'Well, come on down, will you?'

David followed. At least, it was not so bad having this approachable, if rather cross, creature to go down with.

The drawing-room was L-shaped and enormous. Or so it seemed, and its size was increased by the fact that all the furniture, except the large cottage piano, its stool and the musicians' chairs and music-stands, had been taken out of it. Only one or two narrow benches, hired from a caterer, were set close against the walls. The main floor was entirely covered by a large, tightly stretched white cloth. The handsome gilded gaselier, and the gilded wall-brackets were, every one of them, lit. Each flame – shaped like the eye of some fantastic peacock's feather, the outer part golden, the inner part next to the jet transparent purple – shed a mellow, flattering light on girlish shoulders, wasp-waists and elegant bustled dresses, on the one hand; and sleek, black, bewhiskered correctness on the other.

Most of the guests were standing up to make sets of quadrilles. There were four sets and the room would certainly have held a fifth. David's friend Stephen was running about among the guests, getting them arranged.

'Hello, Moorhouse. Glad to see you. Do you mind staying out of this? There's not enough people for five sets.' He was gone before David could reply.

'Have you seen Mother, by the way?' Henry said, still beside him.

'No, I haven't.'

'You'd better come then.'

Henry led the way out of the drawing-room into what was in reality a little study next door.

A stout, elderly lady was sitting by the fire. She looked a very important lady, David thought – partly, perhaps, because he was in a state of mind to be impressed and partly because this lady herself was determined that he should think her so.

She was dressed in black. A handsome cameo brooch held a

white silk shawl about her shoulders, and she wore a snowy cap on her plain parted hair. At her hand was a table with tea-things, for it was then the custom to offer newly arrived guests tea and cakes even at such a formal entertainment as this. Most of the other guests had been offered cups of tea from large silver trays, but Mrs Hayburn liked to preserve the illusion, even tonight when so many were present, that she was still the reigning queen of her own tea-table. And thus she had these things arranged beside her.

For the moment she was sitting alone in the room.

'Mother, this is Stephen's friend, Mr Moorhouse.'

She stood up to greet him. 'Good-evening, Mr Moorhouse. It's very kind of you to come.' Then with the typical Scots belittlement of one's own efforts at entertainment, she added, 'The boys thought they would just have a few friends in to make a little dance. It was kind of you to think it worth while. Sit down and let me give you a cup of tea.'

David murmured as suitable a reply as he could think of while his hostess bent over her tea-table.

Her welcoming speech had been everything that was insincere. She did not think it was kind of him to come. She considered it was an honour for any young man – especially one she didn't know – to enter her house. It was she, not her sons, who had decided to have the dance; for she considered it was time, for prestige's sake, that she should make some kind of social demonstration. The only use David could possibly be to her was that he helped to make up the right number of men.

But now that she had him here she was not averse to finding out something about him.

'Go and see if there are any more people to be looked after, Henry dear,' she turned to her long, gawky son who, having offered David cake, was munching a piece himself.

Henry went, leaving David alone with his mother. The music of the quadrilles started up in loud earnest. Even in the little adjoining room with the doors closed they had to raise their voices.

'Stephen said he had got to know you in business, Mr Moorhouse,' she said conversationally.

That would do excellently so far as Stephen's mother was concerned, so David said, 'Well, yes.' David was grateful to fate and Stephen that his hostess should thus unwittingly have framed this difficult question so that he could answer it.

'He didn't say what you were?'

Her question was impertinent. But David was not to be caught out.

'I'm a merchant, Mrs Hayburn.' That sounded all right. Steel merchants, coal merchants, East India merchants were the lords of Glasgow just at this time.

She was not brazen enough to probe further. Mrs Hayburn was a snob, and snobs are, as a rule, fairly stupid even at their own game. David was very new and very nervous, but he was naturally gifted socially. To an almost excessive degree he possessed the instinct to make the rough places plain. It was by chance a part of him, just as his handsome, distinguished and rather delicate face was by chance a part of him. As he sat there facing this rather formidable woman, and with the relentless beat of the quadrille in his ears, without ever lying, David gave his hostess a very suitable impression of himself. He had been brought up in the country. Mrs Hayburn jumped to – or rather was gently led in the direction of – the conclusion that he was a younger son of the Ayrshire county, not very rich, perhaps, who had come into the City to make his fortune. He was very sensibly living in rooms right in the centre to be near his work. That he was distinguished, her own eyes could tell her for themselves.

No. This was a nice young man Stephen had got to know. About the nicest he had brought home so far. She thought of several others and liked David the better.

The music of the quadrille ended. There was the sound of laughter and talk.

The door of the study burst open and Stephen Hayburn put his head in. 'Hello, Moorhouse. We haven't seen much of you. What are you doing?'

'Mr Moorhouse has been talking to me for a long time, Stephen. Which is very nice of him. I only hope you bother to be as polite to *your* friends' mothers.'

'Well, come on now.'

5

As no one else seemed to be coming into her sanctum, Mrs Hayburn put her arm through David's and led him into the drawing-room. She was doing this entirely to please herself, but the effect she created for David, little as he realized it, was excellent. The dancers, most of them, had not noticed David when first he had looked in. Now they turned to look at this distinguished young man, basking in the sunlight of that old dragon Mrs Hayburn's favour. People, especially the women, asked who he was. They learnt he was a young Ayrshireman, come to live for reasons of his own in Glasgow.

These sons and daughters of industrial prosperity were very ready to be impressed. Was this someone really of the County?

David, in a strange, unreal sort of way, was now enjoying himself. His feelings were those of a highly nervous actor, stepping in, to improvise with little rehearsal, and finding to his surprise that he is doing well – that the part suits him.

There were one or two middle-aged women sitting round the walls, mothers of girls who were also there, personal friends of the hostess. Mrs Hayburn introduced him to these. David had the natural breeding to give them attention. There was a feminine streak in his make-up, and it gave him little trouble to talk easily with women, whatever their age. In turn, they too were pleased with him. They were not averse therefore to see him stand up with their daughters and go through the movements of the lancers, quadrilles and the country dances. Everything he danced seemed to be danced with good taste and decorum. He was so unpossessive-seeming, so unfamiliar. His bearing was one of remote, distinguished shyness. Even when he danced the polka, his almost sad, indulgent smile to his partner seemed to say, 'What is this nonsense to either you or me?' And in the waltz, about which more than one mother had strong views, he appeared to dance with nothing more than a carefulness for the swinging steps, and with none of that abandon that maternal hearts deplored. For had not their husbands – as men of the world – assured them, as stays were laced and beards combed out in the privacy of conjugal bedrooms, that this waltzing was the kind of thing that would do neither young men nor young women any good?

David would have been surprised had he known what was in the minds of all these people. And he would have had sense of fun enough to laugh, and say, that, well, anyway a man couldn't help his face. Yet on the whole he was deliberately, if unconsciously, building up this social picture of himself. He didn't know, really, whether to like these people or not, and yet this playing of a part, or rather this instinctive selection of the right facets of his personality, amused him. He had a feeling that up to now he had been missing something. That somehow he was filling an essential want.

It was with the young women that, naturally, he had most to do. He found that they all said much the same thing. The Italian Opera was now in Glasgow. What did he think of Titiens and Trebelli-Bettini? The Tuesday concert in the City Hall. Didn't he think it was a pity that they were playing so much of this German Wagner's music? 'The New Music! My father says it's the New Noise. And they say London's mad about him now! We'll be having his operas up here next!' Wasn't it exciting that Herr von Bülow would be in Glasgow shortly? David made a mental note to put his deficiencies in this kind of knowledge right.

There was another type of conversation that was more difficult to deal with. Women were not so prone to it. But when, now and then, he found himself standing against the wall with a man, it was never long before it started up. You had only to establish a show of geniality, then it began. It was what he quickly came to call (when talking these functions over with Bel) 'the do-you-know? game'.

'Do you know So-and-So?'

'No, I don't.'

'Don't you really? But you see him about *everywhere*.'

What did the fellow expect you to say? 'Oh, but then I'm not exalted enough to go everywhere ...'? But again you replied meekly in the negative.

'I can't think how you've mised him. You know, he's just become a member of the Western Club. Very young to get in, isn't it? His uncle's Sir So-and-So, the shipbuilder. His mother was a sister of Lord Here-and-There.'

'I can't say I've come across him.'

Coldly, 'Oh, haven't you really? Well you *must* know ...' and so the game began again.

David could not understand what was the use of this kind of conversation. It was senseless and hollow, and certainly not conducive to friendliness. Was it to prove to you that the speaker had impeccable connections? Was it to prove to you that you were nobody at all? Or was it merely vapid talk? He decided it was that.

6

But the evening on the whole continued successfully. Towards its end David felt quite normally jolly. It was, in other words, a dance that had 'gone'. As people became less punctilious he felt more at home. At its end, like the others, he was reluctant to go.

Two of the mothers, quite determined not to let a new and useful young man slip through their fingers, mentioned little dances their daughters were insisting upon giving, and wondered if they wouldn't be too tedious for Mr Moorhouse. They received his card. A note to his rooms would get him any time. In the course of the evening, David's lodgings or digs had turned into rooms.

At last it was time to go. Even up in the gentlemen's bedroom the atmosphere had lost its chill. David got into conversation with a middle-aged man who came from Edinburgh. He was staying in the George Hotel in George's Square. David offered him a lift back into town in his – or rather Bel's – cab.

They had bidden Mrs Hayburn good-night in the drawing-room. The others were saying goodbye at the garden gate. For though the month was November, the prevailing west wind was blowing up the river. Even if it was damp, it was warm. As they stood about waiting for the succession of cabs to take their place, David was conscious of the rustle of the breeze through branches overhead, and the smell of wet country earth. Although it was dark, he was reminded that he was on the extreme edge of the town. But for a terrace or two on the Great Western Road there was nothing further west, only green fields. An incoming ship sounded strangely close. It must be passing near the village of Partick. He thought of Bel and her ambition to live out at this end of the town. He agreed with her. It was not only the right end, it was fresh and pleasant.

The cab arrived. He said goodbye to his friends Stephen and Henry. This last, running up like a great undeveloped colt, assured him it was awfully good of him to come. David felt that the boy really believed what he said. That he regarded things like dances as unpleasant visitations from on high, inflicted through the agency of a restless, self-important mother.

His fellow-passenger mounted too, and they drove off.

'Have you known these boys for long?' he asked him.

'Only Stephen.'

The man did not speak for a little. He sat looking out of the window, as the cab unwound itself down out of the maze which is Dowanhill. When it was safely on Byres Road he went on as though talk had been continuous.

'The young one's the better of the two.'

David could think of nothing better to say than 'I liked him.'

'You would. Anybody with sense would. He's like what his father was. Did you know his father?'

'No.'

'One of the men that made your Glasgow for you. And made a pile of money too. As clever as you make them. A man that wore himself out with his own enthusiasms. A "driver", with a streak of genius.'

David remembered that there had been a good many drivers with streaks of genius in Glasgow in the last hundred years or so. The more money these amassed, the more they were admired and held in awe. He had actually read in a Glasgow weekly paper recently that 'money was the one pass-key that invariably opens the door to success and distinction'. He had wondered. It didn't seem right, somehow, although that certainly was the creed of this wealthy city. No. Glasgow's great inventors, saviours of life, leaders of thought, had not built up their city merely by the money they had earned. It was the spirit that burned within them, surely, that had done that. Besides, he was much too easy-going to like drivers – either with streaks of genius or plain.

'And is Henry Hayburn very clever too?' David asked. Somehow he could not think of that great loose-jointed creature as a genius.

'They say so. They say he's sweeping everything before him. He's at the Anderson College. You'll see. He'll do something.' David's companion said nothing more for a little, then he added as though to himself: 'It would have been better for a boy like that if there hadn't been all that money for him to play with.'

Somehow David gathered that this man did not think much of his friend Stephen nor yet of Mrs Hayburn.

'I don't think Stephen bothers to work much,' he said.

'I dare say not. Their mother doesn't want either of them to work. She wants them to be gentlemen.' He tapped David's sleeve. 'Between you and me she's a bit of a fool. But if Henry didn't work that brain of his would burst. I dare say your friend Stephen's doing everything his mother wants him to do. He's got looks, manner, swell friends and all the rest of it.'

David began to wonder in what category this man was placing himself. But now suddenly he felt very sleepy. Reaction from strain had come, and it was late. For the rest of the way he answered the man in monosyllables.

University Avenue, Woodlands Road, past Mary's house in Albany Place, along a deserted Sauchiehall street, then finally down the hill and into George's Square. Mid-Victorian Glasgow was asleep. Their own wheels and the horses' hoofs seemed to make the only sounds in the City.

'Here's the hotel. And thank you.'

'Good-night, sir.'

'Good-night, Moorhouse.'

Chapter 10

I

The last Saturday in the same month.

It began cheerfully enough. Phoebe, as was her custom, had gone into the nursery several times in the course of dressing. Her nephew and niece had shown due appreciation of her visits. Sarah, who had been with Bel since ever she had set up house in Ure Place, was now promoted from being merely housemaid to nurse-housemaid, receiving some slight addition to her income and occasional help below stairs. Sarah was bleak this morning. With that determined and defeating bleakness that only servants who are beginning to consider themselves indispensables seem able to assume. It was not, however, a manifestation that troubled Phoebe. She was a child who was very little affected by other people's moods. If people showed joy or sorrow, cheerfulness or moodiness before her, as likely as not she would find herself considering them with curiosity, wondering detachedly how they had come to be thus, and how they were likely to behave next.

She took an academic interest, therefore, in Sarah's crossness. But as Sarah was determined to be untalkative, she could not for the moment discover reasons.

Bel, coming down a moment before Arthur, found his little sister sitting on a stool in front of the dining-room fire.

'Good-morning, Phoebe dear, Bel bent down and kissed her with business-like brightness. Bel's attitude seemed rather to imply, 'I am firmly determined that my house is going to be a pleasant house, and to keep it up to scratch I myself shall be the brightest thing in it.'

'Take your porridge while it's hot, dear. There's nothing like porridge for making you a big, strong girl.'

Phoebe felt big and strong enough. Besides, she loathed porridge, as most Scots children do. But she had learnt long since that resistance was useless. And as the fragrance of ham and eggs, rising from the dish set on the brass stand before the fire, was doing all it could to tempt her to reach the other side of her ordeal, she bravely poured milk over her porridge and began.

Bel watched Phoebe. She was growing up a sensible sort of girl on the whole. She didn't give much trouble. If she saw the point of what you told her to do, she did it. And as she was very intelligent, it was easy to make her see the point. But, although Bel was ready to defend her strange independence to Mary and Sophia, she deplored it rather in secret. She believed now that the girl liked her well enough – she had never known her disloyal or thankless – yet she would have been grateful for a show of warmth. For Bel was by nature a warm, pleasant person herself.

Bel sighed a little and poured herself out a cup of tea. She would take her own ham and egg when Arthur came. No. A queer child. But with any luck she would be a beauty in four or five years' time. And the small amount of money Phoebe had from her dead father, that was educating her now, would go to buying a nice dress or two and getting her off. Bel hoped that Phoebe would not be difficult about her help when the time came. Getting her off would put her into good practice for getting her own daughter off. She smiled to herself at the thought of the little year-old Isabel. Goodness knew where they would all be by the time Isabel was looking for a husband. Times were good and looked like getting better. Life was secure. Still – you never knew.

Bel sipped her tea reflectively, forgetting Phoebe's presence now. The idea of getting a sister-in-law and a daughter off had started a train of thought. Ure Place would not be a good centre for the campaign. Why wouldn't Arthur come to realize this? Why wouldn't he go further out? They were putting down tramlines all over the City now. They said it would make it much easier for the horses and that the new trams would be much faster than the old buses. The family could live perfectly well in one of the new terraces in Hillhead. Arthur could come down to his work in half an hour. And it would be so much more healthy for them all. Now that they had children, she loathed the thought of being so near the slum quarters. Only last night she had turned away a wretched, evil-looking fellow begging at the door. She was certain Arthur could afford to move. Of course, he never told her what he had, husbands didn't, but he was free and open-handed – and grudged her nothing within reason. The business must be doing well.

And now the new friendships that David was making. He had come, of course, and told her all about the dance at the Hay-burns'. He had put it all very amusingly. He had made her laugh like anything over this and that. Still, the fact remained that David was making his way. He had already accepted two other invitations of the same kind. She was glad she had helped the boy. And already so far as she dared she had put into practice several little household customs which, she had gathered, the better people always followed.

No. High time they were out of here. They were – all of them – worthy of a better background. She must brace herself once more and have it out with Arthur.

Phoebe stood up to put her empty plate away. Bel's thoughts came back to actuality.

'Finished, Phoebe? I hear Arthur. Put the ham and eggs on the table, dear.'

Phoebe did so, then went over to the window. Bel thanked her and set about her task.

'I hope it's not raining,' she said as she divided out. 'It's dull enough.' She turned to look on her own account, then turned away again. 'You've got to go to your music and your dancing, and little Arthur's going out.'

Phoebe's interest heightened at once. Her nephew's name was enough to do this at any time. 'Where are you taking Arthur?'

'Sarah's taking him to see his granny. He's to stay for his dinner. She's in bed. I promised to send him to cheer her up.'

Old Mrs Barrowfield, sixty-nine now, was suffering from rheumatism. On Friday Bel had called and found her in poor spirits. As a very special treat she had promised the old lady she should have her grandson all to herself next day at her midday meal, on condition that she did not ruin his sturdy little stomach by giving him this, that and the other. The old lady having given her promise, fully intended to break it. For what did a young girl like Bel know about feeding children? Still, better to humour her. Or the child would not be sent.

It was now that Phoebe understood Sarah's gloom. Sarah hated the old lady's officiousness. But she hated more the treatment that was accorded her by the ageing, bad-tempered maids in the Monteith Row kitchen. Bel's young maids and her mother's old ones were in a state of perpetual warfare. Phoebe, now familiar with both camps – for old Mrs Barrowfield continued to like her, and she went there often – heard the point of view of each with interest, and was filled with a detached contempt for all.

2

Arthur seemed preoccupied. He had a sip of his tea, and took up his letters. He looked quite his four years older. His face was, perhaps, a little more set, but his hand, quick and sure as it slit open his letters, showed assurance and vigour.

'Here's a letter from Mungo,' he said presently. 'What's he writing in pencil for?' And then again after a moment. 'He's in his bed. He's wrenched his leg.'

'Mungo? Good gracious. How, Arthur?' Bel exclaimed.

Arthur read aloud: 'I was in the loft of the cartshed looking at some old iron that was up there. I knew there was an old plough and some old chains, and one thing and another. Phoebe will know where I mean. I don't know when they were put there. A scrap-iron man said they might be worth a shilling or two if he could see them the next time he came. Anyway the whole floor was rotten and gave way, with me and the plough and everything else. The old plough half fell on the top of me. I was badly cut and scraped. And a leg was twisted. The boys got me out, and went for the doctor. He got me all cleaned up, and he brought the new assistant and they did what they could between them. That was on Wednesday. But it is just today that I feel like writing. I am all right, but if you could manage to run down I would not be sorry. You could arrange some things for me.' Arthur folded the letter.

'I think you should go, Arthur,' Bel said. 'You could stay and come up on Monday.'

Arthur pondered. He hated being put out of his routine. Besides he was now an assiduous kirk elder. But all common sense, every consideration of brotherliness pressed him to go.

'You must go, Arthur. You must see for yourself how he is. We'll be all right here. I'll pack your bag and send it down to the warehouse.'

'All right. There's a train at Dunlop Street about twelve o'clock.' Being Saturday made it easier from a business point of view.

Mungo now had his special place in the family. As farmers go he was becoming comfortably off. Old rule-of-thumb methods were going one by one at the Laigh Farm. With no one dependent upon him he was able to put back what he earned year by year into his stock. If he were allowed to buy his farm, Arthur did not doubt that he certainly would do so. But so far the laird, although he was on very friendly terms with his tenant, had shown no wish to let him do so. Arthur would certainly have helped Mungo with the purchase. It would be a brotherly act and an excellent investment, for Mungo in his way was as solid as himself.

During the four years that had elapsed since he had been left solitary it had been Phoebe, who had remained in closest contact. She had always gone for part of her school holiday. They had considered it right that she should not be cut off from her old home. She had always come back with her accent broadened and an inclination to be noisy, but Bel had sense enough to see that these were only surface faults, and with a little checking Phoebe lost them again in a week or two. The women servants Gracie and Jean were still there, and Mungo had assured Bel that they were good girls who would not let Phoebe come to harm. Last summer Sophia had implored Mungo to take her children for a fortnight while Phoebe was there. Wil was now eleven and Margy nine. But every day she had sent him letters telling him how to feed them, when they must go to bed, when they must change their clothes, asking if blankets were well aired, and heaven knew what else, until at last Mungo, in a rage, had sent them home. Mary's children, and, of course, Bel's were as yet too young to be an affliction to him.

The consensus of opinion in the family was that Mungo and his surroundings were excellent in their way, but roughening and coarse for those who had profited by the refinements of town life.

Now it was decided that Arthur should go. The bag was to be packed, and in addition, Bel was to make an expedition down to the shops to have a special parcel of delicacies made up for the invalid.

Having a few minutes more before she must go to her Saturday morning dancing class, Phoebe sat down and wrote the following letter:

DEAr MUngo
This is terible news. You should not have gone up there. If I had been there I would have told you, because I knew these boreds were rotten with the damp and the rats. I have climed up often, so I know.

Is your suffering terible? If so, remember we are all thinking about you. Jean and Grace nevertheless will be a very present help in time of trouble. We are all splendid here. Arthur, the second, is going to spend the day with Mrs Barrowfield, and I am very angry, because I wanted to play with him this afternoon. How are Nith and Doon and the new poney doing? If you want me I will come down to you at once. Bel will just have to give me a line to get off the school. Trust in God and your affectionate sister,
PHOEBE MOORHOUSE

She put this in an envelope, addressed it, and sealed it carefully so that Bel should not read it. Great as her secret admiration for Bel still was, Phoebe hated people poking into her affairs.

3

Old Mrs Barrowfield sat up in bed watching her grandson, The child was her greatest joy in life. She kept insisting to everybody that he was the very image of his Grandpa Barrowfield. This may or may not have been true, but the old lady would have it so, for she could not endure to think that he should bear any likeness to his Grandpa Moorhouse, who had been nothing but a farmer. At all events the child had Bel's fine, fair colouring.

She was feeling better than she had felt for some days. For, in addition to her rheumatism, she had been suffering from acute loneliness and boredom – a complaint often to be found among the elderly – and for the time little Arthur had succeeded in banishing this.

The clock on the mantelpiece of her large and comfortably upholstered bedroom overlooking the Glasgow Green chimed two.

'It's time Sarah was coming for you,' she said to the mite, who was hunting lions and tigers at the foot of her enormous bed. She had promised to send the little boy home, to have his afternoon sleep, for it was essential that he, with Sarah, should get home in safety in the daylight. And she herself, comfortable and happy now, would be quite content to drop over until tea-time.

No sooner had she spoken than Sarah appeared. Sarah was grim and purposeful, having just eaten her dinner in the enemy's camp. She began packing Arthur into his little velvet coat, gaiters, muffler, gloves, sailor hat and all the rest of it. His grandmother watched him with sleepy approval. There were not many little boys so well dressed as her grandson. That little coat had been a gift from herself. (In secret Bel thought cornflower blue a little over-bright, but wear it he must when he went to Monteith Row, or there would be no plumbing the depths of the offence her mother would take.)

Affectionate goodbyes were said, and Sarah and her charge set off. The sun was shining through a gap in a wintry sky, but as November sunshine is precious the woman determined to make the most of it. She would take her way across the Green. Probably Arthur would run for some distance, and for the rest she could carry him, for she was strongly built and well able to lift and carry a child of three. For a time after they left the Row it was very pleasant sauntering at a child's pace in the open, grassy expanse, but as they neared the Saltmarket it became unpleasantly crowded with slum children. Sarah picked up Arthur and hurried on into the Saltmarket itself. She was glad she had not come any later in the day, for already this street, famous for its disarray and squalor, was beginning to show signs of living up to its reputation. Men and women – their newly received weekly earnings already being quickly spent in the numberless drinking-shops – were showing signs of becoming boisterous.

But Sarah's honest stomach was not easily turned. You couldn't be brought up in Glasgow, if you were of the working class in however decent a family, without having seen a thing or two. She continued, therefore, cheerful and undaunted, up the Saltmarket.

It was outside O'Reilly's Oyster Rooms that the thing happened.

A younger sister of Sarah's, Peggy by name, suddenly emerged from a provision shop. She was a child of about fifteen. Sarah was annoyed to find her down here, for her family did not live in this low quarter of the town, but in a respectable quiet cottage up at the Monkland Canal. Their father had work in one of the many woodyards by its banks. She stopped to ask what Peggy was doing. Their mother had sent her out to get something, she replied, but she had failed to get it further up the town.

Sarah would not believe this. The girl had reasons of her own for being down here. Sarah decided to find them out. She was filled with what she considered was a just and righteous fury. She set down Arthur and pitched into her. Peggy defended herself badly, for she was a weak sort of girl, but Sarah's reproof was long and heated. Peggy must remember that she came from decent folk. Saturday afternoon was no time for her to be by herself in the Saltmarket. For some moments the sisters became engulfed in their quarrel.

One or two people, hearing, wondered what it was all about. Who was this decently dressed woman talking to this girl? She must be a servant. The rich-looking, golden-haired child in the blue coat, who was wandering round them, must be in her charge.

Two or three entrances up, a hag who dealt in old clothes – and other things – bent down and picked up a kitten that was playing at her feet. She came down towards them, and dropped the kitten near Arthur. He saw it and pattered towards it. She leered at him, picked up the kitten and dropped it again further off. He still followed. She did this a third time. Still he followed. Now he was opposite her own entrance. Again she picked up the kitten and again Arthur followed.

Sarah turned: 'Where's Arthur?'

She could not believe he was not by her side. She refused to believe. She shrieked.

A passing urchin pointed. 'The wee boy went in there.'

She rushed to the doorway. It was merely a passage-way leading through to a narrow close, known as 'Hughie's Yeard'. There were a dozen doors leading up filthy stairways to rooms above. He might have been taken up any of them. There was no one in the yard. She tried one stairway, but it was blocked by two drunken men. She tried a second, tripped and fell on her face, while half a dozen hags yelled abuse and laughed at a decent girl making a fool of herself. At a third a man put his arms about her. She had to struggle to force him to let her go. Out in the middle of the yard again, he stood at the door and smiled a drunken smile. Slowly he withdrew one hand from a pocket. It held a razor.

Again she shrieked and ran out through the passage into the Saltmarket. She had quite lost her head now. Her sister tried to speak to her, but she could get nothing but 'What'll the mistress say? What'll the mistress say? It'll be the jail for me!'

Poor Sarah started to run. Out of the Saltmarket into the High Street, up Kirk Street, past the Royal Infirmary in Castle Street and beyond. In her hysterics she did not think what she was doing, but her instinct was taking her home to her father's cottage.

4

After her midday meal Phoebe had sat herself down in the nursery. Bel had established herself in Sarah's accustomed place while her daughter had her afternoon sleep. Phoebe, lately promoted to serious knitting, was making a pair of socks – black and unspectacular – for Arthur. Her feelings of self-importance were just managing – and no more – to keep boredom at bay. For black is not an interesting colour for a fourteen-year-old to knit.

The sound of voices, quickly distinguishable as those of Sophia and the two children, were not, then, entirely unwelcome to her.

'Go down and say I'll come in a moment, Phoebe. I'll send Bessie up here.' Bessie was the cook.

Phoebe went down. Pompously holding her knitting. Determined that Wil and Margy Butter should see how important she had become.

Sophia's two children had settled down to play an improvisation for four fists at the piano.

'Hello, dear. How are you? I've come across to hear about Mungo. William met David. Children, would you stop it! Aren't they awful! I can't hear what Phoebe's saying! Is it true Arthur's gone down?' There was a crazy kindheartedness and warmth of feeling about Sophia that had always made Phoebe rather like her.

Phoebe walked over to the piano. For the moment, perhaps because of her knitting, she was feeling very much their aunt, even though she was only two years older than Wil. She put a hand on the back of each of their necks and shook them until the din stopped. 'Be quiet,' she said firmly, but without temper. 'You'll waken Isabel.'

Wil and Margy were normal and spirited. A fact which never ceased to astound those who thought about it. For were they not the offspring of a hen and a deaf-mute? Sophia's fussing had made them intolerably impertinent to herself. But apart from that they were much like other people's children.

The three young folks settled down to entertain themselves with Phoebe's scrapbook. Bel came in and greeted Sophia. Her face was a little anxious.

'Do you know,' she said, 'I've just realized it's after three, and Sarah is never home with Arthur yet?'

'I thought Arthur had gone down to Mungo.' It was typical of Sophia to make such a senseless remark. Even with a light cloud of worry blowing up in her mind, Bel could not help seeing this funny. The thought of her serious husband having a day out with Sarah!

'No, Sophia, I mean little Arthur.' She went to the window for a moment. 'I do think it's too bad of Mother to keep him so long. Old people are dreadful. You can't get them to be sensible. And she promised faithfully to send him back after dinner. The streets down there get so nasty on a Saturday afternoon.'

She came back to the fire, however, and talked of Mungo and his accident, showing no more worry until it was after half past three. At last she called to Phoebe, 'Go and look through the house and see if you can see any sign of them.'

Phoebe went, and returned to say they were not anywhere to be seen.

'Well, I'm not going to worry seriously until four o'clock. After that it begins to get dark.'

'Mrs Barrowfield will send them home in a cab now, surely,' Sophia said, trying to be comforting but arousing all kinds of horrors in Bel's mind.

Phoebe was hanging about. Scraps had lost their interest. She had left Wil and Margy to squabble by themselves.

The hands of the clock came, after what seemed an eternity, to four. It was raining slightly, and the light was going.

Bel was now frankly upset. Bessie came with tea, but she could not touch it. 'I wish Arthur was here; I must go across to Mother's. Bessie,' she said to the girl who had come back with little Isabel, 'go and look for a boy to fetch me a cab.'

Bessie went. There was usually a corner boy hanging about in the Place ready to run errands.

5

Phoebe followed her to her room. Watching her in mute misery as she put on her outdoor things, she saw that there were tears in Bel's eyes. For once she did not despise the sight of them. They must be for Arthur, and they filled her with an apprehension such as she had never known before.

Bessie came to say that the cab had come. Phoebe followed Bel downstairs and hung about dejectedly at the open door after she had driven off.

For quite ten minutes she stood gazing into the drizzling rain. When at length she turned to go, she noticed a figure of her own size hanging about the corner. It was Sarah's little sister Peggy.

Peggy was rather a friend of Phoebe's. The girl often came to visit in the kitchen. Phoebe was very fond of her – or rather of her visits – because Peggy was a silly child and allowed herself to be dominated, which Phoebe much enjoyed doing. She shouted to her now.

'Hello, Peggy, what are you standing there for?'

The child came forward. Phoebe could see that she was crying. 'What's wrong with you?'

Peggy's father being a coward himself had sent her down with the news of Arthur's disappearance. Sarah, still hysterical, was quite unfit to come herself. Seeing Phoebe, Peggy took heart. It was easier for her to tell Miss Phoebe than to tell Mrs Moorhouse. Through her tears, and prodded on by Phoebe's increasingly excited questions, the news came out.

Phoebe was appalled.

Arthur stolen! She had heard of such things. When she was younger Sarah and Bessie had told her tales to frighten her. But of course it was a thing that could never really happen to anyone you knew! She hadn't even believed in the stories much.

And Arthur! Her own particular Arthur! Had she not staked her claim upon him on the very first night she came here, months before he was born? Had she not lain in bed on some of those first homesick nights telling herself that there was a baby coming, who would make up for everything she had lost?

She stood trembling. What was to be done? Her contempt for Sarah was measureless. Fancy leaving the place before she had got him out! She told Peggy so roundly.

Peggy, protecting her sister, told her that the people in those places were terrible. Phoebe could have no idea.

Phoebe almost spat back at her. No, she had no idea. But that had nothing to do with it! Sarah would have to go to jail!

But she must think what to do. She told Peggy to come in and wait in the hall. The elder child obeyed.

Sophia too was appalled at the news. But for once she became quite calm and sensible. She called for Bessie – told her to take her own children home at once, and bring back her husband and David, wherever they had got to. She would stay here and look after Isabel and Phoebe.

Bessie went with Wil and Margy as she was bidden.

When they were gone, Phoebe, hanging about miserably, felt herself in the very pit of dread.

Arthur – what could they be doing to him? Why had they stolen him? She had heard that rich children had been taken for their clothes. But that might not be the end of it! This child who despised tears found herself choking back bitter, shocking sobs.

No. She must do something. *She* must think of a plan too! Couldn't she go and try to get him herself? She daren't tell Sophia. Sophia would tell her she was mad, and trot out the usual tales that only slum people could go into these places with safety on Saturday nights.

Very well. She would be a slum child. She would disguise herself. Only last Hallowe'en she had dressed as one and gone across with Sarah to Grafton Square. They had all been taken in. And when she liked she could talk like any of the beggar bairns that came to ask a piece at the Laigh Farm back-door. Suddenly, in her innocence, she was enchanted with the idea. Peggy was here and could show her exactly where Arthur had been taken.

She found Peggy still sitting, miserable, in the hall.

'Come up to my room, Peggy.'

The child followed her.

'Now take off your dress and give it to me, I'll give you this one.'

'Whit are ye goin' tae dae, Miss Phoebe?'

'Never mind, give it to me. This is a better one for you anyway.'

Peggy was the most easily cowed creature in the world. In a few moments they had exchanged dresses. She was standing in Phoebe's little braided serge school dress, and Phoebe was in her plain stuff one. But this was not the end of it, for Phoebe had taken a pair of scissors and ripped Peggy's into rags.

Peggy began to cry again.

'Don't be a silly, Peggy. You can keep my dress.'

Having taken off her own shoes and stockings, Phoebe told Peggy to come. She led her down to the kitchen. As they passed to go out at the back door, Phoebe took down the old sacking apron that Bessie put on when she washed the front steps of a morning. She would wear this on her head as a shawl. In the back green she rubbed her legs and face with mud. It was raining now, so she bared her head that the wet might take the curls out of her hair – curls nightly re-made by Bel with the help of screws of newspaper.

'Now, come on.'

'Where are we goin'?'

'Along the Rotten Row.' Phoebe's tone cowed any further questions.

Now that she had burnt her boats she began to feel that this escapade might after all be regarded as a piece of naughtiness. For the moment she was not so sure of herself. Could the people be so awful as they said? What kind of awful? If it was only drunk – well, she had seen the farm-hands drunk often. Still, she felt a little afraid. Arthur, her brother, when he heard about this, would be furious. But she could not turn tail now. She could not appear frightened before this silly girl crying beside her. And then suddenly she thought again of the unaccustomed sight of tears in Bel's eyes, and again the thought of Arthur the Second and what they might be doing to him made her sick at the stomach. No. She didn't mind about these people that everyone said were so terrible.

They were at the end of the Rotten Row now. At the Bell o' the Brae.

She turned to her companion.

'Listen, Peggy. We're going down into the Saltmarket. You're going to show me where Sarah lost Arthur.'

'No' the night, Miss Phoebe!'

'Yes, tonight. If you don't come, I'll see that Sarah gets taken straight to jail.' And Peggy thus once more frightened into obedience turned to come with her down the hill.

6

It was now about six o'clock, damp and foggy, but the rain was stopping.

The High Street was tumbling with humanity as the two children made their way downwards. The wynds and vennels, it seemed, had emptied their inmates into the main street. Filthy children, their sharp white faces already old and cunning, fought, played, snatched and howled in the gutter. Women hanging round close entrances, many already staggering, enfolded dirty babies in their drab shawls; others shrieked harsh greetings at passing friends, calling obscene pleasantries; again others, though it was still early evening, were already sitting or lying huddled against walls, rendered senseless by whisky. Men stood about in knots, their afternoon's dram causing some to appear lifeless and stupid, others to quarrel fiercely. Younger people of both sexes were parading up and down, thronging the street – pushing and jostling. The shops were busy with their Saturday-evening trade, small shops most of them, their windows lit by one gas-flare. Only the packed public-houses seemed to have enough light. High over their window-screens could be seen gaseliers with lavish clusters of white frosted globes. The children kept to the middle of the street. There it was less crowded, for walkers had to dodge hoofs and wheels, as the buses came and went on the hill. And the drivers, losing patience, were not above lashing out with their whips.

Strangely, perhaps, Peggy was more afraid than her companion. She had had many a stern warning from her parents about these quarters at certain times of the day and week, and she was ready to be terrified. For there was a gulf fixed between respectable working folks and the depraved creatures here.

Phoebe did not understand the meaning of much that she saw and heard about her. She could see the wretchedness and squalor. It was a platitude to her that abominations existed in the slums. But there was no reason that she should know more than this. She was fourteen and from a genteel, Victorian household. In addition, her mind was moving on a single track. Her passionate purpose made her, at this stage, almost unconscious of her surroundings.

They had reached the hurly-burly of Glasgow Cross now. Here the crowd and the tumult were greater than ever, but the lights of the larger shops, the flow of the traffic and the sight of more than one policeman, was, for the moment, reassuring. Peggy would have paused beneath the Tolbooth Steeple, but her companion turned to her, relentless, and pointed across to the Saltmarket.

'Is it down that way?'

'Yes, Miss Phoebe.'

The children crossed over, pushing through.

A little way down the Saltmarket two drunken sailors were fighting. The face and beard of one of them streamed with blood. Peggy screamed, and fresh tears came. Phoebe turned to look at her, and saw that she was again on the point of retreat.

'Come on, Peggy. You can go home in a minute. Where was it they took Arthur? If I get Arthur, Sarah won't have to go to jail.' She seized Peggy's arm and marched her forward.

In a few moments more the older child stopped and pointed.

'It was in there.'

'All right, you can go away now.'

Phoebe loosed her grip on Peggy's arm.

Peggy turned and ran.

Phoebe hesitated for a moment, then she crossed to the other side of the street to have a look at where she had to go. In the foggy gaslight she could see a group of women standing gossiping and cackling at the close mouth. One, very drunk, was leaning against the wall, her bonnet on one side. The others were laughing at what she said. Yet another kept performing vague reel steps, hitching back and forth as though she had a kind of St Vitus' dance. Another, perhaps younger than the rest, with some attempts at dilapidated finery, and with an unnaturally white and pink face and yellow hair, would catch a passing man by the arm now and then and try to stroke his face. This was greeted by howls of laughter from the others, though the woman seemed angry when the man shook himself free. Phoebe did not fully understand, but all her instinct told her she was looking into the abyss of degradation.

She stood pondering. How was she to get past these terrible women? For a moment fear took hold of her. But resolutely she forced it back.

Arthur was hidden away somewhere behind them. If she were feeling afraid, what must he be? No. She could not afford to be frightened.

She must use her wits again. She had already made herself look like a slum child, and she could assume a thick country accent; it was indeed a second language to her. She had gone thus far unnoticed. She must have patience and wait her time.

Another couple of sailors were coming up on the further side singing. The yellow-haired woman danced a step or two before them as they passed. The men shouted, seized her, and, one on either side of her, marched her, screaming with laughter and emitting oaths, off up the street. The other women followed, howling gibes. Only the drunken woman was left, supporting herself against the wall.

The entrance was free. Phoebe had seen the hands at the Laigh Farm drunk. She didn't like it, but she was not afraid. She could get herself past this woman without much trouble. She crossed the street, paused for a moment to look in. The woman gazed at her stupidly, blinked and said, 'Guid nicht tae ye, dochter.'

Phoebe returned the 'Guid nicht', and passed through the dark passage into 'Hughie's Yeard'.

7

If the place had looked disgusting to Sarah this afternoon, it was worse now. Phoebe's eyes had to become accustomed, for it was lit merely by one lamp and by such light as percolated through one or two dirty windows. It seemed to be entirely enclosed, its only entrance being the one through which she had come. She had to go warily, for her feet, though they had often gone unshod in pleasanter places, were sensitive to the garbage upon which she trod. More than once she avoided a broken bottle or tin can. After the rain there was a heavy stench. Several times her feet slipped among that which caused it.

There were a number of people, men and women, in the court-yard and one or two children. Some windows were thrown open, and women were shouting to each other. There was a constant wailing of infants. Yet, for it, Hughie's Yeard was fairly empty. Most of its inhabitants, and many of them were women of a certain trade, were out of it now having their Saturday's fling in the drinking-shops, or walking the streets for business. The people paid no attention to Phoebe. Her childish looks and the rags she had assumed were ample disguise. She stood some minutes bewildered by her surroundings. But noticing she was unheeded, she took courage and began to think what she would have to do. People were going out and in through the dark door-ways that surrounded the yard. She would try them, one after the other. She began with the one nearest to her.

From the entrance on the ground floor itself several single rooms opened off. Most of their doors stood open. In most of them, too, fires were burning in curious primitive fireplaces, built into one corner of the room. Women were working about, some of them cooking. It was Saturday night and there was money to buy food for the pot. By the light of the fires she could see other men, women and children lying on dirty mattresses or on straw, or merely on the floor, which was bare earth. She wondered how so many people could live together in one room. She did not know that the rooms were comparatively empty.

Through each door she peered as far as she dared. For Arthur must be somewhere. Strangely, it never struck her that he might have been taken elsewhere.

This first place was useless. She decided to ascend the stair. The steps of the stair were littered with the same obnoxious filth as the yard outside. It was not only damp oozing through ill-maintained roofs that made the woodwork cracked and rotten. There was one landing, and yet another. The rooms that opened off them and the people inside repeated very much what she had seen below, except that people lay on boards instead of earth. Some rooms had beds. But beds in Hughie's Yeard were places of luxury – and of business.

With a doggedness that had become almost mechanical Phoebe tried stair after stair. Once she was struck aside by a drunken man. Once she had to leave out a top landing because two harpies were locked together, fighting like she-devils, tearing out handfuls of each other's hair. It was amazing how little these things had come to affect her. The more appalling the horrors the greater grew her determination to find Arthur.

She had one more stair to try when a boy spoke to her. He might be her own age, but it was difficult to tell with stunted slum creatures.

'Whit are ye goin' up an' doon a' they stairs for?'

Phoebe started. This boy had been watching her! It was the first time, in what had actually been more than an hour, that she had been addressed directly. At other times she had merely been cursed out of the way. But she must go on keeping her wits about her.

She told the boy in her broadest Ayrshire that she had come up that day from Kilmarnock, and had been told that she would find her aunt here.

What was her aunt's name?

Phoebe invented one.

He did not know it, but then there were so many people here. What did her aunt do?

Phoebe looked blank and said she didn't know.

The boy leered and said something to her that she did not understand. But she thought it best to smile.

At any other time or place Phoebe would have run from this white-faced, undersized creature, but the fact that he seemed to be friendly gave her courage and set her wondering if he might help her in some way. Should she ask about a well-dressed little boy being brought into this yard today? Then fear that she might give herself away overcame her.

He offered to help her to find her aunt on the last staircase. Again it was fruitless. He pointed out to her a corner of an upper room which he said was where he lived. Phoebe made him stare by asking if every family did not have a room to itself. He asked her if they had as much space as that in Kilmarnock, and she had the wit to say they had. But after that she was afraid, and asked no more questions.

Being a helpful sort of boy, it seemed, he offered to try all the yard with her again. Although, as he said, her aunt would probably be out in the streets. Phoebe accepted. But after further endless weary plodding they could discover nothing. He tried several doors that were locked. He told her that when women were having babies they always tried to have them behind doors that locked, for then they would lock the door on the doctor, and the others could force him to give up his money before they let him out. He considered it a good joke. Did they do the same in Kilmarnock?

At the end of his journey he became affectionate and laid his hands on Phoebe. With a brute temper that she did not know was in her she struck him full in the face. Under the lamp she saw his nose was streaming. But, having called her names, the meaning of which she had no idea, he left her.

8

A numb bewilderment settled on her. But she would not leave Hughie's Yeard. She could not give up the idea that Arthur was behind one of those doors. She had no idea what to do now. She crouched down in a corner near the entrance and waited.

A bell, somewhere, tolled nine ... Now and then she could hear the trains roaring on the Union Railway viaduct that cut its way through places such as this to connect with the new College Station. Still she crouched and waited, it seemed for an infinite time. The distant bell tolled ten. The courtyard was getting noisier and fuller. There were endless fights – sometimes between a couple of ill-built, ape-like men, sometimes between drink-inflamed women. Blood flowed freely. But she was past caring. For she was stupefied now with dejection, sick with anxiety and disgust, weak from cold and want of food. Yet even now this child's iron will would not let itself be broken. She must wait here in this terrible darkness. Wait until she could take Arthur with her.

All at once there was a cry at the entrance and a rush of policemen. There were half a dozen of them, of the small, stocky type that at that time Glasgow put on slum night duty. There was a hush in the court. The squabbling stopped and the ranks closed against the intruders.

A raucous voice shouted to ask what they wanted. Phoebe was electrified by the reply.

'Is there a stolen wean in here?'

There was a shout of laughter. 'Ye better come and look.' The yard knew that six policemen would not, in common prudence, dare. The number of scoundrels against them was unlimited.

But Phoebe's heart was bursting her body. So Bel or David

had informed the police! All the windows above were filled with heads. The mob standing back in the yard and the police by the entrance stood glaring at each other. There was no-man's-land between them. Phoebe, near the policemen, could hear what they said. They were not going up 'they bloody closes the night'. It was sure murder. Even if they all went into one together they would be trapped like rats. It would be impossible to fight their way out again. They had obeyed orders and come into the yard. More they could not do. Toffs should look after their own weàns.

The people began taunting them. A woman threw some filth from a window that knocked off a policeman's top-hat, covered his face and ran down his beard. The yard applauded. Another, at a window, showed a child.

'Is it this yin?'

There was yet another roar. A woman carrying a second child danced across the no-man's-land from one close entrance to another. The thing became a game. Women danced across with children or showed them at windows.

At a top-floor window opposite to where Phoebe crouched an old hag and several young women were leaning out, enjoying the spectacle. They seemed, most of them, very drunk, as they howled down abuse in their imbecile delight.

Suddenly the group parted and a child was held out. Its face was smudged and scared. It was wrapped in what looked like a piece of sacking. The woman, seemingly less drunk than the rest, held him up.

'Here! Is it this yin?'

Phoebe's scream was lost in another shout of animal laughter.

It was Arthur.

The numbness had left her. She must decide at once what to do. Should she tell the policemen beside her? Or were the chances of getting him out better if she acted by herself? She had heard them say they would not let themselves be trapped. No. She would act by herself.

There were more howlings, more taunts, more children held up, but at last the policemen went. The inmates of the yard settled down to discuss the affair. From what she could hear, they did not know of the stolen child.

She must go and reconnoitre. She went up the stairs to the top. From its window, it was quite easy for her to decide in which room Arthur must be, although the loathsome landing was almost in black darkness. She pressed against the door gently. It did not give. Presently a woman came out and went downstairs. The door was at once closed, and Phoebe could hear a key being turned. But she had caught a glimpse of a brightly burning fire, a number of women and on one side a bed.

She settled down to wait. She was very excited now, and felt a strange tension in her head; but she felt no fear. People came and went from the other rooms on the landing. She had constantly to be jumping to avoid them. But they were used to crouching children, and they let her be.

Gradually she became conscious of increasing noise in the yard below. There seemed to be more roaring and drunkenness. She did not know that the public-houses closed at eleven, that those who had been turned out were coming home. Several people came up and staggered into the other rooms. At last two women came up dragging two reeling men with them. She had to press herself hard against the oozing wall to let them pass. She could not understand why the women were using words of coarse endearment. They banged on the door, giving their names. The door opened. One man was so drunk that it took a long time to get him through. Phoebe was given ample time to examine the room. Men and women were lying about on straw. Another couple were in the bed. The beasts of the Laigh Farm had taught Phoebe life's straightforward facts. She could have no knowledge of these more terrible ones. It was lucky that her eyes could only look for Arthur.

9

He was there near the fire, sitting on a heap of straw. His eyes were bewildered. Once, he made to move. But the old hag that she had seen at the window struck him. He whimpered, but did not cry. Phoebe felt herself trembling.

The door closed again. It had been no use going in just then, among these furies. But business was becoming brisk, more men and women came up the stairs. The door opened and shut many times. Sometimes, indeed, it was allowed to stand open. Whisky went round freely. They did not bother to turn the key any more. The room was littered with people – stupefied beasts. But still the hag sat on a box by the fire, keeping watch, controlling in some measure her dreadful trade. At first she refused pulls of whisky when they were passed to her. But later Phoebe saw her take one or two.

At last a man came up by himself. Two women greeted him.

Each seemed to think him her special property. They began to fight, tearing each other's hair. The room went into an uproar. Foul bodies were exposed, but Phoebe did not see. She was nothing now but an instinct, calculating its chances to snatch. A little, predatory animal, lurking outside in the darkness.

Now in the turmoil she saw what she wanted. The old woman had risen to interpose. In the fight she was thrust screaming against the wall. For the moment Arthur was forgotten. It was lucky he was near the fire. Even in drink they knew to keep away from that. Phoebe slid into the room. Several times she was crushed by the onlookers as they swayed out of the way of the fighters.

She picked up Arthur and, shielding him as best she might, carried him from the room.

Down the stairs, as quickly as she could. A broken bottle had cut her foot, but she did not feel it. Into the yard. The passage was blocked with people, but she pushed past them. She did not hear their senseless oaths. To them she was merely a slum child carrying another. The pandemonium of the Saturday night Salt-market was at its height, but she did not notice. Several times she tried to speak to policemen, but their hands were full. They would not stop to listen to this filthy girl with the dirty, white-faced child.

Now she was at the Cross. For an instant she halted. Arthur was very heavy for her. She set him down for a moment to think. She would make along the Trongate until she came to a quiet part. At length she came to Glassford Street and turned up. In Ingram Street it was peaceful. She set down Arthur again. His weight was killing her. For the first time she became aware of her foot. She saw it was bleeding freely.

'Walk, Arthur. Walk with Phoebe.' It was the first time she had spoken to him.

But the child merely gave bewildered whimpers and held up his arms.

A policeman passed. She crossed to speak to him, planning to use her usual voice, to tell where she lived, and so prove that she was not what she seemed.

But he turned upon her. 'Away hame. Away oot o' this.' He had had enough of slum brats and their stories.

There was nothing to do but summon all her strength and try to pick up Arthur. Now she was on the low, flat part of Montrose Street. Now at George Street. She set him down once more and looked up the hill. How would she ever get him up there?

She stood, leaning against the wall for what seemed an eternity. She made attempts to encourage herself. Had she not done what six policemen had failed to do? Arthur had said that there were places where no respectable man dare show himself. She had dared. But her pulsing head was past encouragement. They would be so angry with her for going ... Still she had had to go for Arthur ... She couldn't help it ... She had had to go ... And now she must just collect herself and try to make Ure Place. She took Arthur by the hand and dragged him. He began to howl, but she paid no attention. At least, she was getting him to walk. Here was Richmond Street. That was halfway. All was dark. Respectable folk were asleep. She sat down with Arthur on a doorstep to gather strength for the last effort. Arthur's little teeth were chattering as he cried, for he was wrapped in nothing but a bit of sacking.

And now the last effort. Up. Up the steepest part of the hill. She must get there even if she went mad. Now the lower side of Ure Place. Everything was dark but their own house. She could see it through the shrubbery that filled the middle of the square. Its windows were blazing. The door was open, too. Restless figures were haunting the threshold. She moved to get a better view. Against the light she saw the shapes of Bel and David.

With a final effort she gathered the remainder of her strength to shout as loudly as she could.

'Bel! Bel!'

In a moment more her brother David had lifted her up from the pavement, senseless.

Chapter 11

1

It was Christmas Day, an event which was then given little importance by the country folks in Scotland, for New Year's Day was – as, indeed, it still is – the winter feast day. It was the towns, less traditional and less grim, that first became infected by the cheerful spirit of the English Christmas.

But on this dark morning the Laigh Farm was an exception to the rule. Its kitchen, at least, was filled with the Christmas spirit. The great fire, re-lit hours ago, flamed red and cheerful, glowing into every corner and defying the frosty, half-hearted daylight outside. The plates stacked on the scrubbed dresser, on the opposite wall, glittered and blinked. And there was holly about. Along the top of the dresser. Up beside the plates that were put there for ornament. In a white jug on the high mantelshelf. Between the pair of china dogs and the pair of tea canisters, bearing portraits of the young Queen and the Prince Consort. Over the large new portrait of the middle-aged Queen, that last summer Phoebe had persuaded Mungo to buy from a traveller at the door – simply because he had looked tired, and had appealed to her feeling for lame ducks. Over the grandfather clock that placidly ticked out the life of the Laigh Farm in another corner. The farmwomen called all this holly Phoebe's nonsense. For it was Phoebe, versed now in the customs of the town, who had put it about.

Phoebe was an indulged young lady these days. A cloth was laid over one end of the great scrubbed table and breakfast was laid – still awaiting her august arrival, though it was almost nine o'clock. There were parcels, too, by her plate – Christmas presents from the family in Glasgow.

Jean bustled in from work outside. She was a stout, pleasing figure now, with her glowing cheeks, her coats kilted for work, her drugget apron, and her Annan clogs. She took down a frying-pan from its hook and began to bang about.

'Guidsakes,' she said to herself, 'is that lassie never up yet?'

She opened a door to call, but was met by Phoebe coming in.

'Good-morning, Jean.'

'Guid-mornin'. A wis comin' tae look for ye. It's nine o'clock.'

'Well, here I am.' Phoebe was a little spoilt and pompous, for she had been ill. Her face was still pale a little, and now and then a nervousness in her movements, a haunted look, betrayed the fact that she had passed through an ordeal beyond her strength.

'They things are fur yer Christmas,' Jean said, indicating the parcels.

Phoebe, forgetting her dignity, ran to the table. She looked through the parcels and the names of the givers. She had never had so many. Why were they all making such a fuss this Christmas? she wondered. Everybody seemed to want to give her something. All the brothers and sisters. And here was a parcel from Jean and Gracie. Tactfully she opened it first. A box of 'Edinburgh Rock', several pink and white sugar mice with string tails, and a little hymn book.

'Oh, Jean, these are lovely!' And the inevitable Scots remonstrance, 'You shouldn't have bothered.'

'Och, they're jist some bits o' things,' Jean said self-consciously as she took Phoebe's porridge from the fire and poured it into a bowl.

'Is Gracie in the milk-house?' Phoebe ran to thank her, and brought her back into the kitchen.

The two devoted women were all eagerness to see the other presents as Phoebe undid them. A beautiful workbox from Bel with wools and canvas for a sofa cushion, already 'begun' to indicate the correct colours. Books from Arthur. Indoor games from Sophia and William, and a new book to hold scraps from Wil and Margy. An expensive, handsomely illustrated book of religious stories from Mary and George. A book of quadrilles and lancers and a bottle of scent from David (Phoebe was to spend the remainder of her holiday drenched in this). The women went into greater raptures than Phoebe did, especially over the coloured wools.

Phoebe sat down to her porridge feeling very important indeed.

As Jean changed her plate, and set her ham and eggs before her, Mungo came in, and the two women left the kitchen. He was still very lame and used crutches. He lowered himself down into his big chair by the fire. His two dogs curled themselves up under the table at Phoebe's feet. She wished him a Merry Christmas, and pointed to her presents.

He smiled good-naturedly. 'Aye, ye've done very well.' He thrust his hand in his pocket and drew out an envelope. 'And that's from me,' he said, adding, 'Ye see, I couldn't get to buy you anything.'

The envelope contained a gold half-sovereign. Phoebe thanked him, pleased but embarrassed.

'That'll do fine for your bank.' A rather bleak suggestion, Phoebe thought. But he tempered it by saying: 'Unless there's anything particular you're wanting.'

Controlling herself, Phoebe said demurely that she thought there might be, but she would keep it and see; then settled down again to her breakfast.

'I've got something else here for ye,' Mungo said presently, pulling out a neat little parcel and holding it out to his sister. 'They said I was to take charge of it and give it to you myself.'

Phoebe came across and took it from him. 'What is it?'

'Open it and see.'

When she had taken off the wrapping-paper she came upon a small cardboard box, bearing upon its lid the name of a well-known Glasgow jeweller. And inside this was a still smaller black-grained box. Phoebe took it out and opened it. There, mounted on a red-velvet mount, was a handsome lady's gold watch, surrounded by coils of fine golden chain and handsomely engraved with the initials 'P.M.'

She looked bewildered. 'Where did this come from?' she asked her brother, who had been sitting watching her.

'Open and see.'

She opened it. On the inside were the words: 'From Arthur Barrowfield Moorhouse to his Aunt Phoebe. Saturday, 21st November, 1874.'

Phoebe said nothing. She turned the watch about, examining it closely. But her brother could see a deep flush. Bel and Arthur must have bought this for her. At length she put it back into its case, twined the long chain into place, and closed the lid.

'It's a nice watch, isn't it?' Mungo hazarded.

'Yes.'

He could not tell what was going on inside her head. She must realize, of course, that the date marked the day on which she had brought her nephew back from Hughie's Yeard. He tried again to make her speak. 'Will I keep it safe for ye?'

'Yes.' She came over and handed it back to him.

They had all been puzzled, even the comprehending Bel, though the family was, in fact, behaving strictly according to her orders. Phoebe, indeed, was living in the middle of a conspiracy of silence.

When she had come to her senses again on that November Saturday night, she had found herself in her own bed with Sophia and the family doctor standing over her. Sophia, who was holding her hand, smiled when she opened her eyes. 'Yes, dearie, it's me.'

Phoebe looked about her wildly. 'Is Arthur all right?'

'Yes. Yes. His mother's with him. He's all right.'

After they had got her clean and made her drink hot milk, she lay restless. The cut in her foot was pulsing. She could smell carbolic. Sophia sat by her watching. 'Are you all right now?' she asked presently.

Phoebe turned her head and looked at her sister. 'I would like to speak to Bel.'

'I'll get her.'

Bel came, bent over Phoebe and kissed her. The child could see tears in her eyes. 'Do you want to say something to me, Phoebe?'

Phoebe nodded, then raised herself to look about.

Bel, grasping her meaning, reassured her. 'It's all right. There's nobody here but ourselves.' She shut the door.

'Bel, will you promise to tell nobody where I've been?'

'But, Phoebe, why?' Bel was utterly bewildered.

'You see,' Phoebe went on, 'I had to get Arthur. The more bad things I saw, the more I knew I had to stay till I could bring Arthur with me.'

'Of course, dear. You should be proud. Why not tell people?' But she could not get Phoebe to respond.

'I saw – I saw—' Phoebe's voice trailed off. But her look and her tone opened up vistas.

'Don't tell me what you saw, Phoebe, unless, sometime, you feel you want to. We'll all forget about it. I'll tell Arthur. Nobody else. And we'll never talk to you about it again.'

Phoebe looked relieved. 'Does Sophia know where I've been?' she asked presently.

Bel nodded. 'I think perhaps she guessed. But she won't tell anybody either.'

These promises seemed to calm her, and it was not long before exhaustion called her into uneasy sleep. Bel stood by her bed wondering. What kind of mark had the experience of the night laid upon the spirit of this strange child whose wilfulness had so often sorely tried her? And now in a burst of mad courage she had paid her back for her trouble a thousandfold, without, it seemed, even realizing that she had done it. There was nothing, Bel told herself, that she would not do for Phoebe for bringing back her son safely.

But in the days that followed, the days of getting well, Phoebe continued to puzzle her sister-in-law. She kept imploring Bel to keep people away from her. She would see no one. It was as though the child had submitted to some shame in order to rescue her nephew. A shame which even such a motive could not wipe out.

The little boy, apart from lingering night fears and a bad cold, was very little the worse; but Phoebe's was a much more difficult condition. It seemed, at first, as though the slums had laid their blight upon her. Her round face was pinched, and her steady Celtic-blue eyes seemed almost shifty. If she heard a visitor in the hall below she got out of bed and locked her bedroom door.

Bel and Arthur, passionately anxious now to do their best for her, were at their wits' end. But when the time came for her to be about again it was Phoebe herself who solved their problem.

'Bel,' she asked, 'am I to go back to school?'

'Not until after Christmas. And only if you feel well enough.'

'I would like to go and stay at the Laigh Farm.' And then, scrutinizing Bel's smiling and much-relieved face: 'You haven't told Mungo, have you?'

Bel continued to smile. Without hesitation she lied to Phoebe, placidly and radiantly. 'Of course not. What would I tell Mungo for? I think the Laigh Farm would just be the very place for you.'

And so it came that Arthur took her down in a few days' time, cautioning everyone who was likely to come into contact with her against making mention of her exploit.

The entire Moorhouse clan buzzed with talk, of course. Mary agreed that Phoebe had been splendid, but added that no doubt little Arthur would have been quietly turned into the street on the next morning and been little the worse, as other children who had been kidnapped for their clothes invariably were. Sophia told Wil and Margy that Phoebe was a heroine, then realizing that she had gone too far, refused to say any more and was forced to tell them she would whip them if they kept on asking questions. There were many discussions, too, about Phoebe's curious shame over the episode. Sophia said indiscreetly that she could just imagine what Phoebe must have seen. Mary looked so shocked that Sophia should claim any such powers for her imagination that Sophia squirmed a little and said, 'Well – not exactly.' At which Mary looked at Bel and said, 'We hope not.' Then Mary said she thought it would be a good idea if they all three prayed every night that their little sister's soul should be cleansed. Bel nodded a pious acquiescence, but felt in her heart that the air of the Laigh Farm was probably having much the same effect.

3

Jean came back to the kitchen and began to clear away. Phoebe came over and sat herself opposite Mungo. He watched her as she busied herself with the wools and canvas Bel had given her.

'Why are ye taking out the bit that's done already?' he asked presently.

'Because I want to do it my own way.'

'But that's to show ye the right colours.'

'I want to decide my own colours.'

Queer, dour wee thing, with her black hair sternly controlled, her curls pushed back by the large round comb, her wide, braided serge dress spread about her, and her feet crossed on the hassock. There were a lot of things she would want to decide for herself as she grew up.

All at once the dogs got up from beneath the table and began to grumble. 'There's somebody coming in. See who it is, Phoebe,' he said, regretting his lameness.

She rose and went to the window, looking into the farm close. 'It's a lady, with a brown dog, carrying a basket.'

'It'll be Miss Ruanthorpe.'

'Miss Ruanthorpe of the Big House?'

'Aye.' Mungo shifted restlessly in his chair.

'Why is she coming here?'

'She comes often. She'll want me to tell her what to do with some o' her ponies.'

In a moment Gracie came back, followed by a lady and a brown spaniel, at which Doon and Nith continued to show fangs, until they had to be ordered from the kitchen. 'Here's Miss Ruanthorpe,' she said. And Phoebe, with the innocent lynx eyes of a child, saw Jean and Gracie exchange the ghost of a smile.

She was rather an authoritative lady, Phoebe thought, as she took in her strong muddy boots, her rough tweed clothes and her rather mannish hat of the same stuff, skewered to her thick brown hair with several hatpins. Her skin was weather-beaten, but she had fine eyes and flashing teeth.

'Don't get up, Mr Moorhouse. I haven't come to disturb you. How's the leg? Getting on? That's good. I've just come in to wish you a Merry Christmas.'

Phoebe moved to give Miss Ruanthorpe her chair, and herself took the wooden one that Jean had pushed forward.

'So this is the little sister I've been hearing about? A Merry Christmas, my dear. My father has sent you this bottle of Napoleon brandy, Mr Moorhouse – more than sixty years old – and here are some sweets that cook has been making. We mustn't forget our invalids, must we?'

She settled herself and beamed all around her. She was a queer lady, with her booming voice and her 'English' accent, but nice, Phoebe decided, as she opened the package of sweets.

'You see, Sir Charles is English, Phoebe, so that gives us an excuse to hold Christmas, and my mother is Scotch, and so we have to hold New Year too.' She laughed amiably.

Queer, reserved little thing, Margaret Ruanthorpe thought, looking at Phoebe. Was she shy? Or was she merely undemonstrative? That she had character and courage, she already knew: for Mungo Moorhouse had told her.

She sat looking about her, laughing and chatting in the glowing friendly kitchen. This only child of the laird and his lady had left a house full of guests because she could not help herself. Christmas Day was merely an excuse to come across and visit the man who sat there with his crutches beside him. She could not keep away. She looked at him now, his face lit up by the firelight. His accident had taken some of the robustness out of it; it was paler than usual, a little thinner and more distinguished. She had heard the legend of the Moorhouse family's beginnings. She could well believe it. Mungo Moorhouse's natural breeding and dignity came from somewhere. He was an honest Ayrshire farmer, but he was neither obsequious nor arrogant; his poise seemed a part of himself.

From time to time, since he had been left alone, he had helped her with her dogs and her ponies. Their friendship had ripened, mostly in and around her father's stables. At first, she had determined to regard him as an agreeable and obliging tenant. But growing feelings would not hide, and she had come to realize that she had started up more than a casual friendship. She had spent many a sleepless night wondering what to do about this handsome forty-year-old bachelor farmer. She kept inventing endless excuses to bring him to her or to come and see him herself. His accident had been a godsend. She was assailed now by the full passions of a woman in her middle thirties desperately in love. His respectful politeness maddened her. Her situation and his made it more difficult. Could there be no way out? If only she had been the man!

Now she was inviting Phoebe to come and spend the day at Duntrafford. But Phoebe looked troubled, and Mungo excused her on account of her illness. It was always the same. Things conspired to baffle her.

'Well, perhaps you'll both come when our guests have gone

and we're by ourselves again.' She got up. 'No, don't, please, Mr Moorhouse.'

But Mungo struggled to his feet, saw her to the door, then hobbled off to talk to his men.

4

From the kitchen window Phoebe watched Miss Ruanthorpe and her spaniel go out through the back gate. She caught herself wondering vaguely what the smile that had passed between the two farm-women had meant. She must ask them. What was the joke about Miss Ruanthorpe? It couldn't be that she was in love with Mungo, she decided complacently, nor Mungo with her, for she was much too different. Phoebe was still too much of a child and a provincial to realize that even people who had strange, foreign ways might have feelings just like herself.

She gave up thinking about the visitor, and came back to the fire. On the ledge of Mungo's pipe-rack was the case containing her gold watch. Mungo had left it there, forgotten, when he had gone out. She must give it to him to lock up when he came back.

Now that she was alone she could examine it unselfconsciously. She took it out, dangled it, looked at its inscription, put the chain about her neck and slipped the watch, where it should be, beneath her belt. She stood up on a chair to examine the effect in a small square of mirror that hung by the window. Having done this she jumped down, and put it carefully back into its case. She looked at it long and thoughtfully before she closed the lid.

So they had considered it worth while to give her that, because of what she had done for Arthur? Even though she had run away to get him without their permission? She tried now, for the first time, deliberately to cast her memory back into the terrors of that night. She had not understood all, but she had understood enough. And her sensibilities, poised between girlhood and womanhood, had received a bewildering shock. But in these quiet weeks at the farm, her firm will, like her strong little body, had already in great measure come to her rescue. Already the pictures of Hughie's Yeard, the yard itself, the terrible fighting women, the nightmare room where Arthur had been, were becoming unreal – were beginning to haunt her less and less as she lay at night in the darkness. And perhaps in time the strange, unexplained sense of shame would leave her too.

She put the watch-case back where she had found it, and

settled down once more with her canvas and her wools. Anyone looking through the window would have seen a rather prim little girl of fourteen sewing as though her life depended upon it, a girl who had seen nothing more than other children of her age.

Phoebe was well on the way to recovery. Now for the first time she dared to return to her habit of detachment – to view herself as the leading figure in what had been a very unpleasant experience – to prod, indeed, her wounds a little, to see just how sensitive they still might be. And as she sat there examining her feelings coolly, a conviction began to form itself. Hughie's Yeard had scared and terrified her. It had sickened and revolted her with named and unnamed horrors. But it had not driven her from her purpose. It had not broken her passionate will. She, Phoebe Moorhouse, had, even at the most terrible moments, managed to be strong.

Chapter 12

I

There was little that Margaret Ruanthorpe did not know of the doings at the Laigh Farm. Since, in the middle of January, she had heard that Phoebe was not yet gone back to Glasgow, she determined that Mungo and she should pay their visit to Duntrafford. She announced her intention in a roundabout way to her father and mother as they sat at breakfast.

'Now we've got everybody away, I'm thinking of sending someone over to the Laigh Farm to fetch Mungo Moorhouse to see Jupiter. He's not right yet. He ought to be by now, but he isn't.'

Sir Charles looked at his daughter. He was an abrupt old man of seventy-five. 'What does Johnstone say?'

His daughter shrugged. 'Oh, Johnstone! You know what kind of a vet he is.'

Her father reflected. He had an excellent idea of what was in her mind. As a family the Ruanthorpes prided themselves on their lack of subtlety. You said what you thought. You did what you liked. You showed what you felt. And Margaret had shown what she felt about Mungo Moorhouse. He didn't object. When she had been younger he and his wife had thought of her in terms of good marriages and likely young men. And Margaret, not lacking looks, had had such a young man at one time, but he had been killed in a skirmish somewhere out East. And after that she, too, had become a little loud-voiced and abrupt. And she had become louder and more abrupt after her only brother was killed in the hunting-field; an event that had nearly broken the heart of the handsome, tight-lipped woman of seventy sitting at the other end of the table. But they were all tough. Charlie's death had turned poor Lady Ruanthorpe into an austere woman, interested in social conditions. Thus had she managed to go on with life.

'Johnstone isn't bad,' she was saying now as she plunged a knife into the corner of an envelope. 'He was very good with Pansy when she had distemper. I wish he wouldn't drink so much.' Having made this contribution to the breakfast-table conversation, she withdrew the contents of the envelope, flicked it open, and began studying what proved to be a fresh call upon her philanthropy.

Her husband drank his coffee thoughtfully, supporting the cup in his hands, both elbows on the table. No. If his daughter could bring off this strange affair of hers, let her. After all, she was getting on. It didn't matter a curse what the County thought. Damn it, she was a Ruanthorpe, and Ruanthorpes did what they liked. Moorhouse was a fine young man (forty is young to seventy-five), and as straight as you make 'em. She might do much worse. She couldn't have looked anywhere for better, cleaner blood. He was a countryman, and they were country people. Her interests were passionately for the land, and so were his. Good luck to her. But she had better hurry up if she wanted to produce a brood of Ruanthorpe-Moorhouses. And, besides, he didn't want to be too senile to enjoy them. Indeed, the thought of all this warmed you vastly. You wouldn't feel so old and dried up, so discontinuous. If Charlie had lived, of course— Still that was milk spilt long ago now. Sir Charles laid down his cup and looked out of the window. For a moment he saw a young man's set, white face with a streak of crimson oozing slowly over his brow from underneath thick dark hair. For a moment he felt again the agony of trying to tell himself that those eyes that stared up at him were not turning lifeless and glassy, as he held the boy, kneeling there, regardless of the mud in that new-ploughed field. Yes. A brood of children to run about and make a noise before you were too old to care who did what.

'The little sister is still there. A strange kind of child.'

'Is that the child who has been ill? Who went into the Glasgow slums?' Lady Ruanthorpe asked, suddenly pricking her ears.

'Yes; I thought I might ask them both to lunch.'

'Do. I shall ask her exactly what she saw.'

'You can't do that, Mother. It's not allowed.'

Lady Ruanthorpe grunted. 'Ask her to lunch anyway.' She took off her steel spectacles, held them in the light, puffed at them, and rubbed them up firmly with her table napkin, much as her own butler did the spoons. Thereafter she stabbed another letter and was again lost to her family.

2

This time Miss Ruanthorpe persuaded Phoebe to come to Duntrafford. All her life, of course, Phoebe had heard of the people at the Big House, and she had all the awe that still lingered among the country people when they came into contact with the laird and his family. It was strange to her now to find Sir Charles's daughter bothering to be so friendly. There was something canny in Phoebe that put her on her guard against people who were too nice. But Margaret's habitual abruptness breaking through, now and then, her intense desire to please, had the effect, strangely enough, of reassuring her.

The winter-morning drive to Duntrafford was everything that a fine January morning in Ayrshire can be. Farm steadings, crowning rolling hills, shone white in the brief sunshine. Old trees stood up around them, every twig and branch adding to the pattern they made against the duck-egg blue of the sky. Ploughs turning up the long, purple-brown furrows, behind the sleek fat buttocks of the giant Clydesdale horses. Sea-gulls, flapping greedy white wings, following after. On the horizon a piled-up white cloud. Everywhere the smell of the fresh turned earth and rotting leaves – the smell of winter. As they came into the Avenue of the great house, rooks rose from high trees about them. Once there was that heavy scent of a fox.

Miss Ruanthorpe had been wise enough to extract no promise to stay to lunch from either of them, for she knew that Mungo was shy. But when the Moorhouses were driven round to the front of Duntrafford House, unexpectedly – for Mungo thought he was being taken direct to the stables – a man was there with a tray and decanter, and Mungo, unable to refuse, had to take what was offered him, while his sister, bidden to jump down, was taken in charge by Lady Ruanthorpe and led inside to eat cake and drink milk.

Phoebe looked about her. She felt strange, in this great padded room, dangling with tassels, hanging with pictures, and glittering with Indian brass pots filled with hothouse plants. And before her the lady she had so often seen of a Sunday, sitting in the Duntrafford pew in the Big Kirk. Indeed, the very thought of church suggested, in her mind, a musty smell of Bible, coconut matting, a hassock your short legs couldn't comfortably reach, and Lady Ruanthorpe in the front of the gallery. Phoebe didn't believe she was real, that she had an existence elsewhere. When Mr McMinn the beadle dusted the pew and brushed the cushions, he must surely give Lady Ruanthorpe a dust and a brush-down too. Now here she was sitting in a room at Duntrafford, being given plum-cake and milk by the lady from the front of the gallery. Still she was not quite real to Phoebe. She seemed a creature from another world, but the child realized that in spite of her severe expression, and her formidable old-fashioned iron-grey curls and cap, Lady Ruanthorpe was trying to be kind.

'I'm not taking you out to the stables, Phoebe, because I hear you've been ill,' she said.

'I'm quite well now, thank you,' Phoebe said demurely. 'The doctor said I could go out if I kept warm.'

'You'll keep warmer here.'

Phoebe was disappointed. She had hoped to see the Duntrafford ponies. She said so a little timidly.

Lady Ruanthorpe smiled. 'This won't be your last visit, I hope, my dear. Then you can run about everywhere and see everything.'

And so, Phoebe had to stay and talk to this downright lady. She told Phoebe about the dogs and the horses, and insisted that she must come back when it was spring and see the foals and the puppies at the kennels. Phoebe, having formed anew her ideas of what one talked about from Bel, was surprised that the old lady should tell her so much about stud doings. According to her town code it was not ladylike. And yet if Lady Ruanthorpe were not ladylike, who would be?

But the old woman knew that Phoebe was, after all, a daughter of the land and treated her accordingly.

Funny little thing this, with her gentilities of manner, and a slight Glasgow tang in her pleasant voice. Life had written little on her smooth childish face. And yet there was a firmness about her mouth, and her blue eyes were quick. So this was the child who had disappeared for many hours into the worst of the Glasgow slums – the worst in Europe, as she had learnt from missionary pamphlets and special commission reports – and re-emerged triumphant, late in the night, with her stolen three-year-old nephew, safe. What had she done while she was there? What did places like that look like? What had happened? Margaret had said she must not be questioned. Stuff and nonsense. She would ask the child about it now. She was interested in that sort of thing.

It was not extraordinary, perhaps, that an old lady, who counted upon always getting her own way, should ask Phoebe the forbidden question, but it was extraordinary that Phoebe should tell her all the story of her adventure from end to end, answering and amplifying, on being questioned, all that she had already said. When she came to look back on this, as a grown-up woman, she could not explain it to herself. It was not merely that she was well again and able to think of her experiences without nervous revulsion; for when she returned to Arthur and Bel and found that they made no mention of it, she did not attempt to break the taboo. Perhaps it was that Lady Ruanthorpe was nearer reality, was less a creature of her time than Bel. That, somehow, even in the short half-hour Phoebe had known her, she had created about the child an atmosphere of directness – of spades-spadishness – that naturally chimed with Phoebe's own nature; chimed better than the rather stuffy gentility of Ure Place with its polite carefulness. But whatever the reason, there it was. And Phoebe felt much the better for the telling. This odd, over-frank old woman had the effect somehow of a confessor. And when the recital was over and when she seemed to think that what Phoebe had done was not only right but brave, the child felt that something had been washed clean again, that a puzzling inner disarrangement had been set straight. Looking back she was always grateful to Lady Ruanthorpe for inducing her to talk.

3

Their day out was indeed an experience for both the Moorhouses.

Mungo, hobbling about, said his say about Margaret's colt. He looked at the other horses and ponies. He spoke to the grooms whom, in the everyday traffic of the district, he knew well. He had a word for the keeper at the kennels. When he said he must go to find his sister and return home, Miss Ruanthorpe laughed and told him that her mother was keeping Phoebe for lunch, and wouldn't he stay too?

There was nothing for it. No way out. He had been brought hither in Sir Charles's gig and could only get back when he was taken. So Mungo and Phoebe found themselves in the large, heavy dining-room of Duntrafford House, lunching with the laird and his ladies.

His bearing was shy, but he was direct and simple. His manner had no gentilities. The talk at the table was entirely within his range. Sir Charles was an eccentric, as many landlords were; for in these not very democratic days they were little kings and behaved accordingly – but on the whole he was a good laird. His interests went with those of his tenants. And so the meal passed for Mungo in a pleasant exchange of familiar ideas, and – although he did not define this – in an atmosphere of respect and flattery to himself.

Phoebe sat through the meal reserved and quiet, collecting, detachedly as usual, many impressions. At last, in the early afternoon, the gig was sent for and they were allowed to think of going home. She was surprised when Miss Ruanthorpe bent down and kissed her as she said goodbye.

Mungo had limped round to the horse's head to have a look at him. Presently he found Margaret Ruanthorpe's hand in his. In a way, they were, for the moment, isolated from the others.

'Goodbye, Mr Moorhouse.' Mungo's strong, farmer's hand, crushing her own, made Margaret a little reckless. She went on, 'You will come again soon, won't you? Remember, it will always give me a great deal of pleasure.' Her tanned face was scarlet, and the sober farmer's face suddenly caught fire from it. With a little awkward laugh he said goodbye and turned to manoeuvre his lameness up into the gig.

On the drive home Mungo Moorhouse sat utterly dumbfounded. Phoebe, and the groom who drove them, wondered why they couldn't get a word out of him. So the laird's daughter was in love with him? There could be no mistaking her meaning! Strange though it may seem the glaring fact had just occurred to this steady, unimaginative man for the first time. He had no vanity to tell him sooner. Now he was thunderstruck!

What was he to think about it? He didn't know. He simply had no idea. He would have to consider a great deal. He was not in love with her. He had never been in love with anybody, really. He was in his fortieth year, and he supposed he had forgotten to fall in love.

And yet— No, he must think about it. Of course, a man was all right up to forty, but after that it was a dreich kind of life with no woman and no bairns about. Why hadn't he thought about it before? Why had he let things go? Now the laird's daughter! And what would the laird think? And would he, Mungo, have to change his way of life? He couldn't do that at his age. No. He would have to think about it. He would have to think about it a great deal – give the matter great consideration!

Chapter 13

1

It had taken Bel some time to take stock of things. Arthur the Second, and, even more, Phoebe, had given the household in Ure Place much anxiety and much to think about. By the time the little boy had been nursed back to his cheerful, baby normal, and Phoebe had been dispatched to Mungo at the Laigh Farm, Christmas and New Year were upon her. Presents, black bun, plum-pudding and the pantomime with Sophia's and Mary's children, who were now of an age to enjoy it, had put an end, for a time, to her favourite hobby of planning.

Bel, ever the most advanced, announced that this year the Christmas dinner would be given by herself. Mary McNairn claimed the New Year dinner, after the weakest of protests from Sophia, who remonstrated feebly that her emotionless husband, William, would be terribly disappointed that the family weren't coming to Grafton Square.

This arrangement pleased everybody. It was more fashionable to entertain at Christmas – that pleased Bel. It was old-fashioned and kindly to entertain at the New Year – that pleased Mary. It was nice after having protested suitably to have the trouble and expense of neither – that pleased Sophia.

At this point Bel, determined to have everything up to date, had called in her ally David, who was becoming familiar with the uses of society. He had been to two or three more dances in the intervening weeks – and, most impressive of all, he had been to an evening dinner-party. They had actually dined at seven o'clock! In matters of decoration and dress, David was of the greatest use. For such detail his memory was a dry sponge. Though for business detail – as Arthur had pointed out more than once tartly – his memory was much less absorbent.

And so it came about that Arthur took the head of a restrained and elegant dinner-table on Christmas afternoon, while George presided over an old-fashioned and lavish one at the New Year. And at each Sophia, a little guilty at having got out of everything so easily, privately told the hostess that her dinner was the only one to which she had been looking forward.

It was well into the New Year, then, before Bel could really take time to think. But having at last done so, she found herself perfectly clear about one thing – that the Arthur Moorhouses could not go on living in Ure Place. Her motives this time, she told herself, were altogether reasonable, and had nothing to do with worldly ambition. In other words, it came to this: Ure Place was becoming much too near to the slum quarter of the city. The children simply must not again be exposed to the dangers through which little Arthur and Phoebe had passed. Arthur, her husband, must think at once of buying a house out West. She said so to Mary, to Sophia and to her mother; and they, all of them, having no responsibility in the matter, and no reason to contradict her, agreed with her heartily.

She decided, therefore, to open the campaign. The best thing she could do, she felt, would be to make an expedition or two out to Hillhead and Kelvinside, where new terraces were going up steadily; and, having found a suitable house, insist that Arthur should go to see it. He would then be unable to retort – as he had already done – that she would have to find a house first.

But it was to be four years more before Bel succeeded with her stubborn husband. One warm day in February she and old Mrs Barrowfield made a first expedition Westwards. On the journey out she had felt stuffy and overloaded with clothes, and the familiar enough, horsy smells in the tramcar had made her feel sick.

Once arrived, she and her mother trudged about in the sunshine of the early year, noting the clusters of crocus and snowdrops growing before the high terraces above the Great Western Road; and heard the birds chirping in the Botanic Gardens, the cawing of the rooks in its high trees, seen the sparkle of the sun on the glass of the Kibble Palace, which was one of the newest additions to this fashionable private park. But Bel had felt limp and enthusiasm was lacking. On the way home she was overcome again with nausea, and, once arrived at the tram terminus in St Vincent Place, she had found herself strangely feeble and had been forced to sit on while they changed the horses to the other end of the tram. When at last she had had to leave, her mother had sent an urchin for a cab, and thus had got her back to Ure Place.

A fortnight later Bel knew that she was going to have another child. During most of the time of the child's coming she was ill, and, indeed, for nearly a year afterwards. Thus her hopes had suffered, if not eclipse, at least delay while she established her own health and the health of the newly arrived Thomas Moorhouse.

Then Arthur struck a bad patch in his business. Not a very bad patch, but bad enough to plunge a solid Victorian household into deep gloom. The book-keeper of Arthur Moorhouse and Company had pocketed the money of a few accounts paid to him and disappeared. Arthur said it was a disaster. It would take years to repair. The household must save in every way possible. And therefore his loyal wife had held her tongue and saved.

But, as time went on, Bel began to notice that Arthur himself was in no way cutting down. He was giving freely to charity. He had joined the Traders' Club. He did not carp at bills. It was difficult to assess Arthur's prosperity for he was anything but personally extravagant. That he should frankly tel lthe wife of his bosom how they stood for money was, of course, quite unheard of. Yet there seemed always to be money to help outside things.

At last Bel asked David. David replied that Arthur Moorhouse and Company were booming. Even discounting David's congenital optimism she must believe him.

And so once more the push Westwards began.

2

Bel had hoped to enlist Phoebe's help as she grew up – she was nearly eighteen now – but Phoebe continued in her strange detachment. She was, indeed, ready to believe that Phoebe had

come to like herself and the family at Ure Place. Had she not –
well over three years ago – shown amazing devotion in rescuing
little Arthur? And had she not in return been overwhelmed with
the family's affection and consideration, to an extent that would
have drawn love from a stone? But – well, you just had to take
Phoebe's affections on trust, and that must be the end of it.

The girl went about quietly, living her own life. Her school-
days had come to an end, but she had some small talent for
drawing, and embroidery. She studied music with a master, but
made little of it. For the rest, her days were spent learning to
dressmake, to cook, to dust – to learn, in short, to be the head of
that household of her own which every young lady was then
taught to expect. When Bel had tried to fire her with enthusiasm
over the prospect of a new home in a fashionable quarter, Phoebe
had gone no further than saying that it would be very nice, then
seemed immediately to lose interest. Bel sighed and decided to
fight the battle alone.

At first Arthur confronted her with all the usual retorts. Had
she been unhappy where she was?

No. She could not say she had been. But the character of the
locality was now changing.

Did she not realize that a man had to be near his work?

There were endless trams running West now. He could come
and go in no time.

Did she not realize that everything would be more expensive
out there – schools, and shops and everything else?

She replied that if they were dearer they would be better. And
in any case such things, when a man could afford them, were not
to be set against the benefit to his family.

And so it went on. Such bouts usually being wound up by
Arthur declaring with finality that at any rate he couldn't afford
it, so not to worry him.

Bel had to be content with promising herself that she would
return to the attack later.

3

But suddenly, on the same day, two things happened. One sent
Bel into a fit of hot rebellion. The other she did not even hear
about. But both combined to be decisive.

It was again a bright, early spring morning when Sophia
bounced in upon her.

'Good-morning, Bel dear. What do you think has happened?'

'Good-morning, Sophia. What?'

'I've suddenly decided to move out West!'

'I've been decided for a long time, Sophia; that hasn't helped me much, but—'

'Oh, but we've got a house!'

'You, what?' This was really too much!

'Yes, North Woodside Road! The first terrace there, Rosebery Terrace. Overlooking the Kelvin at the bridge. Facing west and everything! They're talking of rebuilding Kelvin Bridge. And I wondered if that would make dust and mess, but both Wil and Margy insist it would be so interesting. Just like children, isn't it? And then it's splendid for the children getting to school. Nothing for Margy to go to the Park School in Lyndoch Street. And the new Glasgow Academy is to be across the bridge, just opposite, for Wil!'

Bel was thankful that Sophia babbled on. It gave her time to hide her intense chagrin. She had had no idea that William and Sophia had wanted to go Westward too. Probably she herself, with all her talk, had put it into their heads! Bel looked at Sophia's thick, rather untidy, forty-year-old figure – and hated her.

The other thing happened to Arthur. That same morning he stepped over from the Candleriggs to the Traders' Club, where he had an appointment with an important business acquaintance. Their affair finished, they remained to smoke and talk, for Arthur felt he could not, at once, leave anyone of such consequence. And presently someone of yet greater consequence hailed them, and asked permission to smoke his pipe beside them.

'You know Moorhouse, Sir William?'

'Fine. Fine.'

Sir William was genial. He set his tall hat, upside down, on the carpet beside him, sat down heavily with his feet stuck out in front of him, his fat hands with the gold signet ring folded over his stomach, his bland face and several layers of clean-shaven chin framed all round by grey bushy hair, and began to suck his carved Viennese meerschaum steadily.

He talked at them continuously, waiting for no replies. Of business. Of the Stock Exchange. Of City Improvements. Of Lord Beaconsfield. Of Russia and the Turks. Then he talked of his garden in Kelvinside, and what his gardener was doing about spring planting. Finally, having sucked his pipe to the end, he got up, lifted his top-hat, and put his meerschaum back into his pocket.

'Well, I've enjoyed my crack. Good-day. Where are ye staying now, Moorhouse?'

Arthur actually felt a little ashamed to have to say Ure Place.

'Tuts! Get out o' there. Bring yer missis and the bairns out my way. The centre of the town's no place to bring up a family. It's time a solid young man like you had a house that gave you some standing.'

And following on these words, Sir William's fat legs and square feet tripped their way among spittoons and leather chairs across the Turkey carpet and out through the double doors.

4

As he made his way up the hill for his midday meal, Arthur was given over to reflection. When Sir William had called him solid he had referred to his bank account, not to his body. And as for being young, well, he was now forty-one – and though he sometimes felt less, he usually felt much more. At all events, Arthur was flattered by the attentions of the great and the rich, as embodied in the squat figure of Sir William. And he was respectfully impressed by his advice. This might, then, be just the time for him to move. It would not be over-stretching prudence – and it would vastly please Bel. He thought of his wife now with affection. Indeed, he had seldom done anything else, in spite of having opposed her dearest wish for many years. Yes. She was a fine girl, Bel. At thirty-two she was a grand, upstanding woman, fit to grace any fine house. He must think of some way of hauling down his flag over this business of moving out West – of some way which would be dignified and not look too much like capitulation.

But Bel made the matter easy for him. For he found her in their bedroom weeping bitterly, face down on the bed.

This was terrible. Arthur had not the faintest idea what to do about it. He was quite unused to Bel making him scenes. This was something quite new. His wife, he had often said with pride, was the steadier of the two of them. Her nature was strong and dependable. He jumped to the worst conclusions. Disaster might have befallen the household. Was it one of the children? Phoebe?

He went over and laid his hand on her shoulder. 'Bel! What's wrong with ye, my dear?'

He received no reply. Bel continued to sob bitterly.

He tried to force her to turn her head, but instead she sat up and looked at him. Suddenly it was borne in upon him that his pleasant, even-tempered wife had become, for once, a flaming fury.

The story of Sophia's visit and her new house out West was flung at Arthur with a force that took him quite by surprise. So the Butters were to have a new house? It had even got through *their* thick heads they they were living in a ridiculous part of the town. It had been all very well living here, even eight years ago. Glasgow was smaller. But now there were modern tramcars running in every direction with the speed of the wind! You could get to the pleasant outlying parts in no time. And now the Butters! Where would Sophia Butter have been if Arthur hadn't brought her to Glasgow and turned her into a lady? Washing out milk-pans in the Laigh Farm milk-house. And Mary too? And David – who was for that matter already in lodgings near the University. Arthur seemed willing enough to do everything for his brother and sisters. It was time he thought about his wife and children.

Arthur bore the storm with a very good show of patience and lordly toleration. He was grateful to his wife. For he saw that she had put him into the exactly right position in relation to herself.

'Calm yourself, Bel. Calm yourself. And listen to what I've got to say to ye.'

For a reply Bel threw herself down on the bed again, and went on howling.

Arthur contemplated her back for a few moments, then addressed her once more: 'It may surprise ye to know that I was just thinking about a new house as I was coming up the brae.'

The sobbing diminished a little.

'Ye see, I was looking at the books this morning, and I find that the last year has not been so very bad. I know ye've had the idea in your head for some time, my dear, but I haven't been just able to see my way.'

Bel sat up again, still weeping, and asked her husband if he really meant that. Her husband assured her that he did. After all, the little story about the books wasn't much – even for an elder of the Ramshorn. Besides, if it came to that, he was an excellent merchant, and knew fairly well the position of his business from day to day.

Bel sobbed a little longer. Indeed, the impetus was such that she had to have time to let it die down. But now her husband was sitting on the bed beside her, his arm lovingly about her as though they weren't married at all. And she was going to have her new house. And she was feeling very happy. And surely it would be bigger and grander than anything William Butter could afford. And she might even be into it before Sophia was into hers. And, anyway, it would be very much prettier, for Sophia had terribly bad taste.

Thus Mr and Mrs Arthur Moorhouse sat together on the edge of their humdrum marriage bed, enjoying the amazing tranquillity of a quarrel just made up. Tender and gentle towards each other, as they had been when they had sat together on the edge of another bed, some nine years before, a newly married pair, come to spend their honeymoon at the Bridge of Allan.

It was Sarah who, all unwittingly, brought these raptures to an end by ringing the dinner-bell loudly in the hall downstairs, and thereafter coming upstairs to the middle landing and shouting on Arthur the Second and Isabel to hurry down, while she looked to the baby.

5

But Bel's day of pleasure was by no means ended. For after the meal, her husband, having looked out of the dining-room window, and having seen that it was going to be a fine afternoon, told his wife to get on her things, because – since he would not have much business to do this afternoon – they might as well take the green car out Hillhead and Kelvinside way and have a look round.

And so the part of the town that was to know them for so many years to come took note, perhaps for the first time, of a lean, distinguished man, clean-shaven but for his greying side-whiskers, discreetly dressed, with his black frock-coat, his grey waistcoat, his black bow tie and his shining tall hat. And on his arm a handsome woman in her early thirties, with a good, maturing figure in a well-fitting bodice and flowing skirt. A smart hat with a piece of white veiling falling elegantly behind set on a fine, fair head. A mouth whose continual smile betrayed dazzling white teeth, and fine eyes that looked steadily about her.

They had come, these two, to find their new home, and they found it in Grosvenor Terrace. A Victorian row, 'commanding a beautiful view of the brilliant parterres of the Botanic Gardens, with the umbrageous woods of Kelvinside beyond', set back from the placid, easy-going traffic of a Great Western Road, where once in a while a green car rattled past on its way to and from

Kirklee; where handsome equipages with their freights of silks and parasols glittered by on fine afternoons; the solemn, liveried flunkies, sitting high above the spanking horses as they flew past brave, new terraces built of the famous Giffnock stone – cream-coloured, and not yet blackened by the smoke of the encroaching city; where milk-carts jingled in the early morning, as they came from the country or passed back in the forenoons out to the green farmlands that lay so near at hand. A Great Western Road, where there was a good deal of mud in winter; and where – in the autumn – fallen leaves lay thick.

It was settled very quickly. Almost that afternoon. For Bel knew that when Arthur had set his heart on something he would not halt until he had got it. And if he wanted this dignified terrace house with the For Sale board, he would do everything, that prudence allowed him, to obtain it.

She was so sure, indeed, that as their tramcar crossed over Kelvin Bridge on its way back to the City, and she looked at the house her sister-in-law would occupy, she felt she could afford to say to Arthur that that was where poor Sophia was going to be, that it was a pity they hadn't found somewhere nicer, for, after all, it *was* the wrong side of the bridge. But that, at any rate, it was nice to think that the families would go on being near each other.

Arthur, well pleased with himself and his wife, merely contented himself by smiling a vague smile of approval. And when he felt the pressure of Bel's hand, as he sat ruminating behind the trotting horses, he thought of his morning encounter at the Club, and decided it would be better, on the whole, not to mention even such august and flattering advice as Sir William's, but to let her think that the decisions of the day had had their source only in his deep affection for herself.

Chapter 14

1

Although the house in Grosvenor Terrace came to be hers in February, it was May before Bel and her family moved into it. For anyone so house-proud as Mrs Arthur Moorhouse a shorter time than this would have been utterly impossible. The house had been bought from wealthy owners, and was in excellent condition. Most of the paint, even, was fresh. But all its four floors had to be painted anew, from the children's flat beneath the slates to the maids' basement bedrooms. As Bel said, 'We can't have the name of going into a house that isn't perfectly fresh, can we?' And then there were endless discussions over furniture. They couldn't have furniture that would make a fool of them. Everything must have the label solid or good. The word beautiful was not often uttered.

Arthur and Bel were at one in this. Their house must be a complete expression of their stability of outlook and circumstance. A house in the West End of Glasgow of that time need not be lightsome or gay, but it must be substantial. Or what would all the other people think? All the other people who were sitting round conventionally in similar houses, wondering, in turn, what people thought of them. All of them equally determined not to be thought arty or trashy.

Bel toiled ceaselessly. It was not all pleasure by any means. She was haunted by the fear that what she bought or what she had decided to take with her from Ure Place might be considered vulgar. And the Arthur Moorhouses mustn't have the name of being vulgar. She spent a night entirely sleepless over a walnut china cabinet that had cost much, and that Arthur had decided was a very handsome piece and would just make their drawing-room. She had not been too sure of it at the time, and now that it stood in its place she had just discovered a thin line of gilded metal inlay. Was that bad taste? What would people say?

Phoebe noticed that Bel was worried. At breakfast she asked the reason.

'It's about that drawing-room cabinet, Phoebe; I'm not sure if I like it. And it's about the most expensive thing we've bought.'

'I think it's beautiful,' Phoebe said, more to reassure her than because she had bothered to think about it.

Bel did not say any more. Phoebe's opinion was of no value, she considered.

Phoebe, really, was perfectly aware of this. But as her sister-in-law went on looking worried to death, she decided to drop down to the warehouse to see David.

David was a creature of great distinction now. Even in an old office jacket he had the art of looking quite special. Sometimes Arthur felt proud of David's appearance, at other times his youngest brother's cool svelteness maddened him. But, on the whole, David had now shaken into a niche in Arthur Moorhouse and Company, and was quite a good business man. He had stood so long in awe of Arthur and been so much forced into regular habits and methodical ways, that his own rather weak character had settled into quite a creditable groove. In other words, Arthur the downright had been the making of this aristocratic young man.

David looked at Phoebe. He hadn't seen her for some time. As a connoisseur he was delighted to note how slender and elegant his eighteen-year-old sister had become.

'Hello, Phoebe, how are you? What have you come down about?'

'David, I want you to help me with Bel.'

'Why? Is she ill?'

'No, but she will be if you don't do something. Could you possibly drop in to Grosvenor Terrace and have a look at the china cupboard in the drawing-room? Tell her how beautiful you think it is. That you admire her taste. And that your friend Mrs Hayburn has got one exactly like it.'

'But that's probably not true.'

'Never mind. If you don't do what I tell you, Bel won't be fit to live with. Remember you're the swell of the family. She thinks you know all about these things.'

David accepted this statement without remonstrance. In the main he agreed with it, though he felt Phoebe was perhaps getting blunt a bit as she grew up. However, he did as she asked him. He met Bel in the new house as though by chance, praised the cabinet extravagantly, and told her that his friend Stephen Hayburn's mother had one very like it. Thus Bel was successfully guided past yet another crisis.

David was not particularly enthusiastic about his family's coming out West. For some years now he had himself been in rooms near the University, where he conducted his discreet and highly selective bachelor existence. Indeed, David was now one of the most respectable of young men. His early visits to music-halls and free-and-easies had merely been to him a reaching away from the humdrum. Grandeur was now his one hobby. No. He felt that his comings and goings might be watched over by the family rather more than he cared about. Not that he had any-thing to hide except, perhaps, a few conceits of dress – a few little affectations of manner, which he had the sense to shed each morning on his way to the Candleriggs. Still, he would be only one of the Moorhouses shortly, not the unique and special Mr David Moorhouse. For he had, by this time, quite lived down cheese. The portrait he had constructed of himself might suffer a little alteration here and there from having the others about. But he was, of course, too honestly fond of them to be anything more than a little apprehensive. Even a snob has his moments, when it is pleasant to sit with his mental waistcoat unbuttoned in the warm company of relatives who love him, even though these may be quite indifferent to the altitudes to which he has soared.

2

Phoebe's attitude to the removal annoyed Bel a little. She kept on being so remote about it. It was not that she was unhelpful – far from it. She was for ever in and out of shops. Running errands. Matching hangings with carpets, chair stuffs with hangings – this with that. But through it all her aloofness persisted. What was the girl thinking? Was she laughing a little? When Bel said how nice it was going to be for them all, Phoebe would smile and agree how good it would be for the children to be near the country. The word 'nice' was never off Bel's tongue these days, she simply couldn't get rid of it. And yet when she used it in Phoebe's presence she always felt self-conscious. Couldn't the child see that she was taking a step up socially, just at the time in her life when such a thing was most important to her?

Yet another annoying thing. She seemed just as interested in Sophia Butter's removal as in the change of her own home. She spent whole days, when Bel did not need her, sewing and making for Sophia. Sophia's plans, like all the rest of her, were in a perpetual muddle. And muddles – especially other people's – can be cheerful things. People who are in a state of confusion usually allow their helpers to do what they like. And Phoebe being strong-minded and clear-headed did exactly what she liked. While the most august of painters' men were applying the very best of paint from garret to basement of the house in Grosvenor

Terrace, Phoebe spent several blissful days with paint all over her hair, applying it at random to rooms that didn't matter – such as the maid's room and the children's bedrooms at Sophia's. She did not show much skill, perhaps, but the work was done amid peals of laughter.

But on most counts Sophia's removal at the same time as her own was a blessing to Bel. For one thing it was the lever that had, at last, dislodged Arthur from Ure Place – or so Bel believed. For another, now that things were in train, it gave her a continual sense of her own superiority in matters of taste and generalship. And for yet another, although she would not admit it even to herself, Bel was a little timid of her new surroundings, and it gave her a feeling of support that her silly, warm-hearted sister-in-law was to be near at hand.

At this time scarcely anybody remembered the existence of the McNairns. Mary's attitude to these upheavals was, throughout, one of indifference. She had no wish, she confided to her husband, to live further West than Charing Cross. It was essential, she said, for children to spend all their growing-up days in one house. It stamped them with the right feeling of permanency. George McNairn agreed – not having bothered much to understand what she meant. But the word 'permanency' was very much in the air and greatly approved of in these days, so George felt that, without unduly agitating his fast-congealing brain, he could agree with his wife wholeheartedly.

George and Mary McNairn had put on weight in the last year or two. George, a fully-fledged baillie now, pursued his platitudinous way greatly respected. Respect, indeed, kept accruing to his character in much the same ratio as fat kept accruing to his waistline. Nor was his wife a skeleton. Her hands were as white, her face was as smooth, her features as good as ever. But none of these could any longer escape the charge of being chubby. Mary kept a good table – and that not merely as a demonstration to the world of her prosperity. The McNairns all liked their victuals. There were twin four-year-old girls now, in addition to Georgie and Jackie, and these likewise, especially the babies, were more than comfortably padded.

George and Mary were on excellent terms with everybody. They were too complacent to quarrel. And they did not see much of their relatives now. The house in Albany Place was pleasant enough if you were really hungry and wanted a square meal well cooked. But if you were in search of spirited talk, then it was a place rather to be avoided. Shafts of wit seemed to bounce off impervious cushions of platitude and to return to you like boomerangs bearing the label 'silly'. The McNairns indeed were kindly enough. But they did not make you feel a success. There was, too, an atmosphere of don't-tell-about-yourself-listen-about-me, which, to say the least, was defeating. In other words, they were just dull.

On the first Friday of May, Sophia moved out. Wil and Margy were given a holiday from school to help, and it was a day of blissful picnicking amid incredible confusion. A meal eaten on Oberon's bank of wild thyme would have given them nothing like the rapture they got from sitting with Phoebe dangling their legs from a newly arrived kitchen table, surrounded by straw, packing-sheets, old newspapers and the remains of Phoebe's paint pots, eating sandwiches. The rush of talk that came from the lips of their over-excited mother was no less constant than the rush of the waters of the River Kelvin as it fled through the bridge that spanned the gap that lay before their front door. It was, indeed, a great affliction to get themselves tolerably clean and go down in the evening to Albany Place to their Aunt Mary who had risen to the occasion and had invited everyone, no matter in what condition, to come and have a good filling meal. Later on David looked elegantly in and asked if he could be of use, but he looked so frail and impeccable that Phoebe told him no, and sent him away again – much to his relief; though he felt a little worried in case the young woman before him with a black smudge on her face should be growing up too unconventionally. For she would, sooner or later now, have to be presented to his friends.

3

But he need not have worried. The next time he saw her she was cool, immaculate and lovelier than ever he had seen her before.

It was on a perfect Sunday afternoon in the latter half of May. He had eaten his midday meal with the Hayburns. It was warm for the time of the year in Scotland, and on Stephen's proposal, he and the two brothers dragged wicker chairs out into the garden. All three young men spent the early part of the afternoon drowsing. At last Henry stirred his loose-boned frame – grown bigger and more mature, but much as it was four years back when David had first known him – and proposed that they should go and have a look at the great hot-houses in the Botanic

Gardens which were then being reconstructed. Stephen was still too sleepy, but David, always polite, agreed to go.

The Botanic Gardens of Glasgow were then owned by a private company of select gentlemen. On Sundays only these shareholders and their friends had the right of a key to their paradise of privilege. And thus on this balmy, indolent afternoon David and Henry found themselves strolling around beds of late spring flowers, among bursting pale green leaves, past rare trees covered with blossom. Clumps of common lilac hung, heavy with perfume. It was pleasant to raise a beige top-hat to girls you knew, as they went by wearing spring dresses frothing with frills that had, perhaps, been taken from their boxes for the first time this very day.

As usual Henry was talking about himself – his plans for Hayburn and Company – his work. His pug face was all animation. David knew him well now, and he realized that a mere show of interest was all that was necessary. You need not worry unduly about Henry. He was a bit of a genius – and geniuses, it seemed, were intense people who talked overmuch about themselves and their interests. On an afternoon like this you could dream along casually, feeling pleased with yourself – the flowers and the sunshine, the spring, and your own elegance. Henry's talk did not do much more to David than the buzzing of the one or two early bumble-bees.

But suddenly Henry received a resounding clap on the shoulder. Both young men spun round. It was Sir William, Arthur's friend of the Traders' Club, and with him, much to David's surprise, were Arthur and Phoebe. He knew they had just moved in, but had seen nothing of them. He had not expected they would be out and about yet awhile. He ought to have known that Bel, when she did come to move, would advance in perfect order – that the thing would be done with the minimum of fuss or inconvenience to her household. And so, on this their very first Sunday, they were in the Gardens, sunning themselves under the tutelage of Sir William, who had met them by chance at the gates.

David was delighted with the encounter. He knew Sir William by sight, of course, and it was most gratifying to be able to exhibit his sister and brother under such august wings. And there was no denying that they did him credit. Today, feeling the weight of his new possessions, perhaps, Arthur presented an appearance that was gaunt, distinguished, and very unvulgar. And as for Phoebe, he had never seen her like this before. Her dress of fine grey stuff lay with extreme elegance to a figure that spoke at once of girlishness and maturity. Her close-drawn waist was small and flexible, and its grace was accentuated by the suggestion of a bustle. A fashionably small hat was set on her small graceful head. Eyes, strangely set and devastating, looked out on the beauty of the spring from under a straight-cut fringe.

'So this is a Moorhouse, too?' Sir William was asking. 'You talk to the young lady, Henry, and I'll see what this young man's got in him.'

So David had to submit to a genial examination, and Phoebe was left to Henry Hayburn.

Queer excitable young man this friend of David's, Phoebe thought, as she sauntered along, beneath her parasol, at Henry's side. There was an attraction about his odd face with its young black beard. She noted, too, his gesticulating engineer's hands. She guessed his age to be about twenty-three or twenty-four. But, good gracious, couldn't the creature stop talking? He was telling her all about himself at an incredible rate. He didn't make you feel of much importance. She tried to stop him once or twice – to draw his attention to some of the beauty about him – but he gave her only the attention of an instant, then off he went again. What he said was not stupid, she had no doubt, but there was so much of it! She had heard that one of the Hayburns was very clever, and she began to wonder if this were he. She came to the conclusion that it must be; he was so peculiar.

At last there was a shout from behind from Sir William. She held out her hand. 'Goodbye, Mr Hayburn!'

Strange creature. His face fell as though he were a puppy that had been whipped.

'Oh, goodbye, Miss Moorhouse. I've enjoyed our talk tremendously.' Then, perhaps because he saw a flicker in Phoebe's eyes, 'Look here, I've been doing all the talking.'

He looked so ridiculously like a little boy that had been scolded that Phoebe found herself feeling sorry for him. 'Not at all, Mr Hayburn, I put a word in here and there, you know.'

'Now you're laughing at me.'

'Nonsense.'

'Shall I see you again sometime?'

'I suppose so. We've just come to Grosvenor Terrace, you know.'

All Henry said to this was 'Goodbye', then he turned and trotted off after David as though David were his nursemaid.

Chapter 15

I

Mrs Arthur Moorhouse was vastly proud of her new house. It was a source of endless delight to 'have things just so', as she expressed it. When Mary and Sophia called during the first days to ask how things were going and to offer help, she was careful that they should not see too much, for she was determined to have a house-warming and to let the full and finished effect burst upon them. She mentioned her plan to Sophia, who was delighted.

'What a good idea, Bel! You see, your house is so much bigger and grander than mine, that a house-warming out here will do beautifully for both of us. But, of course, you must let William and me help with the expense.'

There was, perhaps, a trace of coldness in Bel's voice as she thanked Sophia for her offer. Arthur, she said, would no doubt want to provide all the entertainment himself.

Sophia was only too prompt in replying genially that – oh, well, she dared say he would. That the notion had just then come into her head – she hadn't really thought it out. But anyway a house-warming at Grosvenor Terrace would be lovely for everybody.

There was no further talk of entertainment on her own part, either jointly or independently.

But Bel's entertainment was not to happen for a week or two. By then she would have time to draw her breath, everything would have found its place, and the last french polisher would have given the last inch of mahogany its final rub. She hoped to invite everybody – even the enigmatic and seldom-to-be-met-with Mungo.

For in the last years Mungo had certainly become both of these things. Bel couldn't make him out. He was turning into a different kind of person. It was only at New Year time that Mungo could be counted upon to make his appearance. And last New Year she had noticed a very marked change in him. To the rest of the family he was the same old Mungo, with his sturdy farmer's ways – and his slow Ayrshire voice. And he still seemed not to know, quite, how to behave towards herself and his own sisters. But there were several odd things about him. You would have thought that a bachelor living by himself with no one to tend him would have become more careless in his ways, to show more of the recluse in his manner. But the exact reverse had happened. He seemed to have gained a quiet authority. He still wore the rough clothes of a farmer, but they were well made and unslovenly. His linen, now, was always spotless and of a finer quality than before. And – a detail that she noticed specially – his flat farmer's hands were always clean, and though he still kept his nails cropped, they were neither broken nor in mourning. And yet you couldn't quite put your finger on the real difference. Perhaps it was that Mungo was behaving much more as though he were a person of some consequence in his own circle. But what kind of consequence? What more was Mungo now than he ever was? A bachelor farmer who was prospering. Phoebe, who went most often to the Laigh Farm, reported that things were much as usual. But Phoebe was the worst gossip in the world. She seemed to notice nothing. Perhaps Mungo went about a bit more, that was all. He had taken to breeding a pony or two. The common interest of pony breeding took him, it seemed, to the stables of Duntrafford, and even, sometimes, she had heard, to meals in Duntrafford House. But surely, Bel pondered, there could be no equal friendship between the laird and his tenant. And the shy Mungo was the last person in the world to try to force himself into a friendship above his station. No. Her own husband and David might, in their way, be ascending the social ladder, but when all was said, and whatever change was taking place in Mungo, he would always remain just a plain Ayrshire farmer, without frills.

And frills were the things that counted with Bel. Frills. Any amount of them. A grand house expensively, solidly furnished. A financially solid husband, who went to a financially solid business – it was more genteel not to specify what kind of business – every morning in order to provide more frills. Clothes made by the best dressmaker. Well-fed children at the best local schools taking all the extras, getting all the frills. Good, solid accounts in equally solid banks. Accounts that were never, never drawn to their limit. Seats in a well-built Victorian-Gothic church, where the minister delivered splendid sermons that told you where the unfortunates went who weren't as honest and solid as yourself.

One regret she had, and that was that her mother, Mrs Barrowfield, was left by herself in Monteith Row in the middle of the city. She was as snug and comfortable and – but for occasional attacks of rheumatism – as hearty as ever; but it was bleak for her, Bel felt, to have her only daughter the better part of an hour away from her instead of ten minutes. She never said so, and she was vastly proud of her daughter's fine house, and additional consequence – but she was now a lonely old woman. Bel knew it, and forced herself to make many a trip into town when she would gladly have rested.

As time went on she was to have great reason to be grateful to Phoebe, who, strangely, had always been a favourite with the old lady. There was a downrightness about both of them that seemed to find an echo each in the other.

Mrs Barrowfield's pre-Victorian outlook pleased the young girl. Phoebe found she could talk to Bel's mother with less reserve than she must use with Bel. The old late-Georgian seemed to meet her on a commoner ground. At the time, too, Mrs Barrowfield had been greatly stirred by the Hughie's Yeard incident. Had her eldest grandson been any child she would still have applauded Phoebe's smeddum, as she called it, for she accounted courage the first virtue. But that the girl should have rescued her own eldest and quite special grandson was enough to place her on a pedestal for ever. And so it came about that Phoebe paid many visits to Monteith Row in Bel's place, and always found a warm welcome.

2

On the Friday evening following his chance meeting with Phoebe in the Botanic Gardens, David came to call at Grosvenor Terrace. Phoebe ran down into a nearly completed drawing-room, smelling of furniture polish, to find him with Bel in conversation which, however, stopped when she came in. For a moment, as she greeted her brother, she thought she detected a glint of intrigue in Bel's eye, a glint she was well used to, for Bel was by nature an intriguer.

'Hello, Phoebe,' David said, looking approvingly at his – there was only one word for it now – lovely young sister. He bent down and kissed her solemnly.

'Peculiar young man you had with you on Sunday,' Phoebe said.

'Henry Hayburn? Why peculiar?'

'He seemed very excited.'

'Perhaps he was,' David said, then he seemed to think better of this and added, 'No, I don't suppose he was any more than usual. He's a great talker, Henry. What did he talk about?'

'Himself.'

David laughed. 'He's not really conceited,' he said.

'I didn't think he was.'

'David says the Hayburns are very rich,' Bel said. She was sewing rings on a curtain.

'Then he ought to buy himself a suit of clothes that fits him.'

'Didn't you like the young man, Phoebe?' Bel's head was bent. She was stitching diligently.

'Yes. Quite. Why?'

'Oh, I don't know. You seemed – well – David says he's brilliant.'

'Yes, I've heard all that,' Phoebe stood up again, and, crossing to the window, looked out. The new green leaves of the trees on either side of the Great Western Road looked so virgin, so tender that, for a moment, they laid the restlessness of the spring upon her. The street lamps were already lit, although it was not yet dark. Two hansoms, one following the other, raced past towards the City. A young workman and his girl went by laughing. She watched them until they were gone. People were out and about – doing things. She sighed and came back to Bel and David. 'What a beautiful night it is! It makes me homesick for the Laigh Farm. I would like to go for a walk in the country.'

'It's just what I've come to ask you to do,' David said. 'But not tonight. Tomorrow afternoon.'

'I can't go tomorrow afternoon. I'm taking little Arthur to see the animals at Balgray Farm. I've promised.'

'The children are going to their Granny tomorrow,' Bel said firmly. 'They haven't been to see her since we flitted.'

This was the first Phoebe had heard of the arrangement, which, she thought, was strange. And it was new for David to be troubling about her. Still, perhaps, it was natural. 'All right,' she said, 'I'll come.'

And so it came about that she found herself setting out on the following afternoon.

3

They took the right-of-way known as the 'Khyber Pass' that skirted the west side of the Botanic Gardens and served as a short cut from the Great Western Road through to the Three-Tree Well and the wooded banks of the River Kelvin. There were mills here and there at the water's edge, but the gorge of the Kelvin was still beautiful in parts, though building to the north was in progress. The little industrial village of Maryhill had not yet crept down to the edge of the wooded gulf.

David proposed that they should follow round until they came to the high aqueduct which carries the waters of the Forth and Clyde Canal across the valley of the Kelvin. The great water-bridge and the chain of locks were, he said, things to be seen. Phoebe was very willing to follow.

It was a surprise to her, however, to find Henry Hayburn and a young man, whom she took to be his brother, hanging over the parapet of the Canal Bridge idly looking about them. For a moment she wondered if David had arranged a meeting with these two young men – then she dismissed the idea. Why should he?

'Hello, fellows,' he was saying, now that they were within earshot. 'Out enjoying yourselves? Phoebe, this is Stephen Hayburn.'

Stephen Hayburn was as carefully dressed as his brother Henry was the reverse. He wore fashionable English flannels and a straw boater. In his sporting tie was fixed a gold horseshoe, and he had an eyeglass. Henry gave the impression of being dressed in any old thing.

He flushed as he greeted Phoebe, hat in hand. Stephen's manner was controlled and elegant. He adjusted his eyeglass and tugged at his drooping fair moustache as he greeted her amiably, and said suitable things about his delight at getting to know David's sister. But his eye kept running over Phoebe appraisingly as he talked. She decided that she liked Henry better, stuttering and boyish though he might be.

Which way were they going? David asked.

They had planned to have a look at the locks, then return across the aqueduct upon which they now stood, follow the tow-path for a bit, turn up over the hill and eventually come to the Great Western Road again at North Balgray Farm. They would be pleased if Miss Moorhouse and David would walk with them, if it were not too far.

Phoebe assured them that she was well used to long walks in Ayrshire, and so they moved up towards the locks. Stephen and David went in front, while Henry followed with Phoebe.

Phoebe, in so far as she must choose one or other of the Hayburns, was best pleased with this arrangement. She would have been glad merely to continue her walk with David and let the brothers take their separate way. But all three men seemed determined that they should return home together.

If Henry had spoken overmuch at their first meeting, now he did the reverse. It was left to herself to make desultory conversation as they went along. Now and then she exclaimed at the canal – what a labour it must have been to cut it right across Scotland – building waterways across deep gulleys such as the one they had just crossed. She exclaimed at passing ships. Barges carrying coal or wood to the City woodyards, towed by little smoky tugs. At the Maryhill locks they stayed behind to see a boat go up through, for Phoebe had never seen such as this happen before.

And during all these happenings Henry continued to say little. Now and then he would explain a point to her – usually in highly technical language – as one engineer to another, using terms that Phoebe couldn't possibly know. The working of a tug's steam-engine. The principle of the rise and fall of water in a canal lock. How the level of the canal was maintained. And yet it all seemed as though he were holding himself in. As though he were a little boy who had too much to say, and had been told to remember to let others talk. To every word of her own he gave intense, blushing attention. But there was no ease about him. Only in the shortest possible words did he reply to her questions.

A queer person. She couldn't make him out. Other men she had met talked when they wanted to, and held their tongues when they didn't. And after the torrent of speech on Sunday in the Botanic Gardens! Yet, on the whole, she rather liked him. He seemed such a simple creature.

At last they had regained the Great Western Road, and were coming to the parting of their ways. Again Henry put the question he had put at their first meeting. Would they see each other soon again?

She smiled. 'Well, we're very near you now, you know.'

He blushed again and relaxed a little.

'I didn't talk too much this time, did I?'

'I never thought. No, I don't think you did. Why?'

'Because I talked far too much the first time I saw you.'

'Did you?'

'Yes, I fairly chattered my head off.'

This was really absurd. He couldn't really be grown up. 'I didn't notice. I talk just as much as I feel inclined to. Don't you?'

'Yes, usually. But I can be terribly tedious. You see, I get so interested that I forget people are not so interested as I am.'

She gave him her hand. 'Well, the next time we meet just talk as much as you want to, Mr Hayburn. Say whatever you like. I like people to be themselves.'

'Do you really mean that?' Why did his eyes shine so boyishly?

'Yes. Of course. Goodbye.'

And when Phoebe and David had turned and gone away, leaving him to his brother, Henry could hear nothing but her parting words ringing in his ears. And into these words he read all kinds of meanings that Phoebe had in no way intended.

Chapter 16

I

Stephen Hayburn dropped in upon his mother in her little sitting-room as she sat drinking tea and reading *Good Words*, her practice on Sunday night when she was alone after dinner. She was pleased to see him.

'Will you take a cup of tea, Stephen?'

'Thanks, Mother. If you'll allow me to smoke.'

She smiled. 'I don't mind fresh smoke. But I hate the smell of stale tobacco hanging about in a room afterwards. Still, for once. I'll ring for a cup.' She pulled the china bell-knob.

Stephen returned from his smoking-room with his cigar and a box of vesuvians. He was also wearing a tasselled smoking-cap embroidered in gold and a dark-red smoking-jacket. He took his teacup from his mother's hand, thanked her and set it on a little brass Indian table beside his arm-chair.

'Where's Henry?' Mrs Hayburn asked, looking up at her elegant son.

'Upstairs working, I expect. Or thinking about Miss Moorhouse.'

'Miss Moorhouse?'

'Yes.' Stephen stood watching his vesuvian fizzling, then he lit his cigar with it, settled himself luxuriously opposite to his mother, crossed his feet, which were encased in embroidered house-slippers, on a hassock in front of him, and continued: 'Henry has asked me to talk to you.'

She sat forward. 'About what, Stephen?'

'About Miss Moorhouse.'

'Is this girl the sister of David Moorhouse?'

'Half-sister, I believe.'

'Well. And what about her?'

'Henry has fallen in love with her. Very badly, I should say.'

Mrs Hayburn said nothing. She sat looking into the fire (for like most Scots she insisted upon a fire even on warm spring evenings). She had always told herself that when Henry fell in love he would fall heavily. Everything he did, he did with intensity. So far as she knew he had had none of the tentative, lesser affairs of most young men. Affairs that served perhaps to give them some sense of proportion. With her younger son it would be head over heels or nothing. Now it had come. And not very conveniently.

'Where has Henry seen her?' she asked presently.

'He met her last Sunday in the Botanic Gardens, while he was walking with David. She was with her other brother, the one who is David's partner, and Sir William.'

'Sir William? They know him?'

'Yes.'

That helped a little. Still – the sister of cheese merchants. David was socially established now. Cheese or no cheese. He was an old friend – and quite unstamped by his occupation. Besides, for some reason he had got himself accepted everywhere. And with him the question of marriage didn't enter, nor up till now, had he obtruded his relatives. But now this half-sister—?

'Have you seen her, Stephen?'

'Yes. We arranged with David to meet them yesterday.'

'Arranged? Did this girl know it was arranged?'

'No. We made it look like an accidental meeting.'

'Why hasn't Henry talked to me himself? Why does he ask you to tell me this?'

'He thinks I can persuade you better than he can.'

'Persuade me? Persuade me to what, Stephen?'

'He wants you to invite her here.'

'How can I?'

'She lives with the Arthur Moorhouses. The brother's family

who have just come to Grosvenor Terrace. He wants you to leave cards on Mrs Arthur Moorhouse.'

'I don't know that I want to.' Leave cards on a provision merchant's wife? Her own grandfather had been a crofter in Argyle, but that was two generations back, and merely made her the more jealous for her position now. 'What have you said to David Moorhouse about this?'

'Very little. I don't suppose his family would object if anything came of it.'

'No. I don't suppose they would.' Object to marrying her son? The son of a family that was established, of excellent standing and rich? Stephen and Henry could look to drawing a handsome income from Hayburn and Company all their days. If Henry insisted upon working for his living that was his affair. He didn't need to. (She had already offered to settle him in a country estate. His queer ways would look better in the country, she had thought.) Object? Not very likely. But she was aiming higher than Phoebe Moorhouse for her sons.

'I don't want Henry to marry this Miss Moorhouse,' she said presently. 'I know David's a friend of yours; and I've never discouraged him coming here. I knew you liked him, and I thought he was quite a good friend for you. Even when I discovered what his business was, I didn't let that make any difference. Still, you must see, Stephen, that it's another thing when there's a question of marriage.'

Stephen sucked his cigar and nodded. It made no difference to him what happened. He had merely given way to Henry's importunings in speaking to his mother.

'Besides,' Mrs Hayburn added, 'it's just the sort of marriage your father would have hated.' This was quite untrue. For her husband had been in temperament very like his son Henry – a quick, eager man, over-trusting, uncritical and affectionate. But his widow had a way of dotting her i's and stroking her t's by invoking his memory.

Even Stephen saw this last remark as a little ridiculous, and said, 'Oh, I don't suppose he would. Father wasn't like that.'

She did not, however, bother to reply. Instead, she sat gazing into the fire. At last, the gradual twilight of the north was beginning to make itself felt. The room was growing dim. A flame found glossy reflections in this elderly woman's plain-parted hair. It lit up her prosperous, wrinkled face and the innumerable transparent frills of her snowy cap.

'What do you advise me to do?' she asked him at last.

Stephen considered. Damned handsome girl. He wouldn't mind seeing her about. The old lady was being unduly fussy. And it was not at all likely that Henry would ever be attracted to anyone so presentable again. If she came into the family, at least she would be something to look at.

'Better ask her with David to dinner, Mother,' he said. 'Then you can have a look at her.'

'I can't do that. At any rate, I hope, for her sake, that she's not the kind of young woman who would accept such an invitation. No, I'll have to call on Mrs Arthur Moorhouse first, and I suppose Mrs Moorhouse will have to call here. That means beginning with the Moorhouse family, whether I want to or not.'

2

At this moment Henry came into the room looking as self-conscious as possible. His mother came to the point at once.

'Stephen is suggesting I should call on Mrs Arthur Moorhouse, Henry. He has told me you want to see more of Miss Moorhouse.'

Henry's face flamed. He tugged his unfledged moustache and plunged his hands wildly into his pockets, then took them out again. 'I say, Mother, it would be awfully kind if you would,' he said.

'I don't know whether I am going to or not, Henry. There's a lot of things to think about. I wish your father was here to advise me. I'm sure Miss Moorhouse is a delightful young lady, but after all, you haven't seen much of her, have you?'

'Twice.'

'Twice is nothing at all.'

'Oh yes it is, Mother. I've quite made up my mind.'

Mrs Hayburn laughed. 'Nonsense. How can you have made up your mind? My dear boy, you're only twenty-three. You'll meet a great many more young ladies before you really have to decide.'

Henry, who was leaning his back against the heavily draped mantelshelf, shuffled with embarrassment, kicked the hassock upon which his brother's embroidered feet were disposed, was reprimanded, apologized, then finally said, 'Well, anyway, you *will* call on Mrs Arthur Moorhouse, won't you, Mother?'

Mrs Hayburn was not inhuman. And there were moments when her younger son reminded her sharply of her husband whom, on the whole, she had loved. He was reminding her of his father now – the young, vivid engineer she had married, not the platitudinous ogre it was her pleasure at moments to invoke.

'Do you really want me to, Henry?' she asked, softened.

'Please, Mother.'

'And have you any idea if' – how was she to understate her question tactfully? – 'if Miss Moorhouse wants me to leave cards with her sister-in-law?'

If it was possible, Henry turned a brighter scarlet. 'Oh, no, I don't know anything about that, Mother. How can I?' And then, as his mother did not reply immediately, he added anxiously, 'But you will call, won't you, Mother?'

After all, Miss Moorhouse might not be so interested in Henry as he was in her. The affair might be quite one-sided. Though she could hardly hope for that considering the obvious advantages of the young man. Still, her heart might be given elsewhere for all any of them knew. That would be best, perhaps. At any rate, unless she were going to estrange him, she must do as he asked.

'All right, Henry, I'll go.'

'Will you really, Mother? That's splendid.' And her youngest son bent down and gave his rather forbidding mother a gawky, embarrassed kiss.

Thus it was that Mrs Hayburn came to call on Mrs Arthur Moorhouse. And really she couldn't have done it on a more awkward day. For having got the impression somehow that Mrs Arthur Moorhouse was settled in Grosvenor Terrace much longer than she actually had been, she decided to call at once. Besides, a burning curiosity to know what kind of young woman had succeeded in attracting so violently her callow recluse of a son had begun to take hold of her.

Chapter 17

I

It was three o'clock in the afternoon. Bel was standing in the middle of her new kitchen wearing one of Bessie the cook's aprons and conducting operations with the decision of a general. For on this night she had decided to have her first real dinner-party. Her mother, Mary and George, Sophia and William, and, of course, David, were all to be invited – all the Glasgow clan. She had even made Arthur write to invite Mungo, but they had received no reply. It was to be a gesture. She intended, when she saw fit, to entertain formally after this. She was not going to stand free-and-easiness from the others any longer. None of those terrible droppings in of the wrong relatives that can so effectively ruin the pattern of carefully planned hospitality. And it was to be a dinner-party. No high-teaing or nonsense. The better people out here were going over to evening dinner now. And Bel – so help her God (and her brother-in-law David) – was not going to be left behind. In addition, the house was at last to be thrown open for show – to be the envy of everybody.

But at the moment it was three o'clock, and she was in the kitchen directing a nervous but intensely loyal Bessie in the opening preparations. A young and yet more nervous housemaid, specially engaged for Grosvenor Terrace, was standing beating together much flour and many eggs. Sarah, the reinstated criminal of Hughie's Yeard, now a stout, dignified person well into her thirties, was not to be seen.

One of the long line of bells above the kitchen dresser began to jangle and dance on its spring. It was the bell belonging to the front door.

'Who's that?' Cook said, bending over her work.

'I wish the message boys would learn to come to the back door,' Bel said.

At this moment Sarah, who had been dressing in a maid's room facing the front area, and didn't know that Bel was in the kitchen, burst in, 'Losh, Bessie, it's a cerrige-an'-pair!'

Bel's heart stood still. But she let none of her maids know it. She clung frantically to a show of firmness. 'Go up at once, please, and see who it is. If it's anyone calling, then I'm not at home.'

Sarah started. 'Not at home?'

Bel coloured, but stood her ground. 'Yes. Please. It's what you say if you're not ready to see people.'

Sarah turned and went. After all, who was she that she should question the morality of the best mistress in the world? The memory of a pardon, amazingly granted less than four years ago, made a constant background to Sarah's devoted service.

When she had gone up, Bel left the kitchen and, tiptoeing into a maid's bedroom, stood on a chair behind the net curtain, thus managing to get her line of vision on a level with the pavement.

And there, sure enough, the sparkling wheels of a carriage, and eight shining, well-groomed hooves!

Sarah, more than realizing that the full pride of the Arthur Moorhouse household was, for the moment, in her hands, opened the front door and presented to the critical old woman peering from her carriage the picture of a crisp, sedate and thoroughly superior maid. She regretted that Mrs Moorhouse was not at home, received cards and closed the door. And her mistress, perched on the chair, saw the polished top-boots of a lackey re-cross the pavement, go round to the other side of the carriage, and climb up out of view by the side of, presumably, the coachman.

Bel was standing in her kitchen again, a smothered fire of curiosity, when Sarah came down.

'Who was at the door, Sarah?' Her voice was a model of casualness.

'A Mrs Hayburn, Mam. She left me her cards for ye.'

'Thank you, Sarah.'

David's Mrs Hayburn! What did this mean? She had always understood that Mrs Hayburn was a stiff, exclusive old woman. And yet she had called upon her before anyone else had done so! Were her sons pushing her into a friendship? Was Phoebe the reason? Phoebe! David had hinted that perhaps—! That would be very exciting for everyone! And such a splendid connection. She would take Phoebe with her when she returned Mrs Hayburn's call. She must find out from David which was the exactly correct day.

'Are ye just havin' the potatoes boilt plain, Mam?'

Was it possible that Cook was putting this question to her for the second time? First things first. She must carry through this dinner-party successfully. Mrs Hayburn must be dealt with in her proper order.

Bel drew herself up. 'Yes. Yes, Bessie. I heard you the first time. I was thinking about it. No. I think you'll have to do potatoes in two ways for tonight.'

But having saved her face by giving Cook further minute instructions, human flesh and blood could not wait any longer. So she took herself up the kitchen stairs into the hall, and hanging over her brand-new card-tray she allowed herself to gaze in ecstasy at Mrs Hayburn's cards.

2

By quarter past seven, Bel, in a fashionable and most becoming dress, was to be found serenely, if a little purposefully, putting the finishing touches to the card-tables in her drawing-room. For she had decided that after their meal her guests should play whist. She had thrown embroidered cloths over two tables of suitable size, and was arranging at their corners packs of cards – new, their wrappers still unbroken – and little dishes of sweets, very special ones bought down town, and also, for those who preferred something not quite so fancy, a special make of Russian toffee.

Phoebe and Arthur, severely cautioned not to be late, and consequently unnecessarily early, were standing before the fire watching her. Arthur was looking grave and dignified in his tail-coat, and Phoebe, in white as became a young girl, was looking like a lily.

'Man, Bel, ye think of everything,' Arthur said, stretching out his hands behind him towards the fire.

Bel looked up at the brother and sister for a moment, then went on with her arranging. She wondered if she had detected a glint of amusement passing between them. Members of the same family often possess a telepathy which comes, perhaps, from having the same blood in their veins – a telepathy that even beloved wives do not share. Bel felt that now and resented it a little. For a moment she felt a wave of defiance. Very well. If they were laughing, let them. She was doing her duty by her husband and her children. What did Arthur want them all to be? A family of nobodies? And Phoebe? Who had looked after her and mothered her for the last eight years?

There was the sound of horses' hooves.

'See who that is, Phoebe,' she said, a little tartly.

It was Mary and George. Both looking more portly than ever, Phoebe thought, as she watched them descend carefully from their cab. And her opinion was not altered when, announced some minutes later, Mrs George McNairn, clad in regal red velvet, came in followed by the baillie.

'Bel, I think your house is very nice,' Mary was saying in her flat, unemotional tones. Then having greeted the others and looked about her she went on, 'You know, I once had to go to a committee meeting held in a drawing-room in this terrace. It was just the same shape as this. Of course it would be, wouldn't it? Now what *were* the people called? Anyway, they must have been very well-off. It was a wonderful room. Still I do think you've got this awfully nice, really. Hasn't she, George?'

Mary was prevented from saying more by the arrival of Sophia and William.

'Bel dear! This *is* fun! Do you know it's my first real dinner-party in the West End? William's been so excited about it that you would hardly have known him.' (Bel reflected that she certainly would not have known an excited William.) 'And as for the children, they've been perfect little abominations! Do you know they wanted to drive out here in the cab with us and walk back! I said it wouldn't do at all, and their father had to give them a good scolding. How do you like my dress? It's the one I had last year, with new lace and cut lower. Margy says I'm to be careful it doesn't fall off my shoulders altogether. Isn't she awful? William was just saying the other day he didn't know what present-day children were coming to. Didn't you, William?'

Mr Butter said nothing.

Sophia rattled on. 'Oh, here's Mrs Barrowfield coming in. How are you? Aren't you proud of Bel living in all this grandeur? We could never attempt this kind of thing. As William was just saying the other day – "It's plain Jane for us, Mother. We're not fashionable people, and it's no good pretending to be. We'll leave that sort of thing to Bel." Didn't you, William?'

Again William said nothing.

As David appeared in the doorway at this moment Sophia went on, 'David! How are you? Looking as if he lived in his tail-coat. Of course, so you do. I always forget you're such a social light! And here you are coming to have dinner with all your old dowdy relations!'

Bel was glad that Sarah came up to announce dinner at this point. For she was feeling a little ruffled. First, Mary had struck a wrong note by assuring her how much grander a neighbour's drawing-room was than her own; then next, Sophia had struck so many wrong and unnecessary notes that her performance, even for her, might almost be classed as a virtuoso one.

It was altogether too much. She gave up her original idea of pairing them off in the drawing-room, and allowed them to huddle downstairs to the dining-room as best they might.

3

As she came down the staircase she could hear the front-door bell ringing. Against the frosted panels, with its key-pattern border and its design of an urn of ferns, she could see the vague shape of a man. Who could it be? Anyway, Sarah and the new housemaid, now starched and waiting in the dining-room, couldn't possibly go to find out until the party was arranged and seated.

Arthur being a business-like man said a long, business-like grace. His wife might be getting grand, but he was damned if he was going to let her get irreligious. And so, in quiet, authoritative tones, he pointed out to his Maker at some length that what they were about to partake of would be eaten to His glory, and with humble feelings of thankfulness. Scarcely was the Amen out of his mouth than Sarah swooped down upon the lid of the large and handsome soup tureen, which was standing, ready, in front of her mistress. Clouds of savoury steam ascended, and for a time nothing was seen of Bel but a capable, elegant hand wielding the soup-ladle.

Gradually through their chatter the party became aware of frenzied ringings and knockings.

'There's somebody at the door,' Arthur said to the new house-maid, who happened to pass near him. 'Go and see who it is.'

'The girls can't do everything at once, Arthur,' Bel said, through her cloud of steam. 'It can't be anything important.'

Arthur, as he was at the head of the table and near the dining-room door, got up and went to the front door himself. To his wife's intense annoyance. She must stop Arthur doing this. It was all very well when it was just the family. But this – in her mind – was a dress rehearsal for other, and more important, dinners, when such casual conduct would never do.

The next happening did not serve to soothe her rising irritation. For the party heard loud, brotherly helloings in the hall, and the voices of Arthur and Mungo could be heard greeting each other. In another moment Mungo was ushered in smiling; grubby from his journey, and delighted to see all his relatives, who showed equal pleasure at seeing him. This was really too bad! It smashed the careful formality of this entertainment that

Bel had been planning for weeks! The table which, in great measure, she had decorated herself, had to be pushed about and rearranged, to allow another place to be laid. Mungo, who was looking rougher and more tweedy than ever against the evening clothes of the others, went out again with Arthur to have a wash. They took what seemed an eternity to come back. The carefully timed courses were all at sixes and sevens. She could hear them gossiping and laughing, quite forgetful that they were keeping a roomful of people waiting.

Bel, behind a set smile, felt very much like bursting into tears. Everyone was saying what a lucky chance for Mungo to find them all together like this.

It was Sarah who saved the situation.

'Will I set Mr Mungo's place beside you, Mam?'

Bel raised troubled eyes to Sarah. Suddenly she realized that Sarah was just as upset as she was. There had been sympathy and a full understanding in the woman's honest Glasgow voice. It gave Bel back control of herself – re-established her common sense.

'Yes, of course, Sarah. I must have Mr Mungo beside me. You won't mind pushing round, will you, David?' No. Tonight it seemed she must do with things as things did with her. Formality, for the time, must go.

And when Mungo came back and took his place she was able to welcome him warmly.

4

But after his first burst of greeting, Mungo, it seemed, was – even for him – surprisingly tongue-tied. Bel, David, his sisters plied him with questions. How was he? What of the Laigh Farm? What was the Ayrshire news?

At last, Arthur, looking down the table, said: 'If I were you, Mungo, I would just tell them and be done.'

'Tell us what?' Sophia cried. And all eyes were on Mungo's face, turned many shades redder than his country life warranted.

But Mungo, who was contritely hurrying through his soup shook his head.

'Go on, man, they'll have to know sooner or later.'

'You can't refuse now,' Bel said.

'Oh, well then, you can tell them, Arthur.'

Eyes went to the head of the table.

'Mungo's going to be married.'

'Married!' Mary and Sophia exclaimed together. Mungo? At the age of forty-three Mungo was getting married! It would be one of his farm-girls. The old story over again. No. It was too bad. Just when their children could do very well with a well-to-do bachelor uncle. Sophia had been planning pleasant, endearing little spells of housekeeping for Margy at the farm whenever she was old enough.

Mungo looked up embarrassed but good-natured. 'Well, what's wrong? Any objections? Are ye not marrit yerselves?'

'But tell us who the lady is, Mungo,' Bel said.

It was Arthur who spoke. 'It's Miss Ruanthorpe of Duntrafford.'

'Miss Ruanthorpe!' Again Mary and Sophia exclaimed together, and thereafter sat quite dumb, saying nothing whatever.

It was hardly for Bel – a mere town sparrow – to appreciate the shock of surprise to the two sisters. She had never known, like them, a country child's reverence for the Big House. A reverence which was planted deep in any farm-child's breast. In days gone by Sophia and Mary had hidden frightened, shy little faces in their mother's skirts when Sir Charles, calling at the farm, had bent down to say a word to them.

And now their brother Mungo, the least genteel, most clod-hopperish of all the boys, was going to marry Sir Charles's daughter! No. They sought about for some link that would make this possible, and found none. And typically they did not seek to attribute it to any special qualities in their brother. Mungo was just Mungo. And Miss Ruanthorpe must just be very eccentric indeed.

But it was very exciting. By themselves in the drawing-room after dinner, Mary, Sophia and Bel got their heads together. (Phoebe had gone up with Mrs Barrowfield to visit her nephews and niece.) It would be a great upheaval in Mungo's life. He was to be married quietly in two or three months' time, and he and his wife were to occupy the dower house of Duntrafford. His elder ploughman was to be put into the Laigh Farm-house, but Mungo fully intended to go on looking after his farm, for it was his life's work.

Mary, roused out of her customary placidity, did not really see how this arrangement could possibly work. Sophia agreed with her.

But there were other aspects. Mungo would shortly be as good as laird of the whole of the Duntrafford Estates – for Sir Charles was seventy-nine – and therefore rich! Much richer than any of them. It was a little hard, Bel thought, now adding her theme to the trio, considering how the other boys had worked and how well they had been supported by their wives. Still, she said angelically, it was nice to think of anyone so worthy as Mungo having such good fortune. Apropos of nothing, Sophia said, 'Mungo told me she was thirty-nine. They may have no children, of course.'

All three sat and pondered this for some time. Each working out its implications in relation to themselves and their children.

Presently Bel asked, 'Do you know if she has any near relations?'

'I don't think she has anybody at all,' Mary said, and added, 'I remember when I was a girl, Father and Mother saying so when her brother was killed at the hunt.'

'Was he killed at the hunt? That must have been terrible,' Bel said, but her voice seemed considerably brighter as she added, 'Still, that's all the more reason, dear, to hope they *do* have children. After all, thirty-nine isn't too late.'

And then, as Phoebe had come back into the room, and you couldn't possibly suggest that marriage might result in children before a young girl, she was reluctantly compelled to drop that aspect of the situation.

But, from her point of view, there was an even more immediate, and – though she would never admit it – alarming aspect of this new alliance. They would have to make contact with their new sister-in-law. They would have to meet her. She would have to come to stay. How would she expect to be treated? As the wife of Arthur she must ask her to stay at Grosvenor Terrace first. They had moved out West just in time! As she thought about it, courage returned. Yes. In this house she would be able to face the daughter of a baronet. David was always such a help – you could always go to him, socially naked and unashamed, and say to him simply, 'What do I do next?' and he was much too sympathetic and good-natured ever to mock.

When the men came upstairs they were all in the best of spirits, thanks to the excellent claret that David had said was the right thing to drink *at* a dinner-party. And also thanks to a good deal of port, which he had also said was the right thing to drink *after* one.

If they were all very homely and affectionate, and very much their old selves, without formality or anything else, and did nothing but hang about and chatter, leaving the women to their own devices, Bel did not really mind much now. The family was the family. And she supposed she must let them go on being just that. With the prospect of further social advances to be made, social positions to be stormed in the near future, it was, perhaps, a comfort to her to find herself, for this evening at least, among those for whom she really need make no effort whatever.

Chapter 18

I

At exactly the right moment of exactly the right afternoon, Bel dressed herself in what she considered to be exactly the right clothes and, supported by Phoebe, set out to return Mrs Hayburn's call.

The door was opened by a decorous maid – no detail of whose behaviour or dress escaped Bel – and they were requested to follow her upstairs.

Bel was glad that they were left by themselves for a moment in Mrs Hayburn's large drawing-room, since it let her have a good look round. So this was the room where David had danced upon his first memorable visit? There was much that was old-fashioned and restrained, Bel thought. For Mrs Hayburn's idea of furnishing had been formed when fashion had not yet run to the riot of heavy German drapery and tassels, to the rich, meaningless ornamentation that marked the late seventies; formed when decoration had not quite moved away from Georgian simplicity. Bel liked the room. Much of it appealed to her natural good taste. She found herself determining to eliminate this and that in her own too modern house, and wondering how she could do it without offending Arthur who, of course, had had all the paying to do and was indiscriminately proud of all his new possessions.

Presently the door opened and Mrs Hayburn came towards them.

Her manner was several degrees more genial than it would have been some days ago. For, since she had left her cards at Grosvenor Terrace, David had been here to see the boys and had let fall the information that his brother – the Ayrshire one – was to marry into the County. Up to now the existence of David's country brother had never been stressed, but in the sunshine of his astounding alliance, Mungo, simplest of souls, had budded and bloomed into a social asset.

Still, all that was very well. Henry's mother, however, was not yet by any means sure that she wanted Henry to marry Phoebe. Like a good and tactful parent, she must, of course, avoid all appearance of placing obstacles. But – well – it was surely her first duty to examine the young woman before her and decide for herself. Certainly his taste was excellent. Miss Moorhouse was a beautiful creature. She had never thought that Henry would have eyes for this sort of girl.

Indeed, the two women before her made rather a splendid pair. Miss Moorhouse, dark and slender, with fine tempestuous colouring, and also that indefinable air of distinction that her brother David possessed. And her sister-in-law, fair, elegant and mature – her taste in dress a little too good, perhaps a little too careful – and yet withal, impeccable.

'It's very kind of you to come to see me, Mrs Moorhouse,' she said, begging them to sit down. 'You see, we've known David for such a long time now. Yet it almost seemed as if he had no relatives.'

Bel replied pleasantly that there were her own family, and the family of two married sisters in Glasgow.

'Yes. He did mention you, of course. But for a long time I had no idea that some of your husband's family were still left in Ayrshire. David only told us recently.'

'Oh yes. The oldest of all. And it's so amusing to think – at his time of life! We all thought he was a confirmed bachelor, of course. And now he's just got engaged to be married to the daughter of an old friend, Sir Charles Ruanthorpe.' There were times when Mungo's impending eminence filled Bel with envy. But here, in Mrs Hayburn's presence, she could only be obliged to him.

Mrs Hayburn, who was nothing if not curious, was delighted that Mrs Moorhouse looked like gossiping. She put her hand upon the bell-rope. 'You'll stay for tea?'

Bel, who had heard it was not smart to drink tea upon a first visit, held up an elegant gloved hand: 'No, thank you. I'm sorry. We're going on.'

Phoebe vaguely wondered where Bel thought they were going on to, but dutifully held her tongue.

'I'm sorry,' the old woman was saying; then she added: 'The Ayrshire Moorhouses will go on staying in the country, of course?'

At this moment the devil entered into Phoebe. Or so, at any rate, it seemed to Bel.

'Oh yes, of course, Mrs Hayburn. You see, my brother is just a working farmer. He says he won't let his marriage make any difference to his work.' Too much play-acting had a strange effect upon Phoebe. It made her feel as though she were in an overheated room where she must, cost what it might, throw wide the windows. Bel coloured, but said nothing.

A violent sort of girl this, old Mrs Hayburn thought. She could see that Phoebe had embarrassed her sister-in-law. Why had she done it? Through sheer coltishness? Or was it by intention? Strangely, the sight of Bel's confusion aroused within her a feeling of friendship. She too hated violence. And after all, why was the girl making a fuss? Her brother was going to marry a baronet's daughter. He couldn't just be a ploughman.

And as they went on talking her liking for Bel increased. Mrs Arthur Moorhouse was highly personable and unvulgar, and she seemed anxious to play the social game. She would not mind seeing her from time to time.

But she was not so sure about Phoebe. This child spoke her mind much too frankly. Perhaps that had appealed to Henry, but she, for her part, did not approve of it. There was a fearlessness about the girl that she did not like. No. If it were at all possible she must steer her dreamy, unpractical son safely through this shoal. He had much better take one of the young ladies she had planned for him instead of this odd, stormy creature.

2

But Henry had other views, and Phoebe was to learn them very quickly.

One evening, after a meal at Sophia's, Phoebe found herself with the Butter children on the old Mill Road, down by the waters of the River Kelvin. She had decided to try to go home this way. It was a pleasant walk, she had heard. Wil and Margy had promised to come with her as far as the Flint Mill. A curious little road it was, down there in the gully. High above, on both sides, crescents and terraces were springing up – or stood, already built. But here, down out of it all, the rural past still lingered. It was June and you were in the country, if you didn't raise your eyes. Here there were fresh leaves, the rushing river, and nothing but a white cottage and the mill. And though City sounds were shut out by the flow of the water, you heard the notes of the thrushes and the blackbirds in the bushes nearby. There was no traffic on this little lost road, which was, every day, becoming more engulfed in a thriving Victorian City. It was secluded and remote.

Wil and Margy skipped along by Phoebe's side, showing her this and that. A robin's nest. The wild hyacinths. A flowering lilac bush. Phoebe frisked with them. It was nice to have a rest from being grown up. When they came to the mill they hung about watching; for the men were working late.

Suddenly a voice called: 'Miss Moorhouse.' She turned round. It was Henry Hayburn. He was bare-headed, and carried a book in his hand. His black hair was shaken anyhow over his brow and his eyes were excited. With his dusty coat, his loose black tie, and his boyish beard, he looked, she thought, like the conventional picture of a poet.

She held out her hand. 'I didn't expect to find you down here. What are you reading? Poetry?'

He looked at her solemnly for a moment, surprised, as though he were not quite sure whether she was real, then he grinned. Colour came suddenly into his freckled white face. 'No,' he said. 'It's not poetry. I never read poetry. I can't be bothered with it.' He laid his hand on the pocket into which he had thrust his book and said with sudden earnestness: 'No. This is a book about steam-pressure.'

The difference was ludicrous enough. At another time or said by anybody else Phoebe would have laughed. But the tone of his voice, the lack of any sign from him that he was aware of having said anything comic, the fierce glint of enthusiasm in his eyes, suddenly gave the young girl a glimpse of that strange passion which was Henry's heritage. That fierce, creative obsession. With iron, coal, water-power, electricity, expanding steam. It gave her a glimpse of the importance of these things to this young man. In a flash of unwonted insight – for her peasant blood was not particularly quick – she saw how much it meant to him to be numbered with the old and famous brotherhood of Glasgow's engineers.

Somehow she felt embarrassed. She looked about her. Wil and Margy were hanging over the fence by the mill-stream gazing at the water as it flowed into the mill. She called them.

'Have you seen my nephew and niece before? Wil and Margy Butter. This is a friend of your Uncle David, Mr Hayburn.'

The Butter children shook hands. It amused them to see Phoebe suddenly grown up again. For a moment they stood grinning awkwardly before the unkempt young gentleman, then shortly they turned back to the mill and left Phoebe with him.

'I suppose it's possible for me to get home this way?' Phoebe said conversationally. 'I don't quite know where I am.'

'Yes, it is,' he said. 'But you have to go a bit further up. Look here, I can take you.'

Phoebe protested. 'Oh, no! Please don't let me bother you. I know there's a footbridge somewhere.'

He had become solemn again. He was looking now like a disappointed child. 'I would like to show you the way. You can cross by the footbridge at the Three-Tree Well.' And as he was still looking at her like a spaniel who wants to be taken for a walk, Phoebe accepted.

'All right. It's very kind of you, Mr Hayburn.'

She called the children and they said goodbye.

3

The evening was warm. But the walk through the trees by the riverside was cool and pleasant. Henry paced along by her side, still saying little, though at their last meeting she had laughingly given him permission to talk. But she did not mind. It pleased her to imagine that she was out in the country far from the encroaching City. She could understand why in past days the valley of the Kelvin had been renowned for its beauty. Even now there was much left. They came to the bridge at the old ford. When they stood in the middle of it she stopped and, leaning on the rail, looked down into the water. The young man halted beside her. Midges were dancing. Birds were calling in the wooded bank on the farther side by the Three-Tree Well. Neither of them spoke for a time.

Presently Phoebe looked at her companion. He was not looking down into the water any more. He was looking at herself intently. She smiled at him. 'You can talk to me, you know. I gave you permission the last time I saw you.'

'I remember,' he said bashfully. 'It was very nice of you.'

She tried to read his face, then laughed – a little defensively, perhaps. 'Oh, don't be too serious about it. It wasn't much, really.'

'Yes, it was.'

She did not know what he meant, so she turned away and again gazed into the water as it ran beneath them.

Once more he hung on the rail watching her. Her face was rosy with leaning.

Still looking down, she spoke. 'I've spoiled your evening for you,' and as he made to answer, 'Yes, I have. You came out with your book to read up something and enjoy yourself, and here you are seeing a young lady home because you think you ought to.'

He was incapable of fine speeches, but he cried, 'Oh no, Miss Moorhouse, I wanted to.'

Suddenly she was touched. 'It's nice of you anyway. I'll tell you something. When you told me what your book was about I realized just how much all that kind of thing – I mean your work, engineering – matters to you.'

His eyes gleamed at her. 'Did you, Miss Moorhouse?'

'Yes.'

'How could you possibly?'

'I don't know. Just a sudden look. Something.'

This was wonderful. It was more. It was of great and exciting importance. That she, of all people, should know by instinct what his own people could not, or would not, grasp.

'Mother and Stephen never would have, you know.'

'What a pity!' she said simply.

'I'm glad you do.'

She looked at him quickly and straightened herself. 'It's nice of you to say that, Mr Hayburn, but why you should care what I think, I don't know. We'd better go on—' She was very young and, except in her own virgin thoughts, perhaps, the lands of tenderness were still hidden country, yet the tone of his voice had told her to be careful. She crossed the remainder of the bridge quickly, walking a little ahead of him. But there she had to stop, for she was not sure how next to go. 'Which way?' She turned to him smiling, determined to be pleasantly normal.

'That way. It doesn't matter.'

Without waiting she turned and began going up the hill. Presently she stopped, panting for breath. It was strangely quiet here. Quiet and secluded. Queer to think that it was a stone's-throw from Glasgow's most fashionable Gardens. She stood still and looked back. He was coming up behind her. His face was flushed and troubled as though he were unravelling some conundrum in his mind.

4

When he came level with her he caught her hand and said, 'Miss Moorhouse, I want you to marry me.'

It was said so absurdly simply, with so little seeming emotion, that Phoebe was seized with a mad feeling that she was acting charades – that presently they would have to go back to the beginning, and Henry would be told to put much more expression into it. But she couldn't stand here, her hand in Henry's, thinking about charades. She drew it away and said, 'Mr Hayburn, you're talking nonsense.'

He had turned his back, and saying nothing, was looking out through the leaves across the river.

Phoebe had a strong desire to laugh. It was all so sudden and ridiculous. And she felt she was behaving quite wrongly. As a well-brought-up young lady she ought to have fainted. Bel had fainted the first time Arthur had 'sought her hand', or so, at least, she had once said. But then Bel, even in moments of great stress, always made a point of doing the correct thing. Or if she, Phoebe, hadn't fainted, at least she should have exclaimed that the suddenness of his proposal had taken her completely by surprise – as indeed it had. But instead of causing her a proper maidenly agitation it had only made her want to laugh. The thing was so abrupt, so ill-timed.

She stood for a moment watching his back. Suddenly he turned and faced her.

'Well?' His voice was almost savage. It was gloomy here in the evening woods, but she could see the distress in his face. For a moment this wealthy young man, this spoilt child of fortune, had turned into a lame duck.

'What do you want me to say, Mr Hayburn?'

'I've asked you to marry me.'

'Please, I don't want to marry anybody. You or anybody else. Quite honestly I haven't thought much about that kind of thing. You see, I've only just grown up.'

'Will you promise you'll think about it, Miss Moorhouse?'

'No. I don't think so. Please don't get upset, Mr Hayburn. But why should I?' He was standing looking so miserable, that she added, 'There's a seat by the well, isn't there? Come and sit down.' He followed her, and they sat.

'I wanted to marry you whenever I saw you. You're never out of my mind now.'

'Nonsense. Admit you think a great deal about your work.'

He turned to her, his eyes shining with eagerness. 'But that's it. Don't you see? Down there on the bridge just now, when you told me that you understood about my work, it was wonderful that you, you of all people, should understand what it means to me! When even my own mother and brother don't!'

'If you don't mind me saying so, I think it's possible that neither your mother nor your brother may be very quick in the uptak'. You'll find many people, besides myself, who would realize it quickly enough.'

He shook his head. 'No,' he said. And then, after a long pause, 'Please, Miss Moorhouse.'

Phoebe shook her head. She turned on the seat and looked at him. 'You know, Mr Hayburn, I'm not such a nice person as you think I am. I want to be fair to you, you see. That's why I'm talking about myself. No. There's a hard core to me.'

'I don't believe it.'

'You needn't bother to say that. There is. Sometimes I think I haven't got real affections at all. I find myself standing back and looking at everybody interestedly, as if I was watching – oh, how can I put it? – well, looking at people as if they were gold-fish swimming about on the other side of the glass. You'll see what I mean, if you try.'

He nodded.

'It makes me frightened sometimes. It's not a nice thing really, to feel quite cold when people expect you to feel glad, or sorry, or excited about something. But there it is. I even look at the people I live with and wonder if I really like *them*.' She stopped for a moment, then went on, more to herself than to the young man. 'And yet – yes, I suppose I do. I've done things for my nephew Arthur ... And I still have a kind of schoolgirl's hero-worship for my sister-in-law, Bel. But ... do you know, I'm looking at you just now, and a bit of me is saying to itself, "That's what a young man looks like when he imagines he's in love." ' She put her hand over the large, capable hand that was resting on the seat beside her. 'Oh, I'm nasty and callous, Mr Hayburn. Forget about me.'

He said nothing, but grasped her hand and held it. It was he who spoke first again, after a pause. 'Perhaps your feelings are not developed yet.'

'Perhaps not. Perhaps someday I'll turn into a real woman.'

'For God's sake, don't talk like that, Miss Moorhouse.'

She got up. 'I don't think this talk's leading us anywhere, anyway. I don't know why I began it. Unless maybe to show you how little use I can be to you. At least you can forgive me. Will you?'

He got up too. 'I don't see what there is to forgive. I spoke too suddenly. I believe I've frightened you.'

'Not in the faintest. I wish you had! That would have been something!'

He could not make her out as he followed her up the road to Kirklee. There he said goodbye to her, feeling how desperately unsatisfactory life was, how much he was always bungling things, and how inadequate he had been.

And as Phoebe crossed the Great Western Road and went down towards Grosvenor Terrace she was, perhaps, not far from having the same feelings.

Chapter 19

I

Phoebe's first proposal of marriage left no deep impression on her mind. When she did think of it – which, in a very short space of time, was not often – the incident seemed a little ridiculous, even a little pathetic. Henry Hayburn couldn't, after all, really care much about her. He had met her only twice before in his life. That his proposal had been, at the moment, sincere, she did not doubt. All his behaviour, its very ineffective gaucheness, had shown her that. Yet his feelings couldn't have deep roots.

But, of course, she just didn't want to marry Henry or anybody else. She was only eighteen. On the whole, her family made a pleasant pattern about her; and if she was not conscious of strong attachment to them as individuals, she knew she was, at least, attached to the pattern. Bel and little Arthur were perhaps exceptions. For her sister-in-law, Phoebe's first childish admiration was not diminished, though at times she found herself smiling at Bel's intense preoccupation with the correct thing. Her nephew Arthur was, somehow, a part of herself. He was the one being on earth, herself not excepted, whom she was unable to see objectively.

Now that the excitement of settling in to Grosvenor Terrace was, at last, beginning to subside, it was Mungo's coming marriage to Margaret Ruanthorpe that held everybody's interest.

Bel, dutiful, a little tremulous, but firmly determined to do the honours, asked Miss Ruanthorpe and Mungo to stay. Margaret replied to Bel's letter with great friendliness, and duly arrived for two nights to see her future husband's family. Somehow she filled the house. Bel could make little of her, but what little she made she could not dislike. Even though she stamped through the house in boots made by a village shoemaker, wore rough-cut tweeds from a village tailor, and mannish shirts with collars and ties, she had an indefinable quality that Bel recognized and valued beyond rubies, and wondered how Margaret achieved it.

'I can't tell you what it is,' she said to her mother one afternoon shortly after the future Mrs Mungo's visit, as they sat comfortably together over their cups of tea in the Monteith Row parlour. 'You know, if I wore the same clothes as Margaret I would be ready for the pantomime. But she seems to manage to carry everything off. And when she puts on her dress for the evening – and, mind you, I wouldn't give twopence for it – you would say she was a very nice-looking woman.'

But somehow – perhaps because Miss Ruanthorpe was 'English' – Bel could not approach her very closely. She boomed about with her 'English' accent, was scrupulously polite, impersonal and cheerful, in a manner that defeated Bel's burgher understanding.

There was no sitting down with her and having a good heart-to-heart talk. Margaret, Bel felt, did not make conversation. She issued statements. Not unpleasant statements, but statements nevertheless. It never occurred to Bel that Margaret might in her turn be feeling shy and strange too, and showing it by her abrupt behaviour.

Phoebe and Arthur, having the country in their bones, got on much better. Phoebe, indeed, was of great use to Bel, as she consented to be dragged out by Margaret for a long walk into the neighbouring country, thus giving Bel an afternoon of freedom from her baffling guest. Even Mary and Sophia had more in common with Miss Ruanthorpe, for there were many old interests, memories of their country days, that they were able to recall with the help of this sister-in-law to be. Margaret, being about Sophia's age, remembered their own mother well, as a kindly body in the Laigh Farm kitchen, and she was able to remember pleasant things about her that even they did not know.

It was now high June. The wedding was to be in the early autumn, she said. It was to take place in the drawing-room at Duntrafford, for Sir Charles was no longer young, and it would be too much of an effort to get him to church. She was putting the dower house into order as quickly as possible. They had allowed it to stand empty for some time. There was to be some building, and much putting right. When this was done there would be nothing to wait for. She turned to Mungo with a smile and asked him if there was. It was obvious that she was very fond of him.

And Mungo's family smiled to themselves. It was clear, Arthur said to David, that he had his young lady well in hand. He was letting her do everything. After all, it was being done with Margaret's money. But it was not hard to see that what Mungo said went. There was evidence of affection, even a little complacency on his side. On Margaret's there was evidence of much more. The brothers agreed that, in the circumstances, it was a good thing; and long might it last for his sake.

2

But Margaret Ruanthorpe was very well pleased with her bargain. It had taken a long time – four years indeed – to break down the barriers between herself and this solemn intelligent farmer who was her obsession. During all that time she had known she was following an instinct that was right. The country was in the blood of both of them. They had, fundamentally, common interests, which were bound to make their union, should it come about, successful. And so, without loss of dignity be it said, she had persisted. If Mungo had accepted her enthusiastic friendship slowly, and with extreme caution, at least he had not drawn away from it. Her parents, old and preoccupied with their ailments and each other, let her do as she pleased. She had the sense to move slowly, digging herself in at every new move. He and his little sister had been persuaded to come to Duntrafford to lunch. Later he was induced to come alone. Now that he knew her parents, she consulted him about them – about her father's health, the management of the estate. His advice was invariably good. When she heard Phoebe was back at the Laigh Farm, she came to see her. She made herself familiar and pleasant with the workers on the farm, who, on the whole, came to like her. She stayed for pleasant simple meals in the glowing firelit kitchen. On the first occasion, when Mungo came and found her sitting with Phoebe, waiting for him, he went to put on his jacket. But she protested. She would take it as very unfriendly of him if he made any difference for her.

Thus things had gone on. So gradually indeed, and over such a space of time, that their closer relationship seemed a natural sequel, a growth rather than a thing of violent feelings. But underneath Margaret was steadily determined.

And thus, some weeks ago, the inevitable had happened.

One of Margaret's fillies, a very valuable hackney pony that was not thriving as she should, had, on Mungo's suggestion, been sent over to him at the Laigh Farm. He would keep her in a field nearby and watch over her himself. She would be the finest beast Duntrafford had ever bred, he said, if only he could bring her to a flourishing maturity.

He had had her for some weeks. In addition to improving Margaret's very elegant little animal, he had given Margaret ample excuse for coming across every day. They were on such terms now, however, that this went without remark.

Suddenly disaster fell. The pony entangled a hoof in a coil of barbed wire lying rusty and hidden in a deep patch of grass. The creature, finding herself caught, had danced in a frenzy, wounding herself terribly before they could free her. Round the top of her hoof the flesh was badly torn.

The man who had seen this happen and had eventually succeeded in freeing the pony, was afraid to tell Mungo. The farmer of Laigh Farm was slow-tempered, but they, all of them, knew his temper was there. But told he must be. Mungo went white with rage. It touched his honour, that this animal he had taken into his care, to bring her to her full beauty, should be ruined by mere stupid carelessness. That the beast was not his own made it worse. And that it was Margaret Ruanthorpe's made it worse still. In addition, the idea of the creature's agony tormented him.

For a moment he lost control. Was this a place to look after horses, if the louts about couldn't keep their eyes open for rubbish like a bit of wire? It must have lain there all winter. Surely someone could have seen to it. The man, knowing his master, let him storm; and at last, with a grunt meant to be an apology, Mungo turned and ran.

The pony's condition was as bad as possible. He sent one man for the vet, another to Duntrafford. Margaret and the vet arrived from different directions almost at the same time.

Margaret greeted Mungo. She had never seen him so much moved before.

The hysterical pony, soothed a little by Margaret's voice, allowed some kind of examination. The vet shook his head.

'I'm sorry, Miss. She would 'a' been worth a lot.'

When Margaret was excited her voice went high and harsh. 'You mean she'll have to be shot, Mr Johnstone?'

He nodded.

'Is it no use fighting?'

'The beast's in terrible pain, Miss! An' I doubt – a rusty wire. There'll be poison.'

'Couldn't we try?'

'Well, Miss—' Again he shook his head.

She turned abruptly to Mungo. 'Mr Moorhouse, couldn't we fight with her? For tonight at least?'

Mungo looked at Margaret sorrowfully.

'The beastie will not let ye touch her.'

'She'll let me touch her.' She crossed the box, and standing beside the trembling pony, ran her hand part way down the injured leg. The movement was womanly and gentle. It was not lost on Mungo. The creature threw back its head, its nostrils were wild, but it stood quiet. She held the injured hoof up, painfully tipping the puddle made by the blood that was dripping steadily to the floor.

'Mr Moorhouse, we must try.' Margaret's voice was trembling.

Mungo turned to Johnstone. 'What is it first then? Get it clean? Plenty of rags and boiling water? You stay with her, Miss Ruanthorpe; I'll go an' tell the lassies.'

And thus the battle had begun. All through the first night, Margaret and Mungo – fanatics for horseflesh, both of them – stayed in the box together, scarcely leaving it, dressing the terrible gash, striving to calm the pain-stretched nerves of the high-strung animal and keeping her from doing herself harm. What devotion could do that they did. Sleep hardly occurred to either of them.

In the late evening Margaret sent a scribbled note back to Duntrafford, telling them briefly what had happened, saying she could not come home. In reply the old woman who had been her nurse arrived with clothing and instructions from Lady Ruanthorpe that if Margaret stayed at the Laigh Farm, she, her nurse, must stay too. And so, propriety having been upheld, the fight for the pony's life went on.

For the first days they did not know if the wound had been poisoned. With expert help they did everything in their power to get it clean. But gradually, as time went on and healing showed itself, their fears began to diminish. They would not be able to tell for long, however, if she would be permanently lame. The two discussed the chances endlessly. If the animal had been a brilliant child whose intellect might be permanently injured, and they had been its parents, they could scarcely have been more intense. Whatever happened now, Margaret was determined not to have the filly destroyed. Even if she could never be broken in she might hand down her elegant proportions as a brood mare.

But the leg would be stiff for weeks. How long would it be before they could tell? There was consultation. Endless talks. Animals that have been nursed become affectionate and petted like delicate children. And they tend to forge a bond between those who have struggled with them.

At last there came a day when there was no further chance of the pony losing its life through poisoning. There was a no possible reason, therefore, why Margaret should stay longer. She left the Laigh Farm. But she left it as the promised wife of Mungo Moorhouse.

So it had come. And neither of them knew in the end how it had happened.

Margaret had returned to her own home tired out, but satisfied. It was the fulfilment of a long hope.

And Mungo, too, was pleased. Long familiarity with the Ruanthorpes had broken down his timidity and doubt. He would be at home with this woman he was to marry. For a long time now he had been well aware that Margaret wanted him. But, emotionally slow as he was and uncertain of the wisdom of the step, he had let things take their course. Now their course was taken, and he was content. He could look forward to companionship with a wife of whom he would be genuinely fond.

3

As she said goodbye, Margaret Ruanthorpe invited Arthur and
Bel to come for a weekend to Duntrafford. Bel, she said, must get
to know her parents, and Arthur must renew an old acquaintance. Bel, curious 'to see how people like that did things', was
sorely tempted to accept, but even with her spirit the battle of
getting there, going to the trouble of having the right clothes, and
being on her P's and Q's for more than two solid days was too
much for her, and she was forced to decline. The labour of
getting herself and everybody else into Grosvenor Terrace had
been enough for a time.

And now it was nearly July, which meant, if you were a proper
matron of the City of Glasgow, that you collected your forks and
knives, table and bed linen, the entire supply of old clothes belonging to the household, and heaven knew what else, and locked
or corded them into trunks or hampers. Then, on the first of the
month, you (and whoever you could get to help you – in Bel's
case, Sarah and a man sent along from the warehouse, and at the
last moment, a porter) got everything on to the deck of the Bute
steamer, or the Arran steamer, or the Kintyre steamer, at the
seething Broomielaw. You then sat upon it stoically watching
your children, eating sandwiches and listening to the German
band until you reached your destination. Whereat you disembarked
and lived in extreme primitiveness – and usually, for your children
at least, in extreme rapture – for the months of July and August.

For the last years Arthur had insisted upon their going to Glen
Rosa in Arran. It was a beautiful place, of course, but there had
been times when Bel had thought that it would be nice to have a
smart house at Cove, and, as she put it, 'meet people'. But this
year the idea of Brodick and their house in Glen Rosa (which,
like most Arran houses, was simple to the point of crudeness)
filled her harassed soul with balm. Grosvenor Terrace was very
well and she was delighted at last to find herself established there.
But now, for a blessed two months, she could do and look precisely as she liked. Her time would be pleasantly taken up, running to the beach with the children. Pulling off and on shoes and
stockings, drying little brown bodies and unpacking chittering
bites. And in Glen Rosa there would be the smell of bracken and
bog myrtle, of burning peat, the sound of running water; and of
a morning, as she lay in bed, the cackle of cocks and hens. And
sometimes, in the evening, she would see the Duke's deer moving
on the shoulder of the mountain, frescoed against the sky.

No. A visit to Duntrafford would be too much for her at present, so she thanked Margaret and regretted that she must wait to know her parents until later.

But Phoebe was to be at the Laigh Farm for the summer. Now that she was grown up she must take her share of family responsibilities. On every count it was right that she should be there. She was the only woman of the family who was free to go, and the only one to whom the farm was now familiar. Even in the country she managed to conduct her own very personal existence and live within herself, bothering no one – very much indeed as her own parents had done before her. The farm-hands liked her; she did not interfere. Mungo too was pleased, for Phoebe's independence kept her from being in the way. Indeed, her presence was of great use, for she made it possible for Margaret to come and go without seeming bold.

Chapter 20

1

Phoebe arrived at the Laigh Farm this summer with great plans for improving her mind. She had been reading in a lady's magazine – a truly genteel periodical, with no sympathy for that abhorred creature The New Woman – just how important it was for the refined lady to be well read. There was no reason, it said, why, for instance, a woman of average good intelligence should not grasp the works of Mr Ruskin and Mr Carlyle. A little determination was all that was necessary. Mr Dickens was, of course, a great author, but he was a little helter-skelter if it came to the question of forming style in addition to being well read. Besides, there were moments when he could scarcely be freed from the charge of vulgarity.

Perhaps it was better to leave Mr Dickens to the gentlemen. And talking of style, Miss Austen's books were, as everybody knew, excellent, but on other counts they were a little tame and old-fashioned, perhaps, and lacking in romance. Still, they were the works of a gentlewoman and could safely be recommended. Books like *Jane Eyre* the contributor could not recommend. If a young lady must be romantic, there was always Sir Walter.

Again, before leaving her music-master for the summer, Phoebe had suggested to him he might set her some holiday work. He had perhaps noticed that her practising had not been so regular of recent months, but she had been tremendously busy helping her sister-in-law. Now, however, she was going to bury herself in the country for the whole of the summer, and had every intention of more than making up for lost time. The piano at her brother's farm was an old one, having been bought for her sisters years ago, and perhaps, now, its tone was rather tinny, but she would write to her brother to have it put in order by a travelling tuner. At this point she had looked at her music-master. Would an indifferent piano, did he think, spoil her touch? Knowing her, or rather her youth, better than she knew it herself, he assured her that he thought it would not.

So down into Ayrshire Phoebe came, arrived with many improving books, a fat bundle of pieces and exercises, and a fair amount of fancy sewing, with which she intended to decorate her own bedroom in Grosvenor Terrace.

All of which she at once forgot in the superb July weather. Besides – she lamented later to David who had the temerity to tease her about it – there was so much she found she simply had to do when she got there.

Margaret was always wanting her over to Duntrafford to do this and that. They were for ever in the dower house watching and instructing joiners, plasterers, paperhangers and painters. There was no end to it. And though Margaret had a sewing-woman, of course, there were always little odds and ends that she, Phoebe, found herself promising to do. Then there were all Mungo's clothes to be gone through. She really couldn't let him be married without seeing that he had everything necessary. She had never realized, she said importantly, just how negligent men could be. So David needn't sneer.

Indeed, she built up a very effective picture of herself slaving her way unselfishly through these summer months for her brother and his wife-to-be; the very personification of thoughtful sisterliness, when she had much rather, of course, been sitting in seclusion improving her mind and her fingers.

But she did not tell him of a litter of collie puppies, shocking wasters of time. Nor of the long, solitary walks that took her over field and moor, or across the green holmes and by the wooded banks of the River Ayr – expeditions that she came to make daily.

Almost every evening, too, when Phoebe and Mungo did not dine at Duntrafford, Margaret came across to look at her pony. They were walking the injured leg daily now, very carefully. An ailing animal was a lame duck to Phoebe, and she had become as interested as the others. Would the beautiful little creature yet fulfil its promise? A pony by the same stallion had gone to America, sold, it was said, for a thousand guineas, to pull the governess-cart of a Vanderbilt. Mungo, who had seen this animal, declared its proportions were not so fine as those of the Duntrafford filly. Would she too come, after all, to be of great value?

Or was she to be nothing now but a brood mare? When Phoebe saw her first the filly was still hobbling, hardly putting her hoof to the ground. But by dint of much tending and rubbing the limp began to go. At first she would allow only Mungo's and Margaret's hands upon her. But later Phoebe, having made herself familiar, was allowed to tend her too. Steadily the limp diminished. At last, one afternoon towards the end of August, a farm-boy was given the halter rope and told to trot her. The lad called encouragement and began to run. Margaret, Mungo and Phoebe stood watching. The pony was petted. At first she would only walk, dragging back on the rein. At last, finding this uncomfortable, she hurried her pace and in a moment more her enraptured audience saw her set her elegant neck and begin to trot 'high and disposèdly' round the yard, like the aristocrat she had first shown promise of becoming.

Mungo turned to the women. 'She's all right,' was all he said. Which, to any one but a Lowland Scot, may seem inadequate for more than four months of constant anxiety and labour.

2

A pleasant summer for Phoebe, most of it, and if she didn't carry out the scheme of education she had planned for herself she received, perhaps, some education of another sort. For her constant association with Margaret Ruanthorpe and her parents gave her a glimpse of a different world, a different point of view from the climbing provincialism of Bel's house in Kelvinside. As ways of living, there was not much to choose between them. Sir Charles and Lady Ruanthorpe held to their view of life just as complacently as the Glasgow Moorhouses held to theirs. But their code of life followed a wider tradition, the code of Victorian Britain's lesser gentry; whereas Phoebe's own family, only just emerging – by their own honest effort – from the peasantry, had their outlook sharply limited by that all-absorbing occupation known as 'getting on'. At all events, the world of Duntrafford was something new for Phoebe, and helped her, perhaps, towards finding her own perspective.

The wedding, Margaret had decided, was to be at the end of the first week in September. The holiday-makers would be home again by then. The bridal pair wanted as little ceremony as possible, a fact which suited Phoebe admirably, for thus, until the last moment, she was left free to go her own ways. Late August was lush and beautiful, and her long rambles in the wilds had become more of a rapture than ever.

But her last days were destined to be disturbed. She had called a dog and was setting out one afternoon when, suddenly, as she opened the front door of the farmhouse – a door which had to be unlocked, for it was little used – she was confronted with Henry Hayburn. She drew back surprised.

'Mr Hayburn!' She held out her hand. She was confused, and she knew her face showed it.

He looked hot and tired. He must have walked the three miles from the railway station. He was wearing the same black clothes. The same loose tie. He took her hand.

'I hope I haven't surprised you too much. David told me you were down here.'

So he had come to see her. 'Come in and have a rest,' was all she could think to say.

He shook his head. 'You were just going out. Don't let me stop you. Perhaps I could walk part of your way with you.'

He looked so tired and apologetic now that Phoebe laughed, and laid her hand on his arm. 'Don't be ridiculous. I was only going for a walk by myself. You must come in and sit down. I'll get you something to eat.

'Really – I don't want—'

'If you've come from Glasgow you must be hungry. Come in.' She led him into the cool kitchen.

'You mustn't give yourself any trouble,' he said lamely.

'I won't.' She fetched some bread, new-baked scones and cheese from the dresser, brought a jug of milk and a pat of fresh butter from the cold milk-house, put them on the scrubbed table and set a chair. 'There,' she said, 'that wasn't much trouble, was it?'

She sat watching him while he ate and drank, running her hand over the muzzle of the collie who sat waiting beside her, and playing with its ears.

Strange, gawky young man this, with his hair all about as usual, and his black beard making his cheeks look absurdly young and boyish. There was something appealing about him today, something that pulled at her heart-strings. She felt, somehow, as though she had taken in a beggar man and was giving him food. What else could she do for him to send him happily on his way? That depended on what he had come to beg for. She felt it better not to ask.

She saw that he ate little, but he drank most of the milk she had given him, for he was hot and thirsty. And while he was eating and drinking he said almost nothing. Answering her merely that, yes, he *had* seen David lately, and that he looked well. And again, yes, his mother and Stephen were in the house at Kilcreggan. Stephen had been yachting. No, he hadn't been there much himself. He had been too busy at Hayburn and Company, working on a new idea.

'You look as if you needed a holiday, Mr Hayburn,' she said.

He did not reply directly to this. He rose, struck the flour of the scones from his hands, and asked her if he might come with her on the walk she had intended to take.

3

She was uncertain what to do with him. She did not want to ask him, right out, why he had come. And yet it seemed odd, to say the least, that he should want to make a train journey, then walk for miles through the dust, just to go for yet another walk when he had arrived. She was not really afraid of what he might say to her, but it was a peaceful, sunny afternoon, and she had no wish to be emotional, if emotional he intended to be. Besides, what she had to say to him, if he opened up the topic of their last meeting, would only hurt him. For her mind was not changed.

'Well, shall we go?' he was saying.

'If you want to.' What else was there to do? How else deal with him?

She led him by fieldside paths that skirted hawthorn hedges, untrimmed and high, and with scarlet autumn berries already formed in clusters against the dark-green leaves. By Mungo's fields of corn, ripening fast, as it stood up motionless in the still afternoon sunshine. Then further up to the moorland, across a rough stone wall or two, through beds of rustling brown bracken and seeding dry grasses. Here and there a sheep, with her half-grown lamb, started up, taken unawares.

Phoebe was becoming conscious now of a growing exasperation. She realized that she was hurrying on ahead of Henry out of sheer annoyance with him. And all he did was to tag bleakly after her in his untidy town clothes. What right had he to intrude like this? These Hayburn boys were rich and spoilt. Because they had money and an indulgent mother they thought they were the lords of creation.

Presently she halted and turned round to look at her companion. No. She had to admit it. At the moment the last thing he looked like was a lord of creation. He looked more tired and hot than ever. His hair was over his eyes, and sweat was glistening on his face.

She laughed, and her own laugh, for some reason, sounded to her a little hard.

'I'm sorry to race you along like this, Mr Hayburn. You look desperately hot. But you wanted to come, you know.'

He looked at her – irritatingly, feckless, she thought – and said, 'Yes, Miss Moorhouse, I did.'

'Look. Here's a burn. Lie down and have a drink of water. That'll cool you.' She stood over him contemplating his back, his thick black hair and his long legs, spread apart as he lay flat on the turf by the burnside, putting his lips to the clear surface. She noticed that the seat of his trousers was shiny, and felt sure that his mother would disapprove of this careless shabbiness.

Suddenly Phoebe's irritation evaporated. He was such a child. Like a good little boy, he had dropped down on his knees the moment she had suggested it. He seemed prepared to do everything she told him. She knelt down beside him and, cupping her hands, dipped them into the stream, and drank too. Then she shook the water from them and turned, smiling, to look at him.

He turned too, still prostrate over the little pool, and looked up. His face was red with stooping. Water dropped from his beard and from the point of his nose. A slow smile dawned, in response to her own. He crawled back into a kneeling position, and thus they remained for a moment, both of them, kneeling by the stream, as though they were performing some obeisance.

'Feel better?' she asked presently.

He seized her hand and began speaking rapidly.

'Miss Moorhouse – Phoebe, I still want you to marry me.'

She started, angry, and tried to drag her hand away, but he would not let it go. 'I've been miserable ever since I spoke to you in the springtime. I can't work. I can't do anything.'

She wrenched her hand away and sat back looking at him. 'I told you I didn't want to marry anybody.'

'I thought perhaps you had changed your mind. I spoke to David about you and he said you were down here.'

'Did David send you?'

Henry said 'No', but Phoebe suspected a hesitation. David would hear about this the next time she met him. What did he know about it? A cool, genteel bachelor who cared for nothing but his clothes and his dinner-parties. He was pushing Henry at her, because he considered him a good match. He had no right to encourage this poor boy to come to her once more, merely to be made miserable. Her rage had turned on David. She was sorry for Henry now.

'No, Henry. It's no use. I'm sorry.'

'I can't go on.'

'Of course you can. I'm no great prize, I assure you.'

'I think you're the most beautiful girl in the world.'

She laughed. 'Thank you, Henry,' she said.

'You won't take me seriously.' He complained lamely. 'You don't seem to care if . . . if you break my heart.' His voice broke.

She looked at him quickly and saw that his eyes held tears. Suddenly her sympathy was touched. She was moved to an extent that frightened her.

'Oh, Henry! Please!'

'Phoebe!' He held out his hand to her.

'No.' She stood up, came to him and drew her handkerchief from her belt. 'Look, your face is all wet still, you silly boy. I'll dry it for you.'

He was still kneeling. She bent over him, purposefully polished his face, and put back his hair, as though he were her nephew Arthur.

'Now, promise you won't go on making yourself miserable. It's ridiculous nonsense, you know.' She stuffed her handkerchief back into its place and shook the grass from her skirt. 'Now get up and behave yourself.'

He got up and stood looking down on her. His eyes were burning. Again she was moved strangely. For the first time she became aware that she was standing beside a man. 'When am I going to see you again?' he asked.

She was surprised at her own lack of coolness. 'I don't know. I've no idea.'

'When are you coming back to town?'

'In a week or two, after my brother's wedding.'

'Will you allow me to see you?'

'You're a friend of David's, aren't you?' Then, fearing her tone had been tart, she turned to him. 'Henry, I'm not refusing to see you. I want to be friends. But anything more is hopeless. Please. That's my last word. If you keep bothering me, we'll only be miserable – both of us.'

'Then I suppose I'll see you when you come back?'

He was calm now, and somehow, perversely, his returning poise, if any one so callow as Henry could be said to have poise, irritated her.

'Yes, I suppose so. I think we should go back. The farm folks have their tea at four, before the milking. You'll meet my brother Mungo.' She turned to lead the way home. Henry turned and followed her.

4

Yet to Phoebe that was not the end of it. After Henry had asked her to marry him in early June, she had not bothered about it further. She thought of it merely when something brought it to her mind.

But now this second happening by the burn kept invading her thoughts. It came of its own accord, forcing her to give it endless reflection. She had been sorry, troubled, angry. She tried to puzzle out to herself why he had so stirred her. But she could find no answer. Was it a quality of fecklessness? An appeal to something protective in her make-up? The family told her she ran after lame ducks. Was Henry a lame duck? In a sense perhaps. But then he was said to be very clever in his way. Brilliant, she had heard said. At all events she didn't know. But certainly, whatever her feeling, she was not in love with him she told herself.

Now, as though the thought of him were not enough, he had taken to writing her letters. Long, rambling things, mostly about his work. It was quite plain to her that when she and what she stood for were not obsessing his mind, it was a mind that ran on a single track. Engineering was not only his calling. It was his passion. What would happen to the woman who married him?

Would she find herself, shortly, a mere piece of furniture in his house? A creature, scarcely noticed, who was there to look after his comfort – to liberate his mind from distracting instincts that it might continue upon its own brilliant way? There were many self-effacing women who, if they loved him enough, would accept these conditions considering their lives fulfilled. She was made of different stuff. Often, recently, she had felt purposeless. Had asked herself, indeed, why the Almighty had seen fit to create her. But she was certainly not self-effacing. She kept turning over these things, but her thoughts could find no rest.

The first days of September passed, and now there was a wedding. The family came flocking down, all of them. Mary and George, fat and placid, with their fat, placid children. The Butters. Sophia excited and talking her head off. Wil and Margy, brown and sprouting after their holiday, and looking really quite handsome children. Their father, William, as silent as usual. David, the ever correct and immaculate. And then Phoebe's own people. Arthur, Bel and her nephew Arthur (the younger children had been left behind). Phoebe was delighted to see them. Little Arthur sulked at first and complained that she had never come to 'Glen Rosa, but he clung by her all through the day.

Bel was beautifully dressed. A little too beautifully, too carefully, Phoebe thought, comparing her with the one or two Ruanthorpe guests. Indeed her own family looked, somehow, a little over-prosperous, too defensively confident, too urban, for their surroundings. Now it was Mungo, still countrified, but calm and solemn, who was in place. But the ceremony was a pleasantly simple one, performed, as had been arranged, in the Duntrafford drawing-room before the two families and the men- and maid-servants of the estate. This suited Sir Charles and, somehow, it seemed right that these two should be united in the surroundings to which they were to belong.

And in due course when all was over the Moorhouse clan trooped back to Glasgow, related now, by the bonds of holy matrimony, to a real live baronet, the owner of quite extensive lands. A matter for much secret complacency to most of them, though wild horses would not have dragged this from them. But Providence, they felt, had been kind to them in many ways, and was repaying them even more than they deserved for their devotion to the things that mattered. Such things as the common-sense practice of a good, sensible brand of religion and a strict attention to business.

Chapter 21

I

'Where are you going to, Aunt Phoebe?' Arthur the Second, large enough to be promoted to the breakfast-room, and with a napkin tied round his neck, stopped for a moment from shovelling porridge into his manly mouth. He was a schoolboy now, Bel having sent him to the newly built Kelvinside Academy which had just opened its doors 'to enable pupils to qualify for the University and for commercial and professional pursuits'. It was to be, Bel understood, the most select establishment in Glasgow for the education of gentlemen's sons.

Arthur looked up at his aunt for an instant. He resented that she had come into the room wearing a hat and outdoor things. It meant that she was going to do something he wouldn't be able to share in now that he must go to school.

Phoebe slid an affectionate hand over his round head as she passed him on her way to look out of the window. 'I'm going into town with your Papa,' she said. 'I've got some shopping to do. Then I'm going to see your Granny. I've been home for nearly a fortnight, and I haven't been to see her yet.'

It was a fine autumn morning. The trees in front and across the Great Western Road in the Botanic Gardens had turned to brown and gold.

'Finish your porridge, Arthur,' Bel said reprovingly.

'Couldn't you go on Saturday?' he asked anxiously.

'No, dear. She's going today. Hurry up, son.'

'I'll take you somewhere on Saturday. Where would you like to go?'

Arthur smiled. 'I don't know. I'll have to think,' he said, and attacked his porridge plate once more.

Phoebe, still wandering about, bent over the still empty chair belonging to the master of the house and glanced casually over his folded morning *Herald* to see if there was anything in the way of shop announcements worthy of her interest. The first outside quarter page yielded nothing. Births and marriages of people she didn't know. Bank notices.

She picked up the paper, and held up the front page fully opened out. Wednesday the second of October 1878. An announcement of a new story beginning in the *Weekly Herald*:

'Marguerite: or a Woman's Wit'. A romance from Spanish History. 'The story is essentially modern in spirit; antiquarian research has not been suffered to impair the action of the narrative.' She might spend a penny on that if she remembered. On Monday the seventh October, a return visit of the Comedy Opera Company. They would play 'H.M.S. Pinafore: or The Lass that Loved a Sailor', by Mr Gilbert and Mr Sullivan. She might try to tease David into taking her to that. Royal Botanic Gardens. In the Kibble Palace, 'Mr Cole's Splendid String Band. Tomorrow from seven to nine.' She would keep away from that. She didn't want to run into the Hayburn boys. She had not seen either of them since she had come back. If Henry had written, the letters had not been forwarded. She had, these days, a nervous desire almost, to shut him out of her thoughts.

This was better. 'Mr Copland of the Caledonian House in Sauchiehall Street is just home from Paris, and has made a happy selection of Rare and Beautiful Costumes, the surpassing beauty of which exhausts the vocabulary of ecstatic imagination.' And Millar's at the Cross, and the Polytechnic had autumn shows too. She must really have a look round all these. She had better have her midday meal with old Mrs Barrowfield and make a day of it. It was nice to be back in Glasgow again in this crisp autumn weather, to have all kinds of things to look at, and to be eighteen.

She folded the *Herald* as she heard her brother's step outside the door, and put it back by his plate.

2

The man of business was preoccupied. He was never at his most talkative in the morning. He greeted everybody curtly. Bel hurried to pour out his tea. Phoebe served his ham and eggs. While this was going on he stood warming himself in front of the fire. When he saw that his breakfast was awaiting him, he said 'Thanks', and sat down abruptly. He took his first sip of tea, his first piece of ham, then put out his hand for his morning paper.

'The City Bank?'

Phoebe and Bel stopped to look at him as his quick hands folded the sheets to the news page.

'What is it, dear?' Bel asked.

Arthur read: 'The City Bank of Glasgow has stopped payment. For some time past rumours have been in circulation unfavourable to the position of the Bank; and these have been only too well founded.' He dived deeper and went on reading without comment.

'Is that a very serious thing? What does stopping payment really mean, Arthur?' Bel asked.

He paid no attention.

'I hope we've got no money in it,' Phoebe said.

'If it's a serious thing, that would be dreadful. Arthur, you must tell us! Arthur!'

'What is it?' He put down his *Herald* querulously.

'Have we got any money in the City Bank?'

'No. We haven't.'

'What a good thing!'

'Yes. This may be very serious.' He took up the paper again.

'Will people be ruined?'

'Very likely. There'll be some fun in the town today.' He folded it up and pushed it into a pocket. 'I'll read the rest going in,' he said. He snapped up the remainder of his breakfast with lightning speed. Finished, he pushed himself back and got up. 'If you're coming with me, Phoebe, you'd better come,' he said. 'This bank affair is going to be terrible,' he added. 'It'll affect trade. It'll be a bad autumn for everybody. By the way, I believe David's Hayburn friends are in, up to the neck. Somebody mentioned it at the Club the other day.'

He did not give his sister time to ponder his words, for, in an instant more, he had seized his hat and was out on the pavement waiting for the tram. Phoebe hurried after him, well-used to this treatment. Arthur was the best brother in the world, even if he hadn't time to wait for his ladies.

When they had mounted the tram, however, he remembered he had his sister with him. For instead of swinging himself agilely up the little stairway to the roof, he came inside. This was occupied mostly by elderly men. The conductor rang the bell, the horses were off, and brother and sister settled down to the morning journey into the City.

Presently Phoebe found herself wondering why everybody was talking to everybody else. Tram passengers were not usually so free with their talk. On the few occasions upon which she had to go into town at this hour she had invariably found herself in the company of a tram-load of solemn, bearded, bewhiskered gentlemen; murmuring, perhaps, polite greetings to a new-comer, but for the most, sitting staring in front of them, their hands crossed stolidly over the ivory or ebony handles of their large umbrellas, pondering no doubt the matters of weight which the day held in store for them. But today all was animation and talk. The man next to Arthur had begun talking to him. He was talking of the City Bank. The two gentlemen on the other side of her were talking about the City Bank. Those opposite were talking about the City Bank. What a terrible thing it was! What had brought it about? What would be the extent of the damage done?

To Phoebe, being a well-brought-up young woman, most of this business talk was Greek. The other banks were accepting its notes, one man said. That seemed to be a good thing. An old gentleman shook his head and said *that* wouldn't last long. He had heard talk last night. The Exchange had been humming. He wouldn't be surprised if the affair reached the criminal court. He turned and addressed a passenger sitting on his other side who, so far as Phoebe could tell, had until now said nothing. 'What do you think, sir?'

'I hope it's not as bad as it looks, or I'll be a ruined man.' For this man's benefit the old gentleman immediately became falsely cheerful, but no one who was listening – least of all Phoebe – was convinced by his tone.

As she sat swaying behind the trotting horses, she found herself staring at the gentleman who had said he might be a ruined man. She regarded him with her usual impersonal interest. He must be racked with anxiety. Did people express so little when they were faced with ruin? Did they merely sit quietly and look before them? Was she really hard, that she could not feel more for this stranger? Was there something left out of her make-up? Had she a limited supply of sympathy?

The tram rattled on. Now the brakes were screaming as it descended Renfield Street. Now it had reached its terminus in St Vincent Place. People were getting out. They were preparing to change round the horses.

3

Arthur asked her if she were going direct to his mother-in-law at Monteith Row – in which case she might accompany him by George's Square and the Candleriggs. But Phoebe thanked him and said that she had promised herself to go down Buchanan Street, then by Argyle Street and the Trongate, so that she might see what was showing in the autumn shop-windows. Arthur bade her a hasty goodbye and hurried off.

In Buchanan Street, too, there was an air of excitement.

Phoebe, having been in the country for so long, set about examining each window display with immense relish. But presently she found her attention continually caught by the excited voices of passers-by. The City Bank. Always the City Bank. It was now long past nine. In front of the *Glasgow Herald* office there was a small crowd of people. She crossed over and asked a boy who looked like a young clerk what the crowd meant. They were trying to get further news of the City Bank. As she reached Argyle Street, morning passengers were pouring out of St Enoch's Square from the great, new-built railway station. Urchins selling late editions of the morning papers were doing a roaring trade.

She took her way along Argyle Street. Here in the rush of Glasgow's busiest street the excitement seemed swallowed up. For a time Phoebe let such windows as were worth looking at engross her. Her aim in coming into this undistinguished part was to spend some time in the great emporium known as the Royal Polytechnic, to have an entertaining and profitable look round.

As she came opposite to it she stopped and crossed over. For some time the display in its many windows took all her attention. 'Modes from Paris', 'The very latest from the City of Fashion'. What it had worn at its Great Exhibition this summer. The Polytechnic had sent its buyers, and nothing had escaped their notice. Glasgow's ladies need consider themselves in no way behind in up-to-date elegance. They had merely to put themselves into the hands of the Polytechnic buyers. In one window there was a lithograph of the Prince of Wales and his lovely Princess Alexandra being shown round the Exhibition by deferential Frenchmen.

Phoebe was enjoying herself thoroughly now. She took each of the many windows in turn, gazing her fill. At last she decided to buy some small thing as an excuse for going inside to see the still greater wonders there.

She was turning to go back to the main entrance when she became conscious that people were hurrying along in excited knots on the other side of the street. For a moment she stood looking, and then, anxious to miss nothing, she picked up her skirts and ran over to see what it was all about. Presently she found herself at the corner of Virginia Street, a street which, in the ordinary way, was quiet, business-like, unobtrusive and without interest for a young girl. Some little way up there was a large crowd of people standing. All of them were gazing up at a doorway. In a moment more she had joined them. She saw now that those about her were very excited, pressing forward, it seemed, towards this door. She craned her neck to see better and was able to read the words 'The City Bank of Glasgow, Head Office'.

She spoke to a woman by her side. 'Why is everybody waiting here?'

The woman, poorly dressed in black, turned. 'A don't ken whit *everybody's* waitin' for. A jist ken A'm waitin' till it's ten o'clock, to let me get ma money oot o' that place,' she said acidly.

A man in front of them looked round. 'You'll get no money out o' that place.'

'Aye. 'll get it oot.' The woman's voice broke hysterically. 'It's ither that, or gang to the puirshoose.'

'It's ten now,' the man said, and as he spoke a clock somewhere could be heard striking out ten strokes. The hour when, upon a normal day, all honourable banks threw open their doors and looked the world square in the face. But this one it seemed could not. Voices became more high-pitched and excited. Women began to weep. The special staff of police, who had been sent against serious trouble, kept shouting not to block the street entirely. Their continual cry of 'Move on, please!' could be heard above the din. Here and there a sympathetic policeman could be seen telling a weeping woman to go home; that she was doing no good by standing here, that if she had City Bank notes in her possession she could turn them into coin elsewhere. From time to time people called out that they were ruined. They shouted the words 'Robbers! Thieves! Scoundrels!'

Now the police were forcing the crowd to make way. Phoebe, firmly wedged in now, was swept backwards. 'Keep back there, please! Let these gentlemen through!' Suddenly the crowd went silent. Was the miracle to happen? Was the bank after all to open its doors, just as though it were an ordinary morning? The solemn, black-clad men succeeded, with the help of the police, in pushing their way forward. But the door was merely half opened as they passed inside. The crowd did not like this. Why should these men be the only ones to get inside? Why shouldn't they, too, be allowed to go in and ask for their money? There was a rush forward. Before the police and those inside could quite control them one or two slipped through.

But almost at once the door was forced shut and the people were left murmuring.

At last Phoebe decided she had had enough of it. These people would probably stand here all morning. There would be nothing more for her to see. She turned and began to extricate herself, shouldering her way determinedly among anxious faces. She could not help smiling a little to herself at the thought of how disapproving Bel would be at her boldness in allowing herself to be pushed about in this seedy crowd.

4

She had wormed herself free and was in the act of setting straight her hat and her dress before walking off, when she saw a private carriage swing round out of Argyle Street, and come to a standstill by the edge of the pavement a little way down. A glance at the shining harness and the handsome, well-groomed horses told her it belonged to someone of consequence. Now, as she came nearer, she could see it was in some way familiar. Another step towards it brought complete recognition. It belonged to Mrs Hayburn.

Her brother's words came back to her. 'By the way, I believe David's Hayburn friends are in, up to the neck.' Had they sent someone to find out? She would have turned and gone in the other direction, since, if the carriage contained a Hayburn the meeting would be awkward, but retreat was blocked by the throng. There was nothing for her but to go on. Just as she came up, Stephen and Henry jumped out, and began advancing towards her. Stephen was the first to recognize her.

'Miss Moorhouse!'

Phoebe guessed that both the brothers were very excited. She did not know what to say. She weakly said: 'Good-morning.' Then, feeling she must explain herself, she added, 'I'm just in town shopping. I came up the street to see what all this was about.'

Henry was looking at her dazedly, as though he were trying to remind himself of something. 'We're all here,' he said hoarsely. 'Mother too. She's in the carriage. She insisted on us all coming to see if we've been turned into beggars or not.'

Phoebe noticed the toneless ring of his voice. 'I hope it's not as bad as that,' she said lightly.

'It's just as bad as it can be, Miss Moorhouse,' Stephen said, adjusting his eyeglass with a very good show of calmness.

Phoebe admired him. She had never liked Stephen Hayburn much, but now, in this moment of stress, he was doing well.

'I don't think you'll be able to get any news this morning,' she said, preparing to move. 'The policemen were telling people not to wait.'

'We had better go up, just to please Mother. It was she who made us come here.' Stephen pulled Henry's arm, and they raised their hats and went off.

Having no other choice now but to pass Mrs Hayburn's carriage, Phoebe began to wonder what she could possibly find to say to the stiff old lady in her distress. As she passed, however, Mrs Hayburn took no notice of her. She was sitting forward in the carriage, staring before her, in a terrible trance of suspense. Could worldly possessions really matter so much to anyone? Phoebe wondered, as she gazed at the wide-open, unseeing eyes and the set face suddenly turned frail and marbled with unnaturally blue veins. She wondered if she ought to make herself known and offer to stay until the sons came back, but at once she decided against this. She felt that she would receive no thanks for breaking in. If Mrs Hayburn fainted – as judging by her appearance she might very well do – her coachman could look after her.

Chapter 22

1

In Phoebe's mind the City Bank collapse was inextricably tangled up with the Hayburns. When people talked of it – and for the next month not only Glasgow but the whole of Britain talked of little else; even *Punch* had a cartoon of an erring bank manager awaiting judgement with other common thieves – Phoebe could think only of the two anxious brothers and the terrible white face of their mother as she sat there alone in her carriage. For many days, however, she heard nothing more of them. She knew, of course, that Hayburn and Company had crashed, 'succumbed' (as the papers put it) 'to pressure of money matters'. And this made her wonder. But David, who could, at most times, have told her, had not seen them either and had not liked to obtrude.

Meanwhile the disaster kept piling up. On the first day the depositors had been kept calm by the action of the other banks in accepting City Bank notes and by the exhortations of the newspapers. On the second day the books went into the hands of the auditors. And from then onward the news became more and more sensational. The further the examination went the more shameful was the tale of swindle and deceit. Mouths were full of expressions of contempt. 'Banking run mad', 'Utterly rotten', 'Reckless plungers', 'Cooked accounts'. One newspaper reported that you could hardly go a dozen yards without meeting a friend who had lost everything. Shareholders had not only to pay up in full to the extent of what they held but had to do this six times over. The burden, in most cases, was unbearable. Charity lists were opened for the unfortunate. People like Arthur Moorhouse gave lavishly. In less than three weeks the directors were arrested.

On the day following the arrest, Arthur, scanning his morning paper, read out the announcement of the death of Mrs Robert Hayburn. Phoebe's comment, at the time, was merely that she was not surprised. But as the days went by, this news haunted her. She found herself taken by a strong desire to see Henry and know how he was getting on. She felt he would be defenceless before the blows that had fallen. She did not know whether he had loved his unamiable mother or not. But she rightly guessed that he was one of those who do not bother much about the routine in which they find themselves, so long as it does not interfere with their own intense interests, but who are utterly at a loss if that routine is broken.

At last on the evening of the funeral day, Phoebe, certain that David would have been among the mourners, felt herself impelled to call upon him to hear news of Henry.

2

She found Henry alone by the fire in David's sitting-room. She had expected David and Stephen too, for the landlady had said they were all there. He was sitting forward, his feet on the black, iron fender. His head in his hands.

He looked up casually, for he was expecting the other two. His eyes looked haunted in his white face.

He sprang to his feet. 'Miss Moorhouse!'

Phoebe drew back. She felt she was intruding. 'I'm sorry,

Henry,' she said, using without noticing his Christian name, 'I thought David was here. I've disturbed you.'

'No, no. You're not disturbing me. Come in, David and Stephen went out for a walk. They'll be here any time.'

Phoebe came into the room and gave him her hand. She was distressed to see how crushed and ill he looked. Whether she would or not he had been so much in her thoughts during these last days.

But in her mind she had not seen him so red-eyed, so weary as this. If ever there was a lame duck, it was Henry Hayburn now.

He shook hands formally and they sat down.

'Henry,' Phoebe began. 'You don't look well.'

'I'm all right.' He smiled wearily.

'I was going to write to you,' she said gently, 'but – well, you see, it was perhaps a little more difficult for me than for – most people.'

He nodded.

Phoebe went on. 'Still that wouldn't have kept me. I would certainly have written if I hadn't met you here.' She waited for a moment, then continued, 'I was really shocked to hear about your mother's death. In a way I wasn't surprised. I had seen her, not so many days ago. You remember? She looked ill.'

'Yes. The morning we all drove down to Virginia Street to make sure that we were ruined.'

'It was a shock to me to hear about Hayburn and Company too.'

He appeared to wince at this, but he did not reply directly. He merely asked, 'What were you doing there?'

'I had gone up the street to see what the crowd meant.'

'Your folks had no money in the City Bank?'

'No, Henry. We were lucky.'

'So you had just gone up to see what ruined people looked like? Just as a matter of interest?'

She was not angry with him. She had after all told him she was that kind of person. He was stating now what had been perfectly true. She did not reply, and he went on:

'I suppose you're doing the same now?'

She got up and laid her hand on his shoulder.

'I'm going to speak the truth to you, Henry. You've never been out of my mind since that morning. You may think this queer of me, but I've been really pleased that I could feel so badly upset – over a friend. You see it's not nice to keep on feeling a – a kind of fish with no feelings.' She turned away and leant against David's betasselled mantelshelf, with its black marble clock, its pipe-cleaners, its photographs and the gilt mirror stuck at the edge, with half a dozen cards of invitation, requesting the pleasure of the company of that eligible bachelor Mr David Moorhouse at this ball and that conversazione. Looking down on Henry Hayburn's black mop, she was struck, for the first time, with the eternal see-saw. Henry had been up. Now he was down. It was her brother David's turn.

'You're a queer girl, Phoebe,' Henry was saying.

'I've never hidden from you that I was. Have I?'

'No.' Then after a pause, and with a voice that tried to be hard, but only succeeded in being heartbreaking, 'You needn't bother defending yourself against me now. Beggars don't ask young ladies to marry them.'

Phoebe laid her hand on the mantelpiece. Something told her she was at the parting of the ways. She must get out of here at once if she did not want to be caught – trapped for ever by her own unaccountable self. She saw this so clearly that she felt a little giddy. She had only to turn his last thrust aside, tell him again how sorry she was about everything and go. But after a moment, a moment that seemed to her to stop and hang motionless in eternity, she found herself still here in David's room, looking down into Henry Hayburn's eyes.

But even yet she did not give up the struggle. 'What will happen to Hayburn and Company, Henry?' she said, as though she was attempting to ignore his last words.

She looked down at his engineer's hands. He was wringing the fingers through each other, nervously. When he spoke he seemed to her to be speaking to himself.

'Hayburn and Company was the whole of my life. My father, Robert Hayburn, made it, built it out of nothing. He was an inventor. Other people had to look after the money for him – and you know now what that has led to – but he was the brain, the heart of it all. Stephen and Mother didn't understand about Father's work. What it had meant to him. They weren't touched with the – fire.' And after a long pause, 'If they had given me time I would have taken up his work where he had laid it down.' He turned aside as though to hide his face from her. Again he had tried to harden his voice, and again its tone came near to breaking her heart.

3

She stood looking down upon him fascinated. It gave her a strange, passionate pleasure to hear him say that 'Hayburn and Company was the whole of his life.' Who was she, Phoebe Moorhouse? A strange, not too sensitive young woman who lived without purpose in and for herself. And here was a young man whose mind might be warped and broken by what life was now forcing upon him. She had courage and strength if she had nothing else. At least she could bring him these. It was in her power to save him, to help him to pick himself up and go on. She saw it now indeed as a sacred duty, the reason why she had been sent into the world. She felt now as she did when, a child of fourteen, she had been impelled to go down into the desolation of the slums and rescue her nephew. She had just the right toughness, the requisite lack of feeling, to stand between life and this brilliant, sensitive creature. She alone could let him go on with his life's work.

She was terribly shaken by the decision she had made. Her tears were falling as she bent forward and turned his face up to look at her. She put her arms about his neck and kissed him full on the mouth. He sprang to his feet.

'You *are* going to take up your father's work where he left it off, Henry. I'm going to be with you and see that you do. We'll build up another Hayburn and Company.'

He stood, stupid and speechless, holding her two hands. When he spoke it was to say: 'But don't you see, Phoebe, I'm a beggar?'

'So am I. But we're both strong. Your father started from nothing, didn't he?'

'I can't allow you—'

'Of course, if you don't want me.'

'Oh, my dear!'

He took her into his arms. The faces that came together were both wet. She could feel his beard on her face, smell tobacco, the faint smell of the macassar on his hair, of his linen, of himself. And still, far away, the silent, waiting Phoebe, the Phoebe Moorhouse who had nothing to do with this excited, overwrought girl, sat waiting and wondering.

They came apart. His eyes were shining, and his cheekbones were red. She had made him happy. She had given her life a meaning. She would be happy too.

'Henry,' she said, at length, 'I want to ask something of you.'

'What is it, darling?'

'Let me go home now. You can come and see me tomorrow.'

He kissed her again. Then she turned and hurried away.

Chapter 23

I

Bel came back to consciousness with an odd feeling that someone somewhere in the house was not resting. For a moment she wondered what time it was, and then, as though in answer, the clock on her bedroom mantelpiece struck one. She lay listening. Beside her, Arthur lay peaceful, breathing steadily. A faint autumn night wind caused the lace curtains by the open window to stir now and then. The pale light from a lamp outside made reflections on the ceiling. The clock ticked hurriedly, quietly persistent. She too began to feel restless – on edge. What had happened to wake her up?

She had gone to bed wondering about Phoebe. The girl had come in from David's room. She had asked her how David was and if he had had any news of the Hayburn boys. She said she had not seen her brother, but that Henry Hayburn had been there. Bel had ventured to ask how he was and what his plans were, and Phoebe had answered her casually that Henry didn't look up to much and that she didn't know what his plans were. The girl was in one of her remote, moody fits, so Bel had let her be. She had drunk her evening cup of tea in silence, wandered about the drawing-room aimlessly, played a bar or two standing in front of the piano, then said good-night and gone off early to bed.

Bel lay wondering now, as she had wondered then, if something had happened.

Above her a board creaked. That must be in Phoebe's room, for it was directly overhead on the top floor. Had she got up for something? Wasn't she well? She would wait a little to see if it went on. Was that another creak? Or was she imagining? Was that the handle of a door turning quietly? It was difficult to tell in this solidly built house even in the dead of night. Was there movement now on the upstairs landing? Or were these simply imaginings, born of this unpleasant midnight alertness?

Bel tried to persuade herself that it was nothing. That she had better get off to sleep again. For a long time she lay, trying to make her mind a blank. But it was no use. When the bedroom clock struck two she had to admit that she was wider awake than ever. Should she get up and satisfy herself that all was well upstairs? If it had not been for Arthur she would have done so now, at once. But it seemed unfair to risk wakening a tired, busy man just for a mere whim. In a little time, surely, she would begin to feel sleepy again.

What was that? No. She must go upstairs and see that all was well. Perhaps one of the children—? But if it were one of the two smaller ones, Tom or Isabel, their nurse was with them in the nursery. And if anything was unsettling little Arthur, who was now promoted to a bedroom of his own, he had a way of coming straight downstairs to her or going across the landing to Phoebe.

She slid to the edge of the bed with great caution, listening at every move that her husband's breathing kept steady, and finally found herself standing on the floor beside her bed. Noiselessly she stretched out her hand for her dressing-gown and felt with her bare feet for her slippers. The handle of the bedroom door turned without noise. Like a ghost she slid through.

As she came up the stairs to the top landing she bent close to the bottom of Phoebe's door to see if a light was burning. She could find no sign of one. Over on the opposite side, Arthur's door stood open, and his gas was burning at a peep, for he was a nervous child, and did not like to feel he was shut away in the darkness by himself.

She crept forward and looked in.

2

There in the semi-darkness, in nothing but her white nightdress, Phoebe was sitting by the sleeping boy's bed, silent and motionless, holding his hand.

Bel drew back, alarmed for a moment, as though, almost, she had seen an apparition. The girl had looked so pale and still, with her long, black plaits of hair falling down in front over her shoulders. What did this mean? Had she come there to comfort Arthur, or in search of comfort for herself?

But Bel's practical mind came to the rescue. It was nonsense whatever it was. The girl would catch her death of cold. She looked into the room again, and said quietly:

'Phoebe dear, what are you doing?'

Phoebe started.

'Come back to your room. You'll catch cold.'

Phoebe disengaged her hand gently, and came out of the room after her sister-in-law.

Bel lit Phoebe's gas, turned back the bed, and made her get into it before she said:

'Is Arthur all right, Phoebe? Did he want you?'

Phoebe merely shook her head and said, 'No.'

'What were you doing there, dear?'

'I don't know. I just went.'

Bel stood looking at her, puzzled. It had been a rule with her never to break into Phoebe's confidence. She had always let her tell her what she would. Never forced her. But now it was clear that something was troubling the child. If only she would talk. She looked at her to see if she had been crying. But the eyes that looked out of her lovely pale face shone hot, and strangely clear, like the eyes of a trapped animal.

Bel sat on the edge of the bed beside her and did something that she had never dared do since Phoebe had grown up – she put her arms about her and kissed her.

'Phoebe, my dear, I would like you to tell me what's wrong. You know I don't bother you often, but I would like to know now.'

Phoebe still said nothing. And Bel, holding her, wondered for a time if the girl in her arms resented this show of affection. Presently, however, she felt Phoebe's hand over her own. And thus they remained for some minutes. But things couldn't stay like this.

'I think considering all I've done for you, Phoebe, you might tell me. I don't know whether you're fond of me or not, you've never shown it very much' – Phoebe was amazed at this, though she said nothing – 'but I'm very fond of you. It makes me miserable to see you like this. Did something happen in David's rooms tonight?'

Again Phoebe did not speak. But Bel saw that she was going to now, and waited.

'Yes,' Phoebe said at length, speaking with strange evenness. 'I promised to marry Henry Hayburn.'

Bel withdrew her arms and sat up looking straight at her. All kinds of thoughts crowded in. Henry Hayburn? She would have thought differently of this before the Hayburns had been ruined. But Bel's snobbery was skin deep; like the snobbery of most women when it is set against the happiness of those they love. She dismissed Henry's fall from prosperity. After all, he was young and clever. But why wasn't the child happy? She herself, at the same stage, had been upset, and wept and laughed and been so unreasonable that her mother had been driven to lecture her roundly. But at least she had made some show of emotion, of happiness. She had not gone into this still, dry-eyed trance.

'Phoebe dear, do you *want* to marry Henry Hayburn?' she asked at last.

'I suppose so.' The girl was incomprehensible.

'But Henry Hayburn's a very nice young man. Aren't you happy?'

'I think so. At any rate, I'm going to marry him.'

It was useless. She bent forward and kissed her again. There was nothing else to do.

And now it was Bel who found herself crying. And through the tears she saw the fourteen-year-old Phoebe, ragged and bleeding, carried senseless into the house in Ure Place in her brother David's arms. No. There was nothing she wouldn't do to make up to her for that night. But it was so difficult, so baffling.

Now the girl was speaking. 'Bel, will you do something for me?'

'My dearest, anything.'

'Will you stay with me for the rest of the night?'

Phoebe had no idea of the happiness this gave Bel.

'Of course. If it will help you.'

A minute later they were together in the darkness. She was allowing Bel to hold her hand as they lay.

'Phoebe,' Bel said presently, 'I want you to make me a promise.'

'I'll try.'

'If ever you're very unhappy – any kind of unhappiness – it doesn't matter what or where, will you come as quickly as you can, back home here to me?'

'Why do you say that, Bel?'

'I don't know, dear. But tonight, somehow I feel I must. Will you promise?'

'Yes. Of course I promise.'

'I'm glad, Phoebe. Now try to sleep.'

Neither of them said any more. But, after a time, Bel was pleased to hear Phoebe's breathing come quietly, rhythmically. She did not withdraw her hand. She was afraid to wake her.

Guy McCrone
The Philistines 75p

The Moorhouse family become established in Glasgow town. They are swiftly drawn into turmoil when the dashing and impulsive David falls in love with Lucy Rennie, a professional singer whose trade places her far beneath his family in the social order – especially when he is already engaged to the charms and riches of another . . .

'The authentic stuff of life' TIMES LITERARY SUPPLEMENT

The Puritans 75p

Grown up into a beautiful and elusive creature of the world, Phoebe is drawn away from Glasgow. Destiny sweeps her and her husband to Vienna, the romantic and enchanting capital of the Hapsburgs in its heyday of the 1880s.

'Recaptures the atmosphere of the period most effectively' GLASGOW HERALD

David Toulmin
Blown Seed 80p

A novel two decades in the writing and destined to become a classic of Scottish storytelling . . . The finely-wrought saga of the MacKinnons of Bogmyrtle Farm; of Helen who went out into the world and came home with Audie, her man; and of Meldrum Spark, the tinker, who brought her a wild, doomed passion in the place of a wedlock long turned sour.

'A thing of wild and simple beauty, rippling like corn in the wind' DAILY EXPRESS

Jessica Stirling
The Spoiled Earth 95p

A powerful and exciting love story set against the loyalties and oppressions, catastrophes and ambitions, of a nineteenth-century Scottish mining community. This haunting saga traces the joys and despairs of Mirrin Stalker, radical firebrand and tantalising beauty . . .

'Jessica Stirling has a brilliant future' CATHERINE COOKSON

Selected bestsellers

☐ **The Eagle Has Landed** Jack Higgins 80p
☐ **The Moneychangers** Arthur Hailey 95p
☐ **Marathon Man** William Goldman 70p
☐ **Nightwork** Irwin Shaw 75p
☐ **Tropic of Ruislip** Leslie Thomas 75p
☐ **One Flew Over The Cuckoo's Nest** Ken Kesey 75p
☐ **Collision** Spencer Dunmore 70p
☐ **Perdita's Prince** Jean Plaidy 70p
☐ **The Eye of the Tiger** Wilbur Smith 80p
☐ **The Shootist** Glendon Swarthout 60p
☐ **Of Human Bondage** Somerset Maugham 95p
☐ **Rebecca** Daphne du Maurier 80p
☐ **Slay Ride** Dick Francis 60p
☐ **Jaws** Peter Benchley 70p
☐ **Let Sleeping Vets Lie** James Herriot 60p
☐ **If Only They Could Talk** James Herriot 60p
☐ **It Shouldn't Happen to a Vet** James Herriot 60p
☐ **Vet in Harness** James Herriot 60p
☐ **Tinker Tailor Soldier Spy** John le Carré 75p
☐ **Gone With the Wind** Margaret Mitchell £1.75
☐ **Cashelmara** Susan Howatch £1.25
☐ **The Nonesuch** Georgette Heyer 60p
☐ **The Grapes of Wrath** John Steinbeck 95p
☐ **Drum** Kyle Onstott 60p

All these books are available at your bookshop or newsagent;
or can be obtained direct from the publisher
Just tick the titles you want and fill in the form below
Prices quoted are applicable in UK
Pan Books, Sales Office, Cavaye Place, London SW10 9PG
Send purchase price plus 20p for the first book and 10p for each
additional book, to allow for postage and packing

Name_____
(block letters please)

Address _____

_____

While every effort is made to keep prices low, it is sometimes
necessary to increase prices at short notice. Pan Books reserve the
right to show on covers new retail prices which may differ from
those advertised in the text or elsewhere